BY
MICHAEL CARRIER

A number of very wonderful people helped prepare this book for publication. Each of them contributed significantly. For your help on the interior pages, thank you Evie C., Steve W., Andy A., John B., Charity K., G&G, and numerous others.

For assisting on the cover, a large thank you goes to the amazingly talented members of Grand Valley Artists, Grand Rapids, MI.

DOGFIGHT

BY
MICHAEL CARRIER

GREENWICH VILLAGE INK

An imprint of Alistair Rapids Publishing

Grand Rapids, MI

DISCLAIMER: *DOGFIGHT* is not a true story. It is work of fiction. All characters, names, situations, and occurrences are purely the product of the author's imagination. Any resemblance to actual events, or persons (living or dead), is totally coincidental.

Published 2017 by Greenwich Village Ink, an Imprint of Alistair Rapids Publishing, Grand Rapids, MI.

For additional information visit Michael's webpage at: http://www.greenwichvillageink.com/. Please consider my semimonthly newsletter (http://bit.ly/1kGa9QB). Subscribers receive no more than two emails per month (from a secure site).

Author can be emailed at michael.jon.carrier@gmail.com.

ISBN: 978-1-936092-43-7 (trade pbk) 1-936092-43-3
Printed in the United States of America

Library of Congress Cataloging-in-Publication Data

Carrier, Michael.
DOGFIGHT / by Michael Carrier. 1st ed.
ISBN: 978-1-936092-43-7 (trade pbk. : alk. paper)
1. Supreme 2. Courts 3.Thriller 4. Murder 5. Detective. 6. Michigan's Upper Peninsula. 7. New York 8. Grand Rapids

What people are saying about earlier Jack Handler books

Top Shelf Murder Mystery—Riveting. Being a Murder-Mystery "JUNKIE" this book is definitely a keeper … can't put it down … read it again type of book … and it is very precise to the lifestyles in Upper Michigan. Very well researched. I am a resident of this area. His attention to detail is great. I have to rate this book in the same class or better than authors Michael Connelly, James Patterson, and Steve Hamilton. — Shelldrakeshores

Being a Michigan native, I was immediately drawn to this book. Michael Carrier is right in step with his contemporaries James Patterson and David Baldacci. I am anxious to read more of his work. I highly recommend this one! — J. Henningsen

A fast and interesting read. Michael ends each chapter with a hook that makes you want to keep reading. The relationship between father and daughter is compelling. Good book for those who like a quick moving detective story where the characters often break the "rules" for the greater good! I'm looking forward to reading the author's next book. — Flower Lady

Move over, Patterson, I now have a new favorite author, Jack and his daughter make a great tag team, great intrigue, and diversions. I have a cabin on Sugar Island and enjoyed the references to the locations. I met the author at Joey's (the real live Joey) coffee shop up on the hill, great writer, good stuff. I don't usually finish a book in the course of a week, but read this one in two sittings so it definitely had my attention. I am looking forward to the next installment. Bravo. — Northland Press

My husband is not a reader—he probably hasn't read a book since his last elementary school book report was due. But … he took my copy of *Murder on Sugar Island* to deer camp and read the whole thing in two days. After he recommended the book to me, I read it—being the book snob that I am, I thought I had the whole plot figured out within the first few pages, but a few chapters later, I was mystified once again. After that surprise ending, we ordered the other two Getting to Know Jack books. — Erin W.

I enjoyed this book very much. It was very entertaining, and the story unfolded in a believable manner. Jack Handler is a likeable character. But you would not like to be on his wrong side. Handler made that very clear in *Jack and the New York Death Mask*. This book (Murder on Sugar Island) was the first book in the Getting to Know Jack series that I read. After I read *Death Mask*, I discovered just how tough Jack Handler really was.

I heard that Carrier is about to come out with another Jack Handler book—a sequel to *Superior Peril*. I will read it the day it becomes available. And I will undoubtedly finish it before I go to bed. If he could write them faster, I would be happy. — Deborah M.

I thoroughly enjoyed this book. I could not turn the pages fast enough. I am not sure it was plausible but I love the characters. I highly recommend this book and look forward to reading more by Michael Carrier. — Amazon Reader

An intense thrill ride!! — Mario

Michael Carrier has knocked it out of the park. — John

Left on the edge of my seat after the last book, I could not wait for the next chapter to unfold and Michael Carrier did not disappoint! I truly feel I know his characters better with each novel and I especially like the can-do/will-do attitude of Jack. Keep up the fine work, Michael, and may your pen never run dry! — SW

The Handlers are at it again, with the action starting on Sugar Island, I am really starting to enjoy the way the father/daughter and now Red are working through the mind of Michael Carrier. The entire family, plus a few more are becoming the reason for the new sheriff's increased body count and antacid intake. The twists and turns we have come to expect are all there and then some. I'm looking for the next installment already. — Northland Press

Finally, there is a new author who will challenge the likes of Michael Connelly and David Baldacci. — Island Books

If you like James Patterson and Michael Connelly, you'll love Michael Carrier. Carrier has proven that he can hang with the best of them. It has all of the great, edge-of-your-seat action and suspense that you'd expect in a good thriller, and it kept me guessing to the very end. Fantastic read with an awesome detective duo—I couldn't put it down! — Katie

Don't read Carrier at the beach or you are sure to get sunburned. I did. I loved the characters. It was so descriptive you feel like you know everyone. Lots of action—always something happening. I love the surprise twists. All my friends are reading it now because I wouldn't talk to them until I finished it so they knew it was good. Carrier is my new favorite author! — Sue

Thoroughly enjoyed this read—kept me turning page after page! Good character development and captivating plot. Had theories but couldn't quite solve the mystery without reading to the end. Highly recommended for readers of all ages. — Terry

* * *

Here's a list of all my Jack Handler books (to date):

Getting to Know Jack Series

Jack and the New York Death Mask: http://amzn.to/MVpAEd

Murder on Sugar Island: http://amzn.to/1u66DBG

Superior Peril:	http://amzn.to/LAQnEU
Superior Intrigue:	http://amzn.to/1jvjNSi
Sugar Island Girl Missing in Paris:	http://amzn.to/1g5c66e
Wealthy Street Murders:	http://amzn.to/1mb6NQy
Murders in Strangmoor Bog:	http://amzn.to/1IEUPxX

Jack's Justice Series

Ghosts of Cherry Street:	http://amzn.to/2n3lrRf
Assault on Sugar Island:	http://amzn.to/2n3vcyL
Dogfight:	
Murder at Whitefish Point:	

Murder on Sugar Island was the first Jack Handler book that was set in Michigan. Many readers recommend starting with that book.

—Michael

Dogfight

Judges are like umpires. Umpires don't make the rules. They apply them. The role of an umpire and a judge is critical. They make sure everybody plays by the rules. But it is a limited role. Nobody ever went to a ballgame to see the umpire.

—Chief Justice John Roberts

(*Dogfight* demonstrates that Roberts' statement might be correct, but only in a perfect world.)

Chapter 1

(Some of the characters in this book have appeared earlier in the Jack Handler saga. While I provide descriptive information in the early chapters to help make a reader comfortable, for those who seek more, a brief backstory for all the main characters is included in the "Cast" near the end of this book.)

So, Dana," Sipos said, "what's the *big* story? … Are you taking another run at the White House? That's the first thing I thought of when you called. You sounded so excited. Is that it? Am I right?"

Dana's full name was Dana Reynolds. But, that was not her real name. Her real name was Allison Fulbright, and she was the wife of a former president, Bob Fulbright.

Unlike her husband, Ms. Fulbright did not gracefully retire from the public eye when her husband's term expired. Initially her plans included her own eight-year stint in the Oval Office. But when that hope melted away, she sought out and found various behind-the-scenes methods to stake out her territory as the de facto leader of her party. *If I can't be president,* she reasoned, *then I'll make damn sure the road to the White House passes directly across my desk.*

To accomplish her plan, she was willing to engage in the most clandestine of activities. And that's why she came up with the name Dana Reynolds. She used the fake name whenever she wanted to escape the scrutiny of her Secret Service detail.

And tonight was one of those times she sought this type of anonymity.

The full name of her associate was Alexander Sipos Sr. He was a billionaire businessman and *political entrepreneur*. While born in Hungry, he had immigrated to the United States as a young man. Sipos, as he preferred to be called, had little to prove. He had made his fortune primarily through his hedge fund, and by manipulating international currencies.

In his appearance, Sipos was a very imposing man—but not so much because of his physical stature, however. While at six feet one inch he certainly couldn't be considered short, the fact that he carried about sixty unflattering pounds, coupled with his advancement in years, forced him to fashion his persona as the distinguished older gentleman rather than the handsome young buck. His thick hair was icy silver gray. He wore it rather long showing off a pleasant natural wave. Sipos was imposing because he believed himself to be. For one thing, he always dressed well. Some people mused behind his back that he probably slept in a five-thousand-dollar Giorgio Armani suit. And then, there was that thing about his steel blue eyes. When Sipos turned his gaze on you it would burn a hole right through your head and expose your whole being. It was as though he could look into your eyes and not only read your mind but tell your future.

His tailor contributed substantially to this projected aura. He fashioned for Sipos a dozen elegant gray silk suits that seemed to trim off all of the excess pounds. From his thousand-dollar shoes, to his matching tie and pocket square; from his 18K Gold Rolex Diamond Bezel on his left wrist just peeking from his shirt sleeve of his crisp shirt, to his well-tanned hands and face; Sipos was viewed as a beautiful older gentleman by all who encountered him.

Now, at sixty-nine, he found himself much more at home in a fine leather chair with an Upmann-Magnum Cuban, than driving golf balls.

When he opened his mouth to speak, his deep booming voice made you feel as though you were held captive by the powerful presence of a younger Henry Kissinger. Most people sensed that the only appropriate thing to do in the company of such a force of nature was to remain silent.

Sipos and Dana were not friends. They could not even be considered business partners. In fact, they really did not like each other. Their relationship was based solely on their ability to satisfy one another's needs. Dana's political ambitions required someone with unlimited cash and a dearth of scruples—Sipos was her man on both counts.

Sipos, on the other hand, looked to Dana and her husband for political cover. Even though Bob Fulbright had been out of the White House for over a decade, no one in the country wielded more political clout than did he. That made the Sipos/Dana (AKA Allison Fulbright) relationship a near-perfect *marriage*—not in the literal sense, of course.

"What an intriguing thought—running for president ... perhaps the subject for another day," she said through a carefully controlled smile. "But that's not why I invited you over. ... Here, try one of these."

As soon as she had called him, Dana began mixing the ingredients for her signature *drunk as a skunk* concoction—the Zombie, a drink known in some circles as the *mother of all freak drinks.*

First she poured the ingredients into a large crystal pitcher. These included three ounces white rum, nine ounces golden rum, six ounces dark rum, six ounces lime juice, six teaspoons each of pineapple and papaya juice, six teaspoons of superfine sugar, and, to finish it off red, about four ounces of grenadine. She then added two cups of crushed ice, and stirred.

She poured approximately one-sixth of the concoction into a fourteen-ounce Collins glass which already contained a scoop of crushed ice, stirred it, and then carefully dripped a light ounce of 151 Demerara rum onto the top of the drink.

As a personal touch, she created a garnish for each drink. It consisted of a cube of pineapple sandwiched between two maraschino cherries, all impaled on a toothpick and sprinkled with powdered sugar.

She carefully placed the tasty treat on the top of the drink, and inserted a straw.

That was what the drink looked like when she first offered it to Sipos. Experience told her that by the time she had finished one Zombie, her preparation skills would be substantially diminished. That meant that by the time she was ready for a second, it would be surprising if she were able to poke even the sharpest toothpick through anything. If the pineapple and cherries were going to make the final cut for the second drink, they would most likely be swimming around in it commando.

As far as the third Zombie, were she to get that far, she would not even have to stir it. The waves created by her inebriated quaking would do the job nicely.

Sipos did not trust Dana. And he certainly wouldn't put it past her to poison him. But that was not the vibe he was picking up on this day. It was clear to him that she was well on her way to becoming inebriated. *If she were going to poison me, she would have remained totally sober. She's not going to try to kill me,* he reasoned. *At least not tonight.*

"I think I've tried just about every drink known to man at least once in my life," he said. "But nothing quite like this. What goes into it?"

"Rum, mostly."

"Is this one of those new millennial concoctions?"

"No, not at all. Bob and I first had Zombies at a party in New Haven—back in the '60s. And that was a *very* long time ago. I don't think Zombies have ever become terribly popular because of drugs. While one of these drinks will knock you on your ass, so will any number of two-dollar pills. And Zombies are not easy and quite expensive to make."

"I'll give it a try," Sipos said, appearing to take a healthy gulp. "But, when are you going to let me in on the news? That's how you got me over here, you know. You said you had some *big news*."

"Ah, yes," she said as she set her drink down on the bar. "The *big* news. This is going to be more impressive on the *big* screen. Give me a minute and I'll set it up. And do drink your Zombie. I don't want to be the only one who gets stupid drunk tonight. This will only take a minute."

Sipos took advantage of Dana's distraction to pour several ounces of his drink into the sink, and then to scoop more ice to fill it up.

Sipos found a place to sit on the white leather couch just across from the big screen, then he smiled and raised the drink to his lips. Sliding the straw out of the way, he actually did take a sip this time. *Not bad,* he thought. *But I've got to keep my head. Can't get drunk.* He placed his glass on a square glass and copper coffee table in front of him, and pushed it forward.

"Here, Alexander, slide in a little closer. Do you recognize this fellow?" Dana asked as the first of two videos lit up the screen. She paused it one second before Emma squeezed off the .22 caliber round that struck Jack Handler in the head. Jack was just turning to face her, so the image was a bit blurred.

Dana had for years viewed Jack Handler as her nemesis. He, a retired Chicago homicide detective now working in Michigan's Upper Peninsula as a private security contractor, frequently found the interests of his clients at odds with those of the former first lady. So great was her animosity toward Jack that she hired Emma, a high-priced professional assassin, to kill both Jack and his daughter, Lt. Kate Handler. Kate was an active-duty homicide detective working out of New York City at the Midtown Manhattan precinct.

"I think that's Jack Handler," he said. "Is it?"

"By God, I think you're right," she said with a mixture of sarcasm and excitement. "Watch carefully now as I forward to the next frame. That should leave no doubt as to who the star of my little movie is."

The next frame showed Jack Handler quite clearly. The shock in his eyes suggested he was caught by surprise.

"Where was this shot taken, and under what circumstances?"

"Just hang on and you will see. … Okay, are you ready for this?"

Dana was moving through the video a single frame at a time. The next showed Emma's right hand extended in front of her holding what appeared to be a pistol with a suppressor. And it was pointed at Jack.

The third revealed a small cloud of smoke spurting from the barrel, with Jack's face fixed in a grimace, and his cap appearing to have become dislodged.

The final image showed a greatly distressed Jack Handler slumping to the floor—mouth open, and with his eyes no longer focused on anything.

"That's the last of this slideshow," Dana gleefully announced. "But I do have more.

"As you can see, the first series of images show Jack Handler being shot in the head. In the next series, which is an actual video, we see both his body and that of his daughter being disposed of."

Dana correctly described the second part of her presentation as a video. It started out showing a close-up of Jack Handler's head. Emma narrated.

"Here's Jack Handler's body," she said.

"You can see where the first round struck him," she continued as she zoomed in on his bloodied head. "You can see the entry wound here just above the forehead. The bullet did not exit. The first round was fatal. Unfortunately, my camera glasses somehow became dislodged, so the video does not show my shooting Kate in the upper neck. Both Handlers were killed immediately, but I put a second bullet into each of them for insurance."

The video then jumped to a close-up scene depicting Jack, who was now wearing a baseball cap, strapped behind the steering wheel of Emma's SUV. A blood-covered Kate was visible sitting in the passenger's seat. The video panned to the left to show that the SUV was sitting in a huge vehicle-crushing device.

It then zoomed out and panned back to Jack as the crushing hydraulic hammers compressed the SUV to a cube the size of a refrigerator. Blood could be seen gushing from Jack's head as the vehicle yielded to the pressures of the crusher. The video ended when the compacted vehicle was loaded onto a flatbed railroad car.

"And now it's off to China for the late Jack and Kate Handler," Emma could be heard saying. "Au revoir, you sonsofbitches. Thanks for the nice payday."

With that announcement Emma had ended her video.

Sipos smiled and took a long sip of his watered-down Zombie. "These are actually quite good," he said.

"Give me your glass and I'll freshen it up for you."

"Thank you," he said. "But only if you have another one as well."

"I should warn you. I am going to tie one on tonight," Dana replied walking back toward the bar. "I have enough Zombies in the pitcher to knock out the front line of the Redskins."

"I doubt that I'll be good for any more … after I finish this one, of course. I've got a meeting in the morning. But I'll admit, they are pretty damn good."

"I knew you'd like 'em once you tasted 'em. They just seem to go down easy. Smooth. Like a fruity Southern Comfort."

"The images of Emma shooting him in the head," Sipos said, "that was very convincing. Perhaps even conclusive. The only thing that troubles me is that there is no evidence, at least as far as what you showed me, that Kate is dead—aside from her DNA on Jack's shirt. I saw her in that first video. Or, at least I assume it was Kate standing with Jack. I just wonder how she would have allowed Emma to get two rounds off without doing something. ... Do you have any other reason to think Kate is dead as well? Or is it just Jack?"

"Emma said that she killed Kate as well," Dana said. "They both are dead. But she doesn't have any video of her actually shooting Kate. ... She said she came up on the Handlers in a museum on Fisherman's Wharf, and that she put two rounds in Jack and two in Kate. Apparently her glasses with the camera became dislodged before she shot Kate.

"What Emma is saying makes sense. We saw her kill Jack. And we know that Kate was present when *that* hit went down. Kate would not have stood idly by and watched her father be taken out. Something violent would have happened. It's just logical that after shooting Jack, Emma then shot Kate. Necessity dictates it. Or else Emma would be dead right now."

"And we can see from the video," Sipos said, picking up the narrative, "that Emma was moving in on the Handlers. First two shots take out Jack, followed immediately by a neck shot that killed Kate. It appears that it all happened so quickly that Kate could not react. ... Have you had the video analyzed? Have you shown it to anyone?"

"Bob and Roger said it looks good to them."

"Then all I can say is congratulations."

"It's quite clear that Emma's first shot caught Jack squarely in the head," Dana said, not ready to stop bragging about her accomplishment. "In fact, we can verify that with the video. She told me over the phone that her second shot caught Kate in the upper neck. That would have immediately incapacitated her. It could have taken barely longer than a single second to kill them both. It was after she had shot Kate that she fired the second round into Jack. … Emma is a real professional. That's why I hired her."

"Well, then I say *cheers*," Sipos said raising his glass in a toast. "If Roger and Bob are convinced, then I suppose we have to assume that the contract on the Handlers has been fulfilled."

"All except for the two boys," Dana said. "They were supposed to have been killed as well. I'm pretty sure that they are still alive."

The two boys Dana was referring to were Red and Robby, both fourteen-year-old foster children living with Jack.

"Is that a problem?" Sipos asked.

"Not really. The only reason I included them was because I knew that if Jack thought that the boys were targeted as well it would help draw him out. Apparently it worked, because the boys were also in the museum when Emma shot Jack and Kate. … I've already released payment in full on the contract. Emma is, indeed, now a rich woman."

Dana finished her second Zombie and waved her glass at Sipos.

"Be a dear," she said.

"One more and then I'm on my way," Sipos said as he made his way to the bar.

"Like I said before, I've got an appointment in the morning." he said. "So this will be it for me. … How about we watch the *Killing Jack* movie one more time?"

Dana thought that was a good idea. By the time Emma had loaded the crushed SUV, with the bodies inside, onto the flatbed rail car, Dana had nearly finished her third Zombie.

"I'm sorry, but I have to take another piss," she slurred. "Don't go 'til I get back. Understand? I don't want you to go yet. … Okay? Wait for me? Okay?"

"I'll wait," Sipos said.

Seeing that Dana was going to have a difficult time walking, Sipos offered his arm.

"I'm fine. I'm fine."

Dana, realizing that she was staggering, did not even try to walk. She dropped to her hands and knees and crawled toward the bathroom. But she made it only a few yards from her chair. There, with a big smile, she laid her face down on the carpet.

"I'm just going to rest here for a minute. Don't go. I'll only be a minute."

"Hang on," Sipos said. "I'll get you some water."

He returned in less than a minute with a damp towel, a dry one, and a tall glass of water.

He rolled her over and helped her to a half-sitting position. The room was spinning in front of her, but she was still conscious.

"Here, take this," he said, sliding several pills he had found in her purse into her mouth. "It will make you feel better."

He then held the glass of water to her mouth and encouraged her to drink it.

She smiled at Sipos, and complied. And there in his arms, she fell asleep.

Once it was clear to him that Dana was finished for the evening, he eased her back down to the floor, placing her on her stomach with her face to the side.

The process of positioning her on the carpet caused Dana to wake up. Even though she kept her eyes closed to prevent the room from spinning, Dana was still somewhat aware of what was going on around her. She wanted to tell him that she would be fine in a minute, but her mouth could not form the words.

And then it happened. She opened one eye just enough to see Sipos violently club her on the side of the head with what looked to her to be a lamp.

Chapter 2—Earlier

The rules of "Dogfight" were simple. All a combatant had to do was to wrest a small leather-encased ball from his opponent while keeping both fists and both knees on a ten-by-ten canvas mat. An allowance of 1.5 seconds was made to change position.

Electronic sensors in the kneepads and gloves made it easy for the three judges to ensure compliance—a hand or a knee lifted from the mat for longer than a second and a half immediately ended the contest with the loss going to the offender.

Anthony Pelosi, Associate Justice of the U.S. Supreme Court, was the oldest member of the club ever to have participated. At sixty-nine he was four years over the official fighting limit. But because he had never lost a contest in the past twenty years he was given a special dispensation.

"Fight until you lose," he was told. "But lose once, and you're done—not done for the day, but finished for good."

The ball used was fashioned after those found in Europe dating from as early as the 1300s. It was constructed out of four canoe-shaped pieces of calfskin that were sewn together using nylon fishing line to form a sphere slightly larger than a baseball.

In order to provide for a smooth surface, before the final stitching was completed, the ball was flipped inside out, leaving the rough edges inside, and then stuffed with a compacted mixture of beard trimmings and dried moss.

The component that made the contest captivating was the manner in which the ball was gripped. Combatants were not permitted to touch the ball with any part of their anatomy aside from their mouths. That is, the ball was to be held only by the fighter's teeth.

Before the start of the contest, the champion was permitted to use his hand to position the ball in his mouth precisely where he wanted it. He then would assume his dogfighting position—on all fours near the center of the mat. Four black circles indicated exactly where he was to place his fists and knees.

His opponent would then assume a similar position opposite him. He, however, was not allowed to touch the ball with his hands. Instead, the referee would hold steady the champion's head until the challenger was satisfied with his grip on the ball. Both fighters signaled that they were ready to fight by giving a *thumbs up* with the right hand.

With that, the referee stepped off the mat and blew a whistle. And the contest began.

Before this bout, Justice Pelosi had already determined that this would be his last dogfight—win or lose. At sixty-nine, he was beginning to sense that not only was his stamina beginning to wane, he was worried that a strong opponent might actually rip his aging teeth from his mouth. *I'm too old for this*, he thought, *After tonight, I'm done fighting.*

While gambling on dogfighting was not officially sanctioned, it was deemed as important as the fight itself. At one p.m. on fight day, the contests would be listed on the board. Odds were never posted because they were considered irrelevant. A man would bet on the fighter of his choice not necessarily because he believed that fighter had the better chance of winning, but because he sought to honor that combatant. It just so happened that whenever Pelosi's name appeared on the board, which was almost every time he was registered as a guest, nearly everyone would put their money on him, which only makes sense in that he had never lost.

However, even had he been a mediocre fighter, almost everyone would still have bet on him simply because he was so well liked.

This night was no exception. There were four fights scheduled, and the total amount bet on his victory was greater than all the rest of the bouts combined. It was, after all, going to be his last fight before retiring his kneepads.

In total, there was nearly twenty-five thousand dollars bet on him.

Typically, at the start of a fight, Pelosi would immediately go to his trademark *sleeper* move. Because of his extraordinary neck strength, he would force his opponent's face to the mat, and then he would roll his head over onto the fighter's nose, basically cutting off the opponent's ability to breathe. Within a minute the fight was over.

This time, however, Pelosi decided to try a new tactic.

He knew the challenger would be expecting him to force the fight to the mat, and would therefore tilt his head upward to thwart the attempt.

So, the very second the whistle sounded, Pelosi lifted his large right fist and smashed it into his opponent's exposed nose, and then returned his fist to the mat. The punch, which took less than a second, broke the fighter's nose and caused him to immediately release the ball.

The dogfight was over. Pelosi would retire undefeated.

"Champ, that was the shortest fight in history," Grant Conrad, his second, who was also his close friend, enthusiastically announced as he pushed a water bottle into Pelosi's mouth. "Give me that ball. I'm going to have it bronzed."

"The hell you are," Pelosi said, after guzzling several long mouthfuls of the water.

He then tossed the blood-spattered ball to the referee and said, "Retire this thing in the trash. I don't want any reminders about this foolishness. … I'm just happy to get out of this with all my teeth."

"Got time for a quick drink?" Conrad asked.

"Sure, I just need to make sure Harry is okay. I don't think he was expecting that."

Harry Goldblum, Pelosi's challenger, was a forty-four-year-old attorney from New York. While he was not a novice to the sport, his bout with Pelosi was his first shot at the club championship.

"You asshole! You broke my nose!" Harry complained, reaching out to accept Pelosi's hug. "How in hell did you get that punch off so fast? You fat bastard—you're not supposed to be able to do that. Must have been something wrong with the timer."

"I suspect you're right," Pelosi agreed.

He then leaned over and whispered in the defeated man's ear, "Don't tell anyone, but the system is rigged."

Both men smiled as they shook hands and patted each other on the back.

And then, just as he had promised his friend, Pelosi met Conrad at the bar.

Thirty minutes later, after tossing down two Boilermakers with vodka chasers, Pelosi retired to his bedroom.

When Pelosi did not come down for breakfast the next morning, Conrad went up to check on his friend. Almost immediately he returned with all the color drained from his face.

"Call an ambulance!" he announced from the stairway. "Pelosi's not breathing! I think he might be dead!"

Chapter 3

Kate. U comin?" Red texted. "No fun without U."

Red was Jack and Kate's fourteen-year-old foster boy. Because he was unable to talk due to an injury he sustained to his voice box a few years earlier, the only way for him to communicate was through texting. Even if a person were standing next to him, for Red to make a point, he was forced to rely on his cell phone. When "talking" to Robby, his fourteen-year-old virtually inseparable foster brother, Red would enter his text, but instead of sending it, he would encourage Robby to read it over his shoulder.

The boys were more than just best friends. Not only were they almost exactly the same age, both had been orphaned—Robby more recently than Red—and both had found a home with Jack.

Officially, both Kate and Jack had been awarded guardianship over the boys. But because she spent most of her time in New York, the actual day-to-day operation of the family unit fell into Jack's lap. And that was fine with him.

One of the reasons the two boys tended to function as a single entity had a lot to do with Red's handicap. When more urgent messages needed to be conveyed, Robby stepped forward and spoke for both boys.

It was also beneficial to their relationship that they had other complementing attributes. For instance, Robby was witty and very articulate. That was important, given the fact that Red was unable to verbally express himself at all.

Red was incredibly good-looking. In his younger years he was thought of as cute, but as a fourteen-year-old, that description was yielding to handsome. His mop of red curls and bright blue eyes gave him a charming, sweet appearance that would melt any girl's heart.

But Red's good looks were only an incidental attribute as far as Robby was concerned—Red brought two other qualities to that friendship.

First, he was adventurous. Red seemed always to seek out and find the fun side of every situation. That absolutely endeared him to Robby.

And next in importance, at least in Robby's eyes, was Red's ability to fight. While never a bully, Red did not back down from a skirmish. But even more importantly, he never lost one either.

His physical prowess, however, was based not on his size or strength. As far as his stature was concerned, he was actually nearly an inch and a half shorter than Robby, and about six pounds lighter.

The key to his success in this arena of life was his uncanny ability to quickly assess a situation, and then to take resolute action. He might have looked like Carrot Top, but he punched like Floyd Mayweather Jr.

Today, however, Red was not texting Robby. Instead, he was texting long distance to Kate. She was engaged in a homicide investigation in New York City, while Red, Robby and Jack were exploring the historic Sugar Island estate of Chase Osborn, governor of the State of Michigan from 1911 to 1913.

At his death Osborn had bequeathed his sizable homestead to the University of Michigan. The property, which consisted of over three thousand acres, included the entirety of his so-called Duck Island Preserve, and a large tract on Sugar Island itself. With over sixty thousand feet of waterfront on the two islands, the property on this day was providing the Handler "boys" a hefty serving of adventure. And Red would like to have shared the experience with Kate.

Since she was unable to join them, Red and Robby kept her regularly posted as to their progress.

"Wish I could be there with you," Kate texted, "stuck at work. Case going to court in two days, so tying up loose ends. Let me know what you find. I'll call tonight to get full story. Love you guys!"

Kate would definitely have preferred to be hiking through the Osborn Preserve with her father and the boys. But she was fully engaged investigating the murder of a federal judge. As a lieutenant working out of the Midtown precinct, part of her job as a homicide detective was to make the prosecutors feel comfortable with the evidence they were about to present.

And, as is frequently the situation with high-profile homicide investigations, the case she was currently working on required a carefully nuanced presentation of evidence, one which would leave no openings for the alleged killer's white-shoe attorneys.

While Kate had planned to spend the week with her family at their Sugar Island resort, a steady stream of continuances had pushed this case back, forcing her to postpone her vacation at least for a few days.

"Have Dad give me a call when he can," she texted. "Okay?"

Red saw the message and immediately showed it to Jack.

Without hesitating, Jack dialed her number.

Chapter 4

Dad," Kate said, receiving his call. "Those boys wearing you out?"

The best single descriptive word for Kate was *beautiful.* She had her mother's olive complexion and green eyes. Her trim five-foot-eight frame, with her long auburn hair falling nicely on her broad shoulders, would seem more at home on the fashion runway than in an interrogation room. But Kate was a seasoned New York homicide detective. In fact, she was thought by many to be on the fast track to the top—thanks in part to the unwavering support of her soon-to-retire boss, Captain Lawrence Spencer.

"You could say that," Jack replied to her question. "I'm not fourteen years old anymore. But we are having a hell of a good time. … How about you? You still having fun?"

"Fun's not the word I'd use to describe it. At least, not today."

"What's up?" Jack said, holding a finger up to inform the boys they were going to be taking a short break.

"Well," Kate began to say but then hesitated. "I have no real evidence to support what I'm about to say, but my gut tells me that there is something else going on in the case I am helping the DA put together."

"What does that mean?"

"It's almost too easy. For a high-profile case. The victim was allegedly involved in a relationship with the defendant's ex-wife. So, on the surface, the motive seems clear enough."

"Isn't sex one of the major motives for murder?"

"Absolutely," Kate agreed. "But this is quite different. … I cannot actually put my finger on it, but I seriously question whether sex actually played a part in this crime. For one thing, the defendant and his ex-wife had been divorced for two years. And while it is clear that the victim and the defendant's ex- were seeing each other, the relationship came as no surprise to the defendant. He had been aware of it for some time, and continued to play golf with the victim."

"Is he denying the charge?"

"No. And that's another curious element. He admits pulling the trigger. And he may have actually killed the man. But there is no evidence whatsoever tying him to the crime other than his admission, and the possibility of jealousy."

"What did his lawyers come up with for a defense?"

"Diminished capacity."

"Really? That is very strange. … Do they know what they are doing?"

"He is represented by Smith, Smith, and Rolly."

"Out of Chicago?"

"Exactly. And that doesn't make sense either. There are plenty of excellent lawyers in New York. So why engage a law firm that was based primarily in the Midwest?"

"That is curious," Jack said. "And why diminished capacity? Wouldn't it make more sense to defend the man straight up? If there's no evidence other than his admission?"

"Right," Kate agreed. "I've never defended in a murder case, but I truly believe I could get the guy off. … Like I said, the whole thing just doesn't make sense."

"Tell me, what does the prosecutor think about it?"

"She can't figure it out, either," Kate said. "If his lawyers prevail in the diminished capacity defense, the charge would likely be reduced to voluntary manslaughter—a Class B Felony, with a minimum of five years. Murder One would likely be a minimum of twenty years."

"But," Jack countered, "if there is no evidence against him, wouldn't the prosecutor be willing to plead it down, anyway?"

"Not sure. The DA is a bit of a hard ass about that. Even with a Murder Two—which is probably what it would plead to—the defendant could still be facing a fifteen-year sentence. With an admission like we have in this case, I couldn't see it pleading down to voluntary manslaughter under any normal circumstances."

"What's the diminished capacity defense based on?" Jack asked. "Do they have grounds?"

"Could be. The defendant was mugged last year. And there was significant brain damage—"

"And he's on precisely the same medications as were linked to other cases of diminished capacity?" Jack asked, completing her sentence.

"Exactly. Right down to the specific dose sizes. There is precedent."

"I think I get where you're going with this," Jack said. "You're thinking that this guy's lawyers want to settle the case by offering up their client on this lesser charge. What would he actually do? Three, four years?"

"Possibly as little as two and a half in lockup."

"And that would be the end of it. Case closed. … It's almost as though someone wants this whole matter to just go away. With your defendant as the sacrificial lamb. … And you say that there is really no significant evidence that he actually committed the crime, outside his confession? So, if he retracted his confession, where would you be?"

"Looking for a different suspect. As you can tell, I do not like the way this is going. I think we're being played, and there's nothing I can do about it."

"Where does the DA stand?"

"He seems to just want it to go away, as long as he gets his conviction."

"Not sure why you're calling me," Jack said. "Sounds to me like the fix is in, and you're the only one not happy about it."

"That's about right. This freight train isn't going to stop for me or anyone else. But that doesn't keep me from wondering why. There has to be something very significant going on for these high-priced lawyers to become engaged in so elaborate a ruse. If that's what it is."

"You said earlier that this was a high-profile case," Jack said. "Why so?"

"The victim was Judge William F. Christopher. And, he was not just any judge. He was a lifelong appointee to the D.C. Court of Appeals."

"The *D.C.* Circuit, you say?"

"Yes. The D.C. Circuit handles a lot of the cases involving rules and regulations."

Jack thought for a moment, and then asked, "When does your case go to trial?"

"In three days."

"Three days. So soon? I'm surprised I hadn't heard about it."

"Few have. It's almost as though there's been a media blackout. However, the event occurred over five months ago."

"Jury trial."

"No. Not for a diminished capacity."

"You're still planning on taking a week off afterward?"

"Right."

"Once it's settled, I would like to spend a little time looking at it with you. Be careful not to tip your hand. If there truly is something else going on, and you ask the wrong questions, you might get yourself hurt."

"That's why I'm talking to you."

"Oh shit!" Jack yelled. "Looks like Buddy might have got hold of a skunk. Going to have to deal with that right now. But I would really like to see what's behind this case of yours. We'll take a closer look next week."

"There is one more thing that I think you should be aware of," Kate said.

"What's that?"

"Allison Fulbright's name came up in discovery."

"*The* Allison Fulbright? The former first lady?"

"That's right."

* * *

Jack had a long and memorable history with both former First Lady Allison Fulbright, and her husband, former President Bob Fulbright. It started when one of Jack's close friends, Secret Service Agent Roger Minsk, who at that time headed up the President's Secret Service detail, introduced Jack to his boss. Minsk was recommending that Fulbright enlist Jack's help.

"Jack is a good friend of mine," Roger told his boss. "And I believe he is well equipped to deal with some of the issues that fall outside of the scope of what the Secret Service can provide."

The President trusted Minsk, so that was all he needed to hear. From that moment on, and until the end of the President's second term, Jack worked exclusively for the Fulbrights. However, because of the dark nature of some of the tasks assigned to him by the President, Jack was never permitted to actually enter the White House, nor did his name ever appear on any official records.

While Jack remained on good terms with the former president, his relation with Allison was less cordial. The reason for the strained relationship with the former first lady stemmed from his work a few years earlier to thwart an assassination plot against the sitting president—a conspiracy in which Allison played a major role.

After having destroyed the scheme, Jack never again fully trusted the woman. And she no longer sought out his help or advice. To a large degree, the two of them made every effort to avoid one another.

So, now to hear that Allison might be somehow involved in one of his daughter's cases, Jack was set back on his heels. *This could be a problem for Kate,* he thought as he disconnected the call. *Looks like I'm going to have to get involved, and quickly.*

* * *

"Uncle Jack!" Robby called out. "I think we're gonna need some help over here."

"Damn skunk!" Jack muttered, as he hastily made his way over to the commotion. "Did Buddy physically contact the skunk?" he asked.

He knew that skunks were nocturnal by nature. So, the fact that this one was out wandering around during the day might signal that it had rabies.

"No," Robby replied. "He just sniffed at it from a distance, and then got a face full. But he didn't fight with the skunk or anything. Just sniffed, and then backed off."

The boys had ceased walking along the trail when Jack signaled that he was going to take a call. But that would not suggest that they had switched off their inquiring teenage minds. And the same was true for Buddy, the boys' playful golden retriever. Still a puppy at heart, he had the inquisitive mind of a teenager.

While the boys investigated a hole in the ground next to an old woodpile, Buddy decided he would see what he could find to play with nearby. Buddy drew the boys' attention when he began barking at what the boys immediately determined was a skunk. But before they could convince their beloved four-legged detective to disengage, the skunk raised its tail and shot him with a copious stream of musky fluid. The discharge showered Buddy directly on his snout and lower left front quarter.

It could have been worse had the dog been attacking the skunk. Buddy, however, was only seeking a playful encounter from a distance, so the stream of stink was somewhat dispersed by the time it struck him.

"That's it," Jack barked at the boys, now sporting the broad smile he saved for situations like this.

"Let's head back to the resort … Load Buddy into the back of the pickup. You guys ride back there with him. No point stinking up the whole truck. All three of you are going to need a bath. When we get home, head directly to the river. Don't go *near* the house."

The house where Jack and the boys lived was located on the campus of Kate's Sugar Island Resort. It was set on the bank of the St. Mary's River, the principal shipping channel leading east from the Soo Locks.

* * *

Only moments had passed after Kate's call to her father had ended. She was still sitting in her office contemplating his comments when she received a call from the assistant district attorney she had been working with on the case involving Allison and the dead judge.

"What!" Kate blurted out. "That just can't be! … Have you confirmed that?"

Chapter 5

Jack drove directly to the boathouse, not stopping at the main house as he normally would.

"You fellows jump in the river. Buddy too. I'll round up the chemicals."

Robby flashed a puzzled look at Red.

"Chemicals?" he said. "Do you know what he's talking about?"

Jack, overhearing Robby's question, stopped and turned around to face the boys.

"Don't worry," he said. "It's just regular stuff we have lying around. Concentrated sulfuric acid and bleach. We've got 'em both. I'll only be a few minutes."

Jack turned away quickly to conceal his smile, and started driving toward the house.

For a long moment the boys followed Jack with their eyes, and then they faced each other with looks of concern. Finally, Red shrugged his shoulders and signaled toward the river with his right thumb, and then both boys dove in with their clothes on.

A few minutes later Jack emerged from the house with a bucket of his "chemical" concoction. After setting it in the back of his pickup, he returned to the house and carried out two more buckets.

As the boys were washing themselves down in the river, they could not help but wonder about what Jack was planning for them.

"I don't see any smoke," Robby said. "At least not yet."

"Okay, boys," Jack announced as he parked the truck next to where they were bathing. "A bucket for each of you. Wash yourselves down, and then take turns with Buddy. … And don't worry. It's just a little baking soda, Dawn, with a little hydrogen peroxide tossed in. Won't hurt you a bit, unless you drink it or get it in your eyes."

Red started laughing as he scooped a large handful of the St. Mary's and hurled it at Robby.

Jack set the three buckets down on the bank and took a seat on a nearby bench. But before he was able to get comfortable, he received a call from Kate.

For several moments he listened intently without saying a word. Finally he broke his silence.

"Justice Pelosi?!" Jack blurted. "How'd he die?"

"Preliminary report suggests natural causes," Kate replied.

"When did this happen?"

"Last night, I guess. They found him this morning."

"Really? And how did they conclude that he didn't have some help? Surely they don't have the autopsy back yet."

"Might not be an autopsy. Family doesn't want one."

"On an *Associate Justice of the U.S. Supreme Court*?"

"I understand he had a heart condition. He was sixty-nine."

"So what?" Jack countered. "When a public figure of that stature dies, there should *always* be an autopsy. … Who's running *that* show? Where did it happen? Was he at home?"

"He was up there by you."

"What are you saying?"

"He was staying at an exclusive resort in the U.P."

The term "U.P." to which Kate was referring stood for Michigan's Upper Peninsula.

"What resort?"

"The Huron Mountain Hunting Club."

"I know where that is," Jack replied. "It's about two hundred miles directly west of here. What was he doing there?"

Chapter 6

After ending the conversation with his daughter, Jack did a Google search on "Pelosi." He clicked on the first *Washington Herald* article he found on the topic.

"Associate Justice of the Supreme Court, Anthony Pelosi, found dead at a remote hunting lodge in Northern Michigan.

"The man who in his later years has become known for his commitment to a conservative interpretation of the Constitution, was pronounced dead earlier today by Dr. Frank Roberts, Marquette County Medical Examiner and Coroner.

"Dr. Roberts' preliminary determination listed the cause of death as natural, stating that 'there did not appear to be any sign of struggle, and that there was nothing else to suggest foul play.'

"He did add that 'due to the high profile of the victim, he would, as a matter of standard procedure, order an autopsy.'"

That's the main thing that Jack really sought to know—there *would* be an autopsy.

"Great!" he said aloud. *Now if they do it right, we just might learn something interesting.*

"After you're finished," he shouted in the direction of the bathing boys, "come up here and I'll check to see if you still stink. I can make another batch of that *skunk shampoo* if you need it. If you can still smell yourselves, just keep scrubbing … especially Buddy. He caught the brunt of it."

Jack then leaned back on the bench and dialed his friend Roger Minsk.

"Hey, guy, what do you think about it?"

"I assume you're talking about Pelosi?" Roger asked. "That sure does sound weird. Especially in light of that other judge."

"So," Jack said, "you're on top of the Christopher case?"

"I've been following it from a distance," Roger said. "Up until now it looked like most any other crime of passion. But, with the death of Pelosi, I think it might shed some new light on it."

"Kate's involved with the Christopher case. She called me this morning with some concerns. It's going before a judge in a few days. Likely to plead down to diminished capacity. At least that's what she suspects."

"Little unusual in a case like that," Roger replied.

"That's what we're thinking."

"And you called me … why?" Roger asked.

"Mostly because we have a mutual associate who is somehow involved."

"So, you've heard about Allison."

"Kate caught wind of her name. And she wondered if I had any info as to why Allison might be involved."

"You know, Jack," Roger said, speaking very deliberately, "As head of the former first lady's Secret Service detail, you and I cannot be having this conversation."

"Of course, we both understand that we cannot discuss it," Jack agreed. "But, that having been said, is there anything you *can* tell me?"

"I'm not in *that* loop—not anymore," Roger replied. "Not really.

There once was a time, back when Bob was president, that you and I would both be in this shit up to our eyeballs. But now there's a whole new batch of shady characters. And I've never heard of any of them. … I just keep my mouth closed, and I don't look anybody in the eye."

"Where's Bob come down on this?" Jack asked. He could tell by Roger's tone that his friend was concerned.

"As far as I know, he's not in on it. It's all Allison's show. I know I'd be a lot more comfortable about it if he were. She doesn't command the respect that her husband does. And she doesn't have his savvy, either. … There is one very interesting aspect. Remember, a few years ago, when she moved about using that assumed name? Bernadette Lowery? Well, she's doing it again. Only this time it's *Dana Reynolds*."

Jack remained silent for a long moment. As far as he knew, the last time Allison assumed a secret name was when she and a few of her close associates were hatching a plot to assassinate President Barry Butler, the sitting president."

"What the hell could she have in mind this time around?" Jack finally asked.

"Damned if I know," Roger retorted, clearly agitated.

"You sound concerned."

"I am," Roger admitted. "I have no idea where this is heading. As far as I know, she is not planning another run for the White House. … But, that still could be the case. I know she's convinced that Butler cheated her out of it. That's no secret."

"But all this begs the question," Jack said. "What could the deaths of two judges possibly have to do with her?"

"Four."

"Excuse me," Jack said. "Did you say *four*?"

"That's right. Prior to these most recent events, there were two other federal judges that have died mysteriously. One was only fifty-two, and the other in his early sixties."

"Murdered?"

"Heart failure."

"With or without a bullet?" Jack asked.

Even though Roger could not see his friend, he could picture an incredulous smile involuntarily creeping across Jack's face.

"Depends on your definition of bullet. Some chemicals can be every bit as effective at stopping a beating heart as a well-placed round from a .22 pistol."

"Were there autopsies in these other two cases?"

"One of the judges was autopsied. The other was cremated the day after he died. The family insisted."

"So?" Jack asked. "Was there anything suspicious in the death of the other judge? Did the autopsy turn up anything interesting?"

"It was ruled death by natural causes. He did have a pre-existing heart condition. And a mechanical valve. ... But the autopsy revealed a substantial amount of a rather exotic drug—Phytonadione."

"Never heard of it," Jack said. "What does it do? Does it have any medicinal purpose?"

"It is a type of Vitamin K," Roger said. "Vitamin K occurs naturally in plants and is typically absorbed into the body through dairy products. The body needs Vitamin K to facilitate the clotting of blood. Phytonadione is a man-made form of Vitamin K. Interesting characteristic of the compound is that it does not dissolve in water, but it will in grain alcohol. It is prescribed for patients who suffer from the inability to stop bleeding, and to treat certain liver problems."

"Any info that the judge was a bleeder?"

"No," Roger replied. "In fact, the judge was on warfarin—a powerful blood thinner.

"Not only did the judge suffer from heart disease, he was a prime candidate for a stroke as well. Three years earlier he actually had a brain-stem stroke. For a time he considered stepping down. But, because his recovery was remarkable, and he showed no signs of any brain damage, he remained on the bench."

"Then, what was this Phytonadione doing in his blood?" Jack asked. "If he had already suffered one stroke, certainly no doctor would have prescribed a blood *thickener*."

"No evidence that it was ever prescribed," Roger said.

No one spoke for a few moments, and then Jack said, "Where was this judge when he died? Was he at home?"

"Vegas," Roger said. "Apparently he had been invited to the grand opening of a new casino on the Strip."

"Who invited him?"

"Sipos, the Hungarian moneyman—"

"And benefactor of the Fulbrights' political machine," Jack interrupted.

"That's him. Alexander Sipos. He used to be hitched to Bob's wagon, but lately he's been working primarily on Allison's behalf. And his own, of course. … A good man for most of us to avoid, if at all possible."

"And the judge was the guest of this Sipos character?"

"That's right. Apparently he is heavily invested in some development projects on the Strip. And this judge was not only a principal in the development company, but was a personal friend of his."

"I'm not so sure he has friends," Jack said. "From what I've heard he buys people, uses them up, and then discards them. He's ruthless. … I was afraid of something like this … when Kate tied Allison's name to her case. And now Sipos. What the hell has my daughter got herself into?"

"Be careful, my friend," Roger said.

Jack disconnected the call, leaned back on the bench and gazed unfocused at a squabble of gulls winging about overhead. Their screeching penetrated his ears but not his mind.

And then, after listening to the gulls above and his three *kids* in the river for what seemed a long time, Jack lowered his head and speed-dialed Chuchip Kalyesveh, AKA *Henry*, his Native American friend and all-around handyman.

"Henry. Think I might be needing your help on a little project."

Chapter 7

The men wasted no time. Half an hour after Jack's call, Henry, who also lived on the resort's campus, dropped his duffle next to the bench and sat down beside Jack.

"Boss. What's up?"

"I hope nothing much," Jack answered. "But too much shit is piling up around Kate, and I'm getting a little concerned."

"What stinks?" Henry complained. "You gotta skunk in your pocket?"

"Still that bad, is it?" Jack said with a chuckle in his voice. "I guess I'm just getting immune. … Buddy tried to make friends with a striped kitty cat."

"But the skunk wanted no part of it," Henry said. "I can see that. Did you try peroxide, baking soda and Dawn dish soap?"

"That's what they're doing right now."

"Sometimes tomato juice will help cover up the smell."

"Uncle Jack," Robby called out. "You and Henry gonna take a trip? Can Red and I go?"

"You think I'd take you anywhere the way you stink?" Jack said. "And, besides, you and Red need to be minding your own business."

"Sorry," Robby said. "It's just that since we had to call off our hike today, we thought that maybe we could tag along with you and Henry. That is, if you were going somewhere."

The boys could read Jack like a book. They could see that he was preoccupied about something. That, along with the fact that he was enlisting Henry's company/help, suggested to them that there just might be something interesting about to happen.

But, when they observed Henry plopping down his bulging duffle—that nailed it. The boys knew that Henry's bag of tools signaled that an adventure was unfolding before their eyes.

"You boys are going to stay with Mrs. Fletcher. Henry and I have some business to take care of, and it might take us a day or two."

The boys knew better than to argue their case. Instead, they just stood silently in the St. Mary's allowing their pathetic eyes to plead their case.

Henry leaned forward so the boys could not see his lips move, and he mumbled to Jack.

"I'm not so sure she is going to want to deal with that stink—not in her house. And I know you don't want it in yours either. Maybe you ought to reconsider. … A little campfire smoke might do wonders."

Jack thought for a moment and then said, "Dry off. Put on your clean clothes. I'll gather up your camping gear. Meet me at the house, but don't go in."

Bounding to his feet and glancing at his watch, he announced, "I want to get going within the next fifteen minutes."

Henry jumped up, snatched his duffle and tossed it in the back of the pickup. *Fifteen minutes? Jack's in some kind of hurry. Must be an important mission.*

"Are you good for three days?" Jack asked Henry.

"Definitely."

Fifteen minutes after Jack's announcement, the five of them—Jack, Henry, Red, Robby and Buddy—were loaded into Jack's Tahoe and headed toward the Sugar Island Ferry. As was always the case with adventures such as this, Jack pulled a flatbed trailer with two John Deere Gators.

Chapter 8

One thing for sure," Henry said, "I'm not too sure about what you have in mind, but we're not gonna be sneaking up on anyone. Unless *eau de skunk* is an effective cover for this sort of mission. ... And, by the way, what exactly is the nature of the operation at hand?"

"Fact finding," Jack replied. "We'll gather some information, if we're lucky. Nothing more than that."

"Information about what, exactly?"

"Did you turn on the news this morning?"

"I thought that might be what you were up to," Henry said. "This has to do with that Supreme Court justice that died yesterday. Isn't that right? ... Do you suspect foul play?"

"Not necessarily," Jack said. "But I just learned that four federal judges have died within the past few months. Pelosi, who was an associate justice, is just the latest."

"I understand that he was staying at this exclusive hunting camp up on Huron Mountain, overlooking Lake Superior. That place is guarded like Fort Knox. How are we going to get in there?"

"It's not a crime scene yet," Jack said. "And it will probably never become one. Not if I'm correct about how it was pulled off. Of course, it could be purely coincidental. The justice was sixty-nine. And he did suffer from heart disease. He might very well have died from natural causes. But there was another judge who died in Las Vegas, and he had a trace amount of a drug that caused the blood to clot. That was a very unusual way to die. … If that was, indeed, what led to his death. Or, at least it is unexpected to find that drug in a person's body. The name of the compound is *phytonadione.* It's a synthetic form of Vitamin K. Ever heard of it?"

"Never. I've heard of *Special K*, but I'm sure it's not the same thing."

"Not at all."

"If it enhances blood *clotting*, does that mean it would be a drug of choice for hemophilia?"

"I don't know about that," Jack said. "But it would seem logical. At any rate, from what I understand, we would not expect to find it in a healthy person's body—at least not in any quantity."

"So, I think I'm getting it. You would like us to find out if there is any evidence lying around this resort camp that would suggest Pelosi was murdered."

"That's about it."

"Where are we going to look? It's going to be virtually impossible to even reach it … from *any* direction. I've heard that they've got armed guards stationed throughout the forest surrounding it, and especially around the main building. We'll be lucky to get within sight of the camp, much less search it."

"I'm thinking we will start with the trash," Jack said. "There'll be a dumpster. That should be relatively easy to find. All we should have to do is crack the first line of defense. The trash will certainly be located a good distance from the lodge itself."

"And what do we look for?"

"Anything that looks suspicious, I suppose. That's the best answer I've got at the moment. … We'll start with the trash. If we come up empty, and still haven't been detected, we'll consider entering the main building. It's just that there will undoubtedly be a lot of private security inside the camp. And if we do go in, we'll be even less sure about what we might be looking for."

Jack glanced up to see if the boys might have been tuning in to their conversation. First he checked Red, who was sitting directly behind Henry. And then he adjusted the rearview mirror so that he could see Robby. *Both sleeping*, Jack said to himself, as he readjusted the mirror. *That could mean a late night around the campfire.*

Jack always stowed his camping equipment, complete with three days' worth of clean clothes, water, food, and camping supplies, inside one of his John Deere Gators. And he kept that vehicle, along with a second Gator, securely strapped down on a flatbed trailer. That level of preparedness allowed him to be on the road within minutes.

It took them almost an hour and a half to reach Newberry, and another hour and change to hit Munising. They stopped at a gas station in Munising to fill up, and to use the restrooms, and then on through Marquette toward the thick forests surrounding Huron Mountain Hunting Camp.

"Wake up," Jack said, turning to face the sleeping boys. "We're almost there. Time to wake up."

"Did you bring a gun?" Jack asked Henry.

"I'm a convicted felon," Henry said as he popped open the glove compartment and removed a Glock 17. "You know I can't get caught with any type of firearm, or I'll go back to prison."

He pulled back on the slide to load a round into the chamber, and then verified that the clip was fully stocked.

"Got another clip in here?" he said, rummaging through the compartment until he located a second full clip. He leaned back enough so that he could slide the magazine down into the bottom of his jeans pocket.

"Where are we going to pitch our tents?" Henry asked.

"As close to the camp as possible."

"And where might that be?"

Just then two men stepped out from the forest and blocked them from proceeding. Each of them was armed with what appeared to be a fully-automatic carbine.

"Right about here," Jack said. "It looks like this might be the end of the line."

"They do look like they mean business," Henry said as he slid the Glock under his belt and covered it with his jacket.

"You boys are gonna have to turn around here," the man in charge barked at Jack. "From here on in it's private property."

"We just wanted to visit the camp," Jack said. "Can't we do that?"

"It's private. Unless you are an invited guest, or a member, this is all the further you can go. Are you a member?"

"No, I'm pretty sure I'm not a member. So, we'll just turn around right here and head back."

After Jack managed to get the Tahoe and trailer turned around, Robby asked, "Is that really it, Uncle Jack? Do we have to go back home already?"

"Not exactly," Jack said.

The sun had set less than an hour earlier, so there remained a slight glow in the western sky. Jack did not want the guards to see him pulling off into the woods, so after a safe distance, he found an old lumber trail that led into a clearing. He cut off the headlights and steered the Tahoe through the deep grass until he had reached a safe distance. He then turned on his headlights and proceeded until he found a suitable place to set up camp.

"This is it, boys," Jack said. "Time to get to work."

Excitedly, the boys, along with Buddy, jumped out of the truck and began pitching their tents.

But, there was a problem that they did not know about. Fifteen hundred feet above their vehicle circled a large drone. Because it had no lights on, and flew so high, no one in Jack's group was aware that they were being observed by infrared cameras. After a few moments the drone increased its altitude by another two hundred feet, and disappeared into the northern sky.

Just as Jack had suspected, the boys did not want to turn in. So they all sat around the campfire and told stories until it was nearly four in the morning.

Finally, the boys surrendered to their respective tents.

"Well," Jack said. "Are we ready to move in?"

"Absolutely. Let's do it."

Using the coordinates he had compiled from Google Maps, and a map of the terrain, he and Henry headed out of their camp on foot toward the Huron Mountain Hunting Camp. Little did they know that their presence had also been detected by a second drone, and now their every movement was being observed and recorded.

Chapter 9

"Where to first?" Henry asked.

"Their dumpsters. They've got a few of them. But they all appear to be at the rear of the building. Off the service road."

"How do you get all your information? That's not all on Google Maps. At least I don't think it is."

"A lot of it is, actually. But I also have an application, one that Roger gave me, that hooks me into the military's mapping satellites. They're a little more accurate."

"Does it show you if there are locks on the dumpsters?"

"We should just assume there are. That's why we've got bolt cutters."

"Okay," Henry said as they approached the wooden gate that blocked casual traffic into the area housing the four dumpsters—they were on foot. "Exactly what will we be looking for?"

"Really don't know," Jack said as he cut the lock from the gate.

"Let's hit this one first," Jack said. "You climb in, and toss the bags out. … All of them."

Henry complied with Jack's directive and began dropping the large clear plastic trash bags over the side. After the tenth bag, he lifted himself over the side and dropped down to where Jack was working.

"You're making one hell of a mess, boss," he said.

"It'll give them something to do in the morning," Jack quipped. "Besides, I'm sure the bears have done worse."

With only two bags remaining from the first dumpster, Jack abruptly put an end to the process. "Check *this* out, I think it might be what we're looking for."

"And I was just beginning to enjoy digging through their trash," Henry said as he leaned against the edge of the dumpster to see what Jack was talking about. "Whatcha find?"

"We've got a couple things going here," Jack said. "First of all, we've got a totally empty bottle of phytonadione. And in the same trash bag we have an empty vodka bottle.

"And not only is the bottle empty," Jack continued after he'd sniffed the top of the bottle, "it has been rinsed out with water. ... How many times have you ever rinsed out a vodka bottle before tossing it?"

Henry processed what Jack was saying, but he did not comment.

Finally, Henry said, "This might not relate, but in one of the bags we haven't gone through yet I can see what looks like about fifty or more warfarin pills just dumped in the bag. I don't see a bottle, just the pills."

"Really?" Jack said. "That could be significant as well."

"Should I gather them up?"

"Not all of them," Jack said. "Grab a few. I think that will give us what we need, along with this empty bottle of phytonadione, and the vodka bottle."

He slipped the evidence into separate plastic bags that he had brought for this purpose, and then sealed them.

"What's this?" he asked himself. "Looks like some sort of weird baseball. Almost. Hand stitched."

"Ever seen anything like this?" Jack asked Henry. "It's a little strange because it's got some serious blood stains."

"Can't say that I have."

"I'm ready to head back," Jack said as he tucked the ball in a small Ziploc bag, and then into his jacket pocket. "How about you?"

"Definitely."

Just as Henry turned to leave, the muffled crack of what sounded like a suppressed .223 sniper round broke through the silence of the night.

The bullet struck Henry in the left side of his upper chest. The force of the impact spun him around and he toppled to the ground.

"I'm hit, Jack," he said. "Leave me here and go. I'll just slow you down."

Chapter 10

Let me take a look at that wound," Jack said as he ripped open Henry's shirt. "Small caliber. I wouldn't be surprised if it were a .223. … Can you sit up? I want to see the exit wound."

Jack helped Henry lean forward enough so that he could determine whether the bullet passed all the way through Henry's chest, or if it was lodged inside.

"Not bad," Jack said after observing a relatively clean exit wound. "Probably a newer rifle."

Henry knew the significance of what Jack was saying. The older Vietnam era M-16's employed a 1:14 barrel. That meant that the bullet made one full turn every fourteen inches. This relatively slow twist caused the round to be substantially unstable. So, when it struck human flesh, it would almost immediately begin tumbling. This slowed the bullet dramatically as it passed through the body, producing damage to surrounding tissue to a radius of six or seven inches in every direction. Often the bullets from the older models lodged within the body, causing additional damage.

The new M-16's have a rotation ratio of 1:7—meaning that the bullet makes a full spin every seven inches. Not only does this result in a more accurate rifle shot, but rounds fired through a 1:7 barrel will strike their target at a velocity of up to 3100 feet per second, thus causing them to pass straight through a human body leaving a path of substantially less destruction. Such was the case with Henry.

"Not so bad, given that you were hit in the chest," Jack said. "This could have been a whole hell of a lot worse. We've got a relatively clean exit wound. Provided it didn't clip a major artery or vein, you should be okay. We've just got to get you out of here quickly—before they close in, or you will bleed out. ... Don't even think about staying behind."

Jack keyed his Garmin Rino 650 GPS 2-Way Radio using GMRS. "Robby, do you copy?"

There was no response.

He tried again.

Still nothing.

"Robby, do you copy?"

"Uncle Jack."

"We've run into a bit of a snag," Jack reported. "Need you to fire up a Gator and come pick us up. *Quickly*."

"Be right there."

"You can read our coordinates. Right?"

"Yes."

"Start out heading in that direction. Henry and I hiked straight in. Pretty clear, so you shouldn't have a problem. But stop two hundred yards short. We'll move in closer too. You should not pull all the way in—stop two hundred yards out. Henry's taken a round to his chest."

Jack had met Henry when both were serving time at a Federal Prison Camp. They first hit it off when Henry found out that Jack lived on

Sugar Island. While Henry was originally from Arizona, and currently resided in Missouri, part of his family had settled on Sugar Island. He even thought that he might have relatives still living there.

But their enduring friendship was cemented when Henry came to Jack's rescue after he had been severely beaten by other inmates.

Henry had found Jack unconscious and bleeding on the shower room floor with four thugs standing over him. They had dragged Jack underneath a showerhead, covered his head with a towel and were trying to suffocate him—sort of like water boarding without the board.

Henry took them all on at the same time, totally whipped them, and then called for medical assistance.

Jack was aware from the beginning that Henry had a reputation at the prison camp as one of the toughest inmates, but he did not know just how competent his friend was with his hands.

"He'll be okay," Jack replied to Robby. "Just don't come in too close. Two hundred yards, no closer."

"We're on our way."

"Great. Remember. No closer than two hundred yards."

"Got it."

"How's this going to work?" Henry asked.

"All we have to do is hit those woods," Jack said. "Fifty yards. Once we reach the woods we'll be tough targets. … I think that shot was fired from a substantial distance. For certain the shooter was using a suppressor. But I barely heard a thing. He undoubtedly has a great vantage point. So he will likely stay in place and wait for another clean shot. We just have to get out of here, pronto."

Jack then noticed a sizable pool of blood running out from under Henry's back.

"Looks like you're bleeding a little too much from the exit wound.

At least it's external, where we can get at it."

Jack placed his fingers on Henry's neck to check his pulse.

"Damn!" he barked.

It's way too rapid, and way too weak. Jack was thinking. *And he's getting cold. Got to stop the bleeding before he goes into shock.*

Jack ripped his own shirt off and tore it into several strips. He tied two of them together, end to end. He rolled up the third one and forced it into the hole in Henry's back. While holding it in place he wrapped the first two around Henry's chest, looping it over his right shoulder so that the knot was directly on top of the exit wound. He then tied the ends together as tightly as possible.

Jack scoured the area with his eyes looking for a suitable object to create a tourniquet. He spotted a broken oversized pallet lying at the opposite end of the fenced-in area. Without thinking Jack stood to his feet to retrieve it. As his head rose above the top of the fence the sniper fired. Fortunately, Jack was moving quickly and the bullet merely ricocheted off the dumpster.

Jack immediately dropped to his belly.

"Damn, that was close!" he muttered as he crawled on all fours over to the pallet. He ripped off a ten-inch piece of a broken board, and scurried back over to where Henry was lying. He slid the wood under the tourniquet and twisted.

Henry cringed in pain.

Jack continued cranking up the pressure until he observed that the bleeding had virtually stopped. He then placed Henry's hand on the piece of wood and told him to keep the pressure on the wound.

Henry complied.

"I've got to get you out of here right now," Jack said. "Before those boys get here. I'm afraid they just might keep heading this way and get themselves in some big trouble."

Jack helped Henry to his knees as he prepared him to make a run for it.

"I don't think I can stand up," Henry said. "I'm feeling pretty weak."

"Won't have to," Jack said. "I've got a plan. All I want you to do is to keep the pressure on that wound. Can you do that?"

"Yeah, but I can't run."

Chapter 11

The thought came to Jack when the round fired at him bounced off a dumpster. *Apparently the range is great enough to sufficiently drop the velocity,* he reasoned. *That's why the round didn't penetrate the steel.*

There was one dumpster that had wheels. *What if I can get Henry loaded in that one and roll him across the parking lot toward the woods. It could work.*

Jack scrambled on his hands and knees over to the wooden pallet and dragged it over to the dumpster. He tipped it up on end and leaned it against the dumpster like a ladder.

"There," he said aloud but to himself. "That ought to do it."

"Okay, Henry," Jack said to his friend. "Your limousine awaits. This is what I need you to do. I need you to slither up this ladder like a snake and drop into the dumpster. You can't raise your head at all. I'll be pushing on your feet. Ready?"

Henry was nearly out of it.

This has got to work perfectly, Jack reasoned. *And quick. Henry's about to go into shock.*

Jack helped drag Henry over to the makeshift ladder.

"Let's do it," he said.

Henry released his grip on the tourniquet stick, using his hands and arms to pull himself up the ladder. All the time Jack was pushing his feet.

"Okay, Henry, let's get out of here," Jack said. "Get yourself up that ladder. But, keep your head down. Pretend you're a snake."

Inch by inch Henry struggled his way to the top. As soon as he could get a good grip on the edge of the dumpster, he pulled himself over the top. Soon he was dangling into the steel box with only his legs remaining on the ladder.

Jack lifted his legs slightly and Henry tumbled in.

"There, that wasn't so bad now was it?" Jack said as he tossed the bags of evidence into the dumpster with Henry.

Jack took a look. The dumpster was almost facing the right direction—but not quite. "Damn," he muttered as he struggled to yank it clockwise a few degrees. "This would have been much easier before I loaded you in it!"

After a dozen efforts he satisfied himself that he had it pointing in the right direction.

He then removed his belt and looped it through one of the handles on the dumpster. Gripping the other handle in his right hand, he started the big box moving.

As soon as the sniper saw what was going on he opened fire. Round after round bounced off the black steel, and off the asphalt. Jack was able to position the dumpster between himself and the shooter. Little by little the downward slope allowed Jack to pick up speed. So, by the time the escape vehicle reached the end of the parking lot, Jack was running at nearly full speed. … *Full speed*, that is, for a guy pushing sixty from the wrong side.

Just before the wheels hit the soft earth, Jack wrenched the rear of the dumpster around. By doing that, he was able to use its momentum to cause it to overturn. Henry and the evidence bags came tumbling out. Jack grabbed the evidence in one hand, and ran his other under Henry's arm and helped him to his feet.

"This is it, Henry. We're going to have to make a run for it. You *have* to do it."

Within minutes, Jack saw what he assumed was the headlights of the Gator with the boys onboard. However, he was in for a disappointing surprise.

Chapter 12

The sniper fire had ceased several minutes earlier, as the two men were now hidden by the trees. Jack and Henry made their way as quickly as possible, approaching the point where they anticipated meeting up with the boys, and the Gator.

Jack called the boys again, allowing them to pinpoint his location using GPS.

Henry was preoccupied with his pain. Each step was an accomplishment. While Jack was supporting much of Henry's two hundred pounds, he was at the same time keeping a keen eye on the Gator's distinctive headlights.

The vehicle that was approaching was definitely a Gator. So, under Jack's guidance, the two of them continued on their approach.

But then something happened. The Gator stopped—totally stopped.

"Why would the boys do that?" Jack asked out loud. "They've got our coordinates. Why would they stop so far out?"

Then, upon hearing a noise above them, Jack immediately dropped to his knees in the wet leaves. He pulled Henry down with him.

As soon as they hit the ground, a beam of light shone down from above, illuminating them where they attempted to hide.

Jack quickly surmized that they was dealing with a low flying drone. He spun around and fired off three shots with his Glock. His rounds disabled the spotlight, and more. Within fifteen seconds the drone came crashing down only a dozen yards from where they were lying.

By that time the occupants of the Gator had opened fire on them with two fully automatic rifles. Fortunately, the shooters did not know their precise location, so all they could do was randomly spray the area with little accuracy.

Jack and Henry did not move. *No point in giving away our location*, Jack surmised.

When one of the shooters stopped to reload, Jack spotted a welcome sight. Bearing down upon the attackers from the rear was a second Gator. As they drew near the driver cut the lights, but did not slow down.

The gunmen were so intent on shooting up the entire forest they never saw it coming.

But Jack did.

The impact was devastating. Just seconds before the Gators collided Jack jumped to his feet and ran full speed toward the entangled vehicles.

"Boys!" Jack shouted. "You okay?"

"Seatbelts, Uncle Jack," Robby announced through the smoke. "We had our seatbelts on. … *They* didn't."

Jack reached the first shooter just as he was beginning to stand. Jack planted a roundhouse right to the side of his head, knocking him unconscious.

"Where's the other one?" he asked.

"He's in our Gator," Robby said. "He looks like he's coming around.

What should I do?"

"You've already done enough," Jack said. "I'll take care of him."

Jack dragged the second shooter over the side of the boys' Gator and laid him out with his friend.

"Toss me the Zap-Straps from my glove box. Think I should slow these fellows up a little."

Jack secured the men's hands in front of them and to each other. That way he concluded they could find their way out of the woods safely, but not quickly enough to present a problem to him or the boys.

"Who was driving this thing?" Jack asked.

"Why?" Robby asked. "Are we in trouble?"

"Oh, I should think so," Jack said. "Look at all the damage you did."

The boys just looked at each other but said nothing.

"I'm pulling your leg," Jack barked with a big smile. "You just saved Henry's life. That's what kind of trouble you Huckleberries are in. If you were old enough, I'd give you a cigar. A Cuban. ... C'mon. Let's get Henry to a hospital. ... Or something."

Jack's good mood quickly turned black when he drove the Gator up to where Henry was lying.

"Clear out that back seat," he commanded. "Make room."

Henry was a very large man. And he was now unconscious. So, the boys had to help Jack load him in the Gator.

"We don't have time to drive him. The hospital is going to have to come to us."

"Roger," Jack said after dialing his friend. "Henry took one in the chest. A .223 straight through. He needs serious attention right away."

"I show you in the middle of the woods near Powell. In the U.P. Does that sound right?"

"Not for long. As soon as we transfer Henry from this Gator into the

Tahoe we'll be headed for Marquette. If you could arrange for an escort. I'll be driving with four-ways flashing."

"Done."

"And this needs to be off the record. Can't have the locals getting involved."

"Are you leaving any bodies in the woods?"

"No."

"Then consider it done as well."

* * *

The boys helped Jack transfer Henry from the Gator to the Tahoe, and within minutes a Marquette deputy, with lights and siren, pulled his patrol car in front of Jack on Big Bay Road to provide escort.

"Be sure to keep that bandage pressed against Henry's back," Jack told Red.

"He's got it real good," Robby responded for his friend. "Henry opened his eyes for a second," Robby said. "I think he smiled."

Those words came as welcome relief for Jack. *He just might make it*, he thought to himself.

Less than ten miles from Marquette General Hospital, Jack's phone vibrated.

"Kate. You're up late. What's up?"

"Dad. I just got word from the prosecutor in this diminished capacity case. The suspect hanged himself. Or so it would seem."

"Kate. I've got Roger calling. Can I call you right back."

"I'm home. Call me when you can."

"Roger. What's up?"

"We've got another one, Jack."

"Another one what?"

"Another Supreme Court Judge has died. Chief Justice James Sutherland was just found dead."

"Same as Pelosi?"

"He was lifting weights in his basement. He dropped them and they crushed his throat."

"Rog, I've got to go. Almost reached the hospital. We'll talk later. Okay?"

"Kate," Jack said, calling his daughter back. "Just heard. Chief Justice Sutherland is dead. An accident, supposedly. … I'd like to see you get out of Dodge for a few days. Can you arrange it?"

Chapter 13

Now, with the defendant dead in the case she had been working, Captain Spencer, Kate's boss, had no problem allowing her to take an early leave for her anticipated vacation.

The boys were particularly pleased that she was headed up to Sugar Island. They thought that perhaps she would be willing to take them on the hike through the Osborn Estate—the one so abruptly ended when Buddy tried to make friends with the skunk. They always enjoyed it when Jack took them on adventures, but Kate was special in their eyes. She added a dimension of excitement Jack could not deliver, at least when it came to spicing up the more mundane of activities.

Of course, they'd be the last to minimize the exhilaration of playing bumper-car tag, in the middle of the woods, at night, with two men firing semi-automatic rifles. But that was the exception. That was just hanging out with their Uncle Jack while he was working.

But, to take the day off, pack a sandwich, and venture out on a hiking trail with no particular mission in mind—that sort of exercise was best carried out by Kate.

Getting Henry admitted to the hospital was a breeze. Roger had made all of the arrangements.

Jack and the boys stuck around until the doctor assured them that Henry had stabilized.

"Let's hit the road," Jack said. "Kate's eager to see you guys—I'll never know why."

Jack called Roger to fill him in on some of the pertinent details regarding their trash bin raid. Once Roger knew that Henry was doing well, he laughed out loud at the picture Jack painted of his high-speed dumpster rescue.

Roger's reaction: "I'd given my left ... pinky finger to have witnessed you running fifty yards. You're too old to be doing shit like that."

Roger also provided Jack with all the details regarding the death of the Chief Justice.

The boys were totally engrossed in the thought of having Kate home.

The next day, from the moment she got in their car at Chippewa County International Airport, they started their sales pitch coaxing her to take them on the skunk-interrupted expedition to Duck Island and the Chase Osborn Preserve.

And, understanding that a good salesman stops pitching as soon as the client says *yes*, the second Kate agreed to their request, they dropped the subject.

"About the Chief Justice—you don't buy that it was an accident, do you, Dad?"

Jack glanced over at her. She read his eyes.

"Is it even *possible* that no foul play was involved?" she asked.

"Here's the deal," Jack said. "Sutherland had just purchased a ten-thousand-dollar universal gym—four stations.

"He was found lying on an old weight bench. ... With his larynx crushed by a two-hundred and fifty pound barbell."

"That's a lot of weight for a guy his age, don't you think?" Kate asked.

"Exactly. Especially when he had the same capability on his new equipment. And, the weights didn't match. He had been working out with one hundred and fifty on the universal. And suddenly he's doing two fifty on the weight bench. That's a very unlikely scenario."

"And how many people would be pushing their limit on a weight bench without a spotter?" Kate asked. "I know I wouldn't."

"Not only that," Jack added, "if something gives out when you're lifting, like you develop a cramp, or feel a pull, you can shift the bar down and land it on your stomach. And then slide it off. I've had that happen, and never did I come close to dropping it on my throat. ... Too much doesn't make sense.

"So, to answer your question, no, I don't think it was an accident. In fact, it doesn't even appear that the killer wanted it to look like one, either. He was sending a message."

"Crush a man's throat," Kate continued Jack's thought, "and you discourage people from talking."

"Exactly."

"Who do you suspect?"

"Well, from what you said earlier, it sounded to me like Allison was somehow involved in your case. I would like to know more about her role in that. Whenever she has her hands in something, people seem to die. ... And then, I heard from a reliable source that Alexander Sipos has been spending a lot of time with Allison of late."

"Sipos. That Hungarian businessman?"

"That's him. But he's a lot more than a businessman. He is a major powerbroker—not just in this country, but throughout the world."

"What could they be up to? Hasn't Allison given up on her quest for the White House?"

"Never know about her," Jack said. "But think like this for a moment. What if someone ... someone like Sipos ... could come up with a plan to control—to manipulate—the makeup of the federal court system? Remember, back in the 2000 presidential election. The Supreme Court virtually handed the election to the younger Bush with their ruling on the Florida ballots. Sipos is a student of history. That event would have made an impact.

"And then consider that all the appointments to the federal courts are for life—all thirteen lower courts, and the Supreme Court. All those judges are appointed until they die, resign, or are impeached. They are not elected.

"So, just imagine the power a clever man could attain by controlling the makeup of those fourteen courts. Wrap your head around that."

"You think that's what's happening?" Kate asked.

"If a man is power hungry," Jack said. "If he wants to control the world. And if he is aging. Sipos is pushing seventy. He has to have started to realize that his days are numbered. If he is going to accomplish his goal, he needs to bet on a sure thing."

"And anyone who controls the courts in this country," Kate said, "can virtually run the show."

"Right. And America is the big enchilada. Rule America, and you will rule the world. That is, if you know how to play your cards right. And no one understands international currency manipulation better than Sipos. He's been doing it for years. He would rule the world right now were it not for the United States of America."

"And if he runs the federal court system, he will rule America."

"That's my theory," Jack said.

"What does Roger think?"

"Roger is in charge of protecting the former first lady," Jack said. "If he ever did *anything* to jeopardize that gig, and she were to find out, we'd be attending his funeral. … And probably mine, because she knows we're friends. And then there's the matter of his job—he is the head of her Secret Service detail. He takes that responsibility seriously."

"Aunt Kate," Robby said, leaning forward and tapping her on the shoulder. "Red and I were wondering if tomorrow would be a good day to go on that hike."

Kate looked over at Jack.

"How could you say no?" he said. "That's all they've been talking about. Besides, I think it's time for you to meet Mr. Skunk."

"I think I already have, unofficially. I can smell skunk in your truck."

"Really? I thought we had that licked," Jack chuckled.

"I need to go visit Henry, too," Kate said. "Maybe we can see Henry later today, or first thing in the morning, and then do the hike tomorrow afternoon. Mr. Skunk will probably be sleeping in until at least the afternoon. No promises about tomorrow, just best efforts."

The boys had what they wanted—an *almost promise* for the next day. So they sat back in their seats and allowed Jack and Kate to talk.

Jack told her about the evidence he had gathered at the hunting club. Kate told him she could expedite the lab work. She explained that, as a lieutenant, she now had the authority to put through *rush requests*.

Jack considered her offer, and then said, "Not so sure it would be good for your career to become so intimately connected with *this* evidence. Better to have Roger take care of it."

They discussed what their next step might be … after the hike, of course. They decided not to personally try to investigate the death of the chief justice, mostly because they were both certain that the FBI would be all over it.

Instead they would concentrate on Associate Justice Pelosi's recent demise. They knew that the FBI would not take over until the autopsy came back.

But that's all the further the discussion went, at least for that day. Even though Jack was driving five over the speed limit on Highway M-28 between M-123 and Paradise, a dark SUV with tinted windows sped past them. As it did, the passenger's window opened just as it drew even with Jack. A Glock 17 emerged from the SUV and four shots were fired in rapid succession, followed by a fifth.

As soon as he had seen the barrel emerge from the window Jack immediately slammed on the brakes.

The first four rounds struck the door of Jack's Tahoe. The last one was aimed at his head. It struck and shattered the driver's door window.

Three of the first rounds pierced the Tahoe's door and struck Jack. One bullet hit the door handle and did not penetrate further.

Because he had nailed the brakes so quickly, the fifth round missed hitting Jack directly. It passed through the glass beside and in front of his head, and then exited through the front passenger window, narrowly passing behind Kate's head when she was launched forward by the rapid braking.

While that final shot did not hit Jack directly, it did propel thousands of tiny splinters of glass, with many of them pelting the side of his face, including his left eye.

Even though he was in immense pain from the bullets he had taken to his side, Jack guided his truck to the shoulder of the road.

"Dad!" Kate screamed.

"Check on the boys," Jack said, forcing the words out of his mouth.

"Are they okay?"

After Jack slammed the shifter into park, he removed a pen from the visor and wrote the plate number down: BHI 3712. It would not have been necessary for Jack to log the number, but he did not yet know the severity of his wounds.

"You guys okay?" Kate asked as she turned to physically inspect each of them.

Both nodded.

"Buddy's okay, too," Robby said.

"Don't try to brush the glass off your clothes. You'll cut your hands. I'll take care of you when we get home."

"Where are you hit?" Kate turned back to her father and asked.

"At least twice in the side. Maybe three. It hurts like hell."

He then took a few deep breaths, checked his mirror and shoved the shifter into reverse.

"What are you doing?" Kate asked.

"That was a Glock 9mm. There's going to be some casings. I want to get one before they get run over."

Chapter 14

Sit tight, Dad," Kate ordered, as she slipped on a pair of latex gloves. "I'll find your casings."

Jack did as his daughter said and remained behind the steering wheel.

"Uncle Jack," Robby said. "How bad are you hurt?"

"I'm fine," Jack responded, forcing a smile as he turned his head back to make eye contact. "The door slowed them up a lot, and the Kevlar did the rest."

By *Kevlar*, Jack was referring to the synthetic material used in bulletproof garments.

Earlier that day Jack had received five new Kevlar vests, and one K-9 Ballistic Vest. Roger had express shipped them upon hearing about Henry's getting shot.

Even though Jack's current stock of personal protection was only three years old, upon receipt of Roger's gifts he immediately donned one of the new vests. He also made each of the boys and Buddy put one on as well. He correctly assumed that Kate would be wearing her NYPD issued protective garment. However, he did bring one of the new ones for her *just in case.*

Ever since Jack worked with Roger during the Fulbright administration, the former president made sure Roger kept Jack's protective garments up to date. It was common knowledge that the fibers in Kevlar products begin to separate with age and heat, so when he heard about Henry's misfortune former President Fulbright had Roger ship the newest products available.

Jack recognized immediately that his life might have been saved because of the switch. While his old vest was still well within the expiration date, Jack could easily see that the newer unit provided substantially greater protection against an attack from the side.

As he sat waiting for Kate to secure evidence from the scene, Jack held his tingling left hand out in front of him and flexed his fingers. He then felt around to see if he was bleeding from his left side.

Observing that he detected no blood on his upper arm, he began to examine the flesh beneath the vest.

Carefully using the fingers from his right hand to probe the injuries to his left side, he was again relieved to discover that there was no evidence of entry. While he was suffering from an enormous amount of pain, he was quite certain that the vest had protected him.

Kate, walking up to the gaping hole that had been the side window, announced that she had located two of the spent 9mm. casings.

"Besides your face, how are you?" she asked.

"Bruised and battered," Jack sighed. "But I don't think there are any bullet holes. … What do you make of my eye? I can't open it. How does it look to you?"

"I think you might have some glass still stuck in your face. So you probably took a piece or two in the eye. If you can manage to take a seat on the passenger side, I'll drive you in to the hospital. But you need to keep that eye closed until the doctor can take a look at it."

When Jack stepped out of the Tahoe Kate took a closer look at his side.

"Two of the rounds are stuck firmly to your vest," she reported. "One probably dropped to the floor. We'll locate it later. But, good news, there are no entry wounds. Some very red flesh, but nothing made it through or around your vest.

Jack would not allow the boys to observe his suffering, so he stood tall as he walked around the front of the Tahoe. He did, however, drag his right hand along the hood of the truck to help maintain his balance.

He breathed deeply as he tried to get comfortable in the passenger seat.

"Let me help you with that seatbelt," Kate offered.

Jack just smiled and said, "Thanks, but I can handle it. I'm a little slow right now, but I'll be fine."

It took him a minute to attach the ends of the seatbelt. Once he had accomplished the sought-after *click*, he reached his right hand back and pulled the lever allowing him to put his seat back a few degrees.

"I trust you're not reporting this. Right?" Kate asked.

"No point. The investigation will do better without interference. … My big takeaway from yesterday, and today, is this—I've got to do a better job with the boys. I cannot continue exposing them to harm. It's just not right for me to keep doing stuff like this."

"I don't know what you could have done," Kate said trying to console her father. "This attack occurred in broad daylight and on a public high—"

"Stop and pull off right here!" Jack commanded as he grabbed a full magazine for his Glock out of the glove box.

Kate did not question him. She slammed on the brakes and pulled off.

"Stop here for a second and let me out. I've got something to do. Drive up to that house and take the boys inside!"

With his Glock in his right hand, and the spare magazine gripped gingerly in his painful left hand, he sprang out of the Tahoe, nearly losing his balance as he hit the ground.

"Go!" he shouted. "Get out of here!"

Jack had spotted a dark vehicle heading toward them from the opposite direction. He was watching for it. *The shooters don't know whether or not they got me,* he thought. *They're going to want to confirm their kill, or they will not be able to collect.*

There was a culvert under the driveway where Kate had dropped him off. Jack thought about using it as cover should he be right about the approaching vehicle, but when he observed just how much his gun hand was shaking from the pain his body was suffering, he thought better. *If they're the shooters I'm going to have to get in close or I'll never hit them,* he reasoned.

So, instead of ducking into the culvert, he started walking on the side of the road facing the oncoming vehicle, but on the opposite side.

If that is indeed them, he thought, *they will recognize me and stop. The actual shooter is not the driver, so it will make it awkward for them. They'll have to stop, and the driver will be forced to confront me, unless the passenger gets out. He's going to want to get a clean shot at me, and he can't do that unless he gets out.*

Jack carried his Glock at the end of his extended right arm, keeping it slightly behind his right leg. His face was pointing straight down the road, while his eyes were fixed on the vehicle.

Just as he suspected, the dark SUV screeched to a stop directly opposite him. The driver opened his window and pointed a semi-automatic pistol at him.

Jack turned abruptly and ran toward the driver's window, squeezing off as many rounds as he could as he approached.

The driver managed to fire only once before Jack's bullets killed him.

Jack observed the passenger door opening.

Jack knew that the gunman was out of the vehicle, *but is he coming around from the front or the rear?* he asked himself.

Jack moved toward the rear of the vehicle and took refuge behind the rear wheel. There he dropped to his knees and peered beneath.

He spotted the man's feet.

I've got eight rounds left, he reasoned.

Without wasting another second Jack fired six rounds into the man's ankles and feet. The man began screaming in pain.

"Toss it where I can see it!" Jack shouted.

"Help me!" the gunman shouted. "Here's my gun. You blew my feet off. I need help."

Jack heard the Glock strike the pavement and slide toward the rear of the vehicle, but he did not move.

"Who hired you?" Jack asked.

"I need a doctor! I'm bleeding out!"

"Tell me who hired you and I'll get you a doctor."

"I don't know. Someone out of New York. *I don't know who it was.* I'm dying! Get me a doctor!"

Even though Jack knew that multiple rounds into a man's feet could easily cause him to go into shock, and that he probably would die, he still didn't move.

"How'd you get the contract? You have to know something."

"A woman from New York. I never saw her. She sends me a text, and I take care of it. She goes by the name of Dana, but that's not her real name. I have no idea who she really is. But I think she's very important.

"She has a woman who works with her. A real looker. Her name is Emma. I call her Legs. I usually deal with her.

"Now. I've answered your question. Will get me some help?"

"*Dana?*" Jack quizzed him, recalling his earlier conversation with Roger regarding the woman they both knew who sometimes went by the name of Dana. "How do you know she's from New York?"

"Damn it! I *don't* know. Not for sure. I've just heard *that* she is. *Oh, God!* Are you gonna get me some help?"

Jack could tell by the amount of blood the man had lost that he was going to die, so he kept pressing for more information.

"What's *your* name?" Jack asked.

"James Bond! ... Oh my God. This hurts!"

"Who else did she have you kill? And what can you tell me about this Emma woman?"

"Damn you! I'm as good as dead if I tell you any more."

"If you ask me," Jack said. "I'd say your fortunes are not so good as they stand right now. Not without my help."

"I helped poison a guy. Further upstate. ... I think he was some kind of a judge. An important one. As for Emma, I just know she works for Dana. ... Now, are you going to get me a doctor?"

"Poison?" Jack quipped. "You don't seem like the *poison* type."

"That's how she wanted it done."

"How'd she pay you? Check? Cash?"

"Gold, damn it! She sent me gold bullion."

"Got any of it with you?"

"You sonofabitch. You're shakin' me down. … Yes, as a matter of fact I do. It's not bullion. I have five twenty-franc Napoleon coins. She gave them to me as a tip for a good job. Come here, I'll give them to you. Just call me a doctor. An ambulance."

"I'll call you an ambulance. But first take them out of your pocket and toss them one at a time under the vehicle and over to me."

Jack removed a pair of latex gloves from his pocket and gathered up the coins as the wounded man whipped them in his direction.

"Five?" Jack said. "Did you say there were five?"

"Handler. You picked up five. I saw you. You know how many there are. … I've lost a lot of blood. If I don't have a doctor soon, I'm not going to make it."

"Yeah, I'll take care of that. But tell me, who's your next target?"

The man didn't respond.

Jack, looking down under the vehicle to make eye contact, smiled and said, "After me, of course."

"Another judge. This one in California."

"Where in California? And what's his name?"

"Thompson, I think. He lives on a mountain just outside San Francisco."

"Did you have the contract by yourself?"

"I own the contract, but I've farmed it out to a buddy. … Actually it's my brother. He's gonna take care of it."

"When does that go down?" Jack asked. "The Thompson hit?"

"I'm not going to say another word until you call me an ambulance."

Jack slid over enough to take a peek at the dying man. *What the hell is that?*

Jack said to himself. *Looks like an empty ankle holster to me.*

"Okay," Jack said, "have it your way." He then leaned over again and shot the man squarely in the forehead.

Jack then raised himself up enough to lean back on the wheel. He tried to take a deep breath, but his ribs hurt too much.

He could see Kate approaching on foot, but still well up the driveway, gun drawn.

He managed to raise himself to his feet by leaning against the still-running SUV.

After he had reached through the open window and turned off the ignition, he unhooked the driver's seatbelt and pushed him over so he could remove the man's wallet. As he tucked it in his pocket, Jack's foot brushed against the driver's Glock where it had fallen on the road. He picked it up and slid it under his belt.

Jack then walked around and seized the same items from the man on the ground.

"Kate, pick up the boys and drive back out here," Jack said as Kate approached.

"Everything okay?" she shouted.

"All's well. I just want to scoop up a little of the evidence from inside the vehicle, and there appears to be too much for me to carry."

It took Kate a few minutes. Jack wasted no time. He gathered up everything that was visible, including the vehicle rental papers. He then went through the glove compartment, and the center console. He opened one of the two suitcases that were lying on the back seat and tossed the two wallets and the rest of his findings in it.

By the time Kate reached the road, Jack was standing alongside it looking more like a hitchhiker than Harry Bosch. He walked to the rear of the Tahoe and tossed the suitcase he had opened into it, and then returned to the front passenger seat with the other one.

"Let's get out of here while we still can. ... Were there any people in the house?"

"No, it was empty and unlocked. Did anyone see you?"

"No one could identify me. A couple cars passed when I was going through the vehicle, but no one got a look at my face."

"What's up with the suitcase?"

"It's locked. Pretty good, too. It feels much heavier than the other one. I'd like to get a look inside."

"Is it booby-trapped?"

"Not likely," Jack said. "These guys were contract killers, not spies. But it does feel much heavier than clothes. I'll wait until we get home."

"Firearms?" Kate asked.

"Could be, but I suspect something much more sinister."

Kate did not ask a follow up, but she did frown. *What could be worse?* she asked herself.

The boys were wondering the same thing.

* * *

As soon as they arrived at the resort Jack spirited both pieces of luggage off to his shop, which was located inside the boathouse about a hundred yards from the house. Not only did he wish to inspect the suspicious suitcase far enough away from Kate and the boys in the event that his worst suspicions were correct, but he wanted also to dispose of the Glock he had just used to kill the two men.

So, before he endeavored to pick the lock on the suitcase, he fired up a small Oxy/Acetylene clay-lined smelting crucible—one he maintained for just such a purpose.

While the unit heated up, he went into the bathroom to inspect the damage to his face and eye.

Holding his left eyelid up with his right hand, using the edge of a facecloth he managed to dislodge the small piece of glass that had knifed into his eyeball during the initial attack. He blinked several times.

"Damn, Handler," he said. "Your face looks like shit."

Using a dampened washcloth he wiped off most of the blood and glass.

"Much better," he proclaimed.

He then removed the magazine from his pistol, as well as the round that was in the chamber, turned on the vent fan, and tossed the gun into the melting pot.

After he had pulled the prints from the shooters' guns, he test fired each of them in a tank of water, logging the cartridge and bullet to the serial numbers of the two pistols. He then stripped them down and dropped them in with his Glock.

It will take a while to melt them down, he said to himself, *let's see what I can find out about this suitcase.*

"Okay, boys," Jack said, addressing the two men he had just killed. "Let's see what it was that you were hiding."

Chapter 15

Might this be a bomb? Jack wondered as he examined the suitcase as objectively as possible.

"Who would spend two and a half thousand dollars on a high-quality piece of luggage like this, only to blow it up?" he asked himself.

He reasoned that no one smart enough to make a bomb would use a suitcase that might get stolen. *Anyone with a brain would use a cheap suitcase—a piece of junk. So, I don't think this is a bomb. ... But, it would not surprise me if it is being used to transport explosives, or some other compound. Perhaps, even gold? It's too damn heavy for it to be much else.*

Jack then powered up an airport security grade explosive detection device—known in the vernacular as a "puffer." Jack's unit utilized mass spectrometry technology, which can detect sixteen explosive compounds with ten to a hundred times more sensitivity than devices using the less sensitive ion mobility spectrometry technology.

"I'll just bet we've got some bad stuff here," Jack said aloud as he began to analyze the contents of the suitcase. "I wonder what it is."

As soon as he saw the results of his testing he immediately set the puffer sensor down and stepped back.

"Holy shit!" he exclaimed. "TATP!"

Just then Kate opened the door to his shop and said, "Knock. Knock."

"This is insane," Jack said, looking over at his daughter. "Why in hell would anyone even consider using a piece of expensive luggage like this to transport cheap, homemade explosives?"

Kate stopped.

"So, it is a bomb?"

"TATP. The explosive of choice for suicide bombers."

Kate just stared at the suitcase for a moment, and then said, "Triacetone triperoxide? Is that what's in the suitcase? Don't they refer to that as the *Mother of Satan*? Because it's so unstable. … Are you sure?"

"I'm no bomb expert," Jack said, taking another two steps away from the workbench, "but this very expensive piece of equipment just told me that's what it is. I'm not about to question the results. … I think it's going to be right."

Jack fully understood the dangers associated with triacetone triperoxide. This meant that he was aware of the extreme volatility of the explosive. Had he even suspected that he was dealing with TATP, he would never have removed the luggage from the shooters' vehicle in the first place, and he most certainly would not have transported it in the Tahoe with Kate and the boys.

It is ideally suited for suicide vests and shoe bombs for a number of reasons, not least of which is its simplicity—and can be made in your kitchen using materials you can purchase at any Walmart store.

All you need to buy is hydrogen peroxide, salt, and acetone. And then remove the acid from your car's battery, and ice from your freezer. If you want to get fancy, you could purchase a model rocket igniter to detonate the bomb, but it would not be necessary because TATP devices can be exploded by using heat, fire or impact.

For twenty dollars a bomber can produce enough highly volatile explosive material to kill a hundred people at an airport.

"TATP?" Kate said with an incredulous furrow of the brow. "Aren't these characters supposed to be *professional* killers? What would they be doing with something like that? … I should think that they'd be using C-4, or some more sophisticated explosive. Not something as unstable as TATP."

"So it would seem," Jack said, still standing at a distance from the suitcase. "This stuff is so volatile it's even used to make detonators."

"Wasn't it TATP that the terrorists recently used for their suicide vests in Paris and Brussels?"

"Right," Jack replied. "That's what makes me wonder just what they were intending to use this for. … Hell, dynamite is even more effective than this stuff. Harder to obtain, I suppose. But it's more stable. I would think that a real professional contract man … he'd be using something more high-tech. … Unless, of course, he wishes to make people *assume* it was an act of terrorism. To disguise its origin."

"That's just what I was thinking," Kate said. "But where? And to kill whom?"

"Just before he died," Jack recalled, "the main shooter told me that he had been contracted to take out a judge in San Francisco. I believe him. He even gave me the judge's name. Thompson."

"Judge Lawrence Thompson. Of the Ninth Circuit," Kate said.

"Then you've heard of him?"

"Yes. Most definitely. He has been the topic of discussion with my girlfriend—the prosecutor. Discussion, or debate. I'm not sure how best to describe it."

"I've never heard of him," Jack said. "So, what's the scoop?"

"He's a relatively recent appointee—seven or eight years ago. Started out conservative. But, as soon as he began to find his way around, he started voting with the progressives. That was totally unexpected. … Some thought he was being groomed for the Supreme Court. But that's never going to happen now. But, get this, now he's aligning himself again with the conservatives. Something has to be very wrong with him. He can't seem to find himself."

"And he probably never will, especially if he's dead," Jack said.

"Do you think he's been targeted for his judicial views?"

"Would seem so. If what you say is correct, some people are undoubtedly disappointed in him. They expected him to lean in one direction, and he rules the other way. And, if he was being considered for the highest court, then that has to be particularly frustrating to the powers that put him on the bench in the Ninth."

"Do you think that these explosives were to be used to take him out?" Kate asked.

"No. That would be very unlikely. I doubt that those guys would have attempted to transport this sort of explosive for any great distance or across any state line. TATP devices are manufactured in the area where they are intended to be used."

"How about a bridge?" Kate asked. "We've got the International Bridge, and the Mackinac Bridge nearby. Or the Soo Locks. Could any of them be the target?"

"Wrong type of explosives, and not enough of it. This would likely be used in an anti-personnel device. … We should be looking at airports, museums, political gatherings, theaters—venues like that. Since the psychological impact would be greater downstate, I think targets like Detroit International Airport, or the Gerald R. Ford International in Grand Rapids—both of them would make sense. Anywhere that there is a large gathering of people, and media coverage. Terror never occurs in remote areas. Think about it. And this bomb is designed for terror."

"Could there be a timer in it?"

"Possibly," Jack said. "But I'm thinking that this bomb could be a ruse to cover up the judicial assassinations. … What if someone were to carry it into an airport? It could kill a hundred people without even going through security. It would look like your garden-variety act of terror. So, if a judge is killed in Detroit or Grand Rapids the day of or the day after a bombing, which event gets the media coverage? The bombing, of course. Especially if the assassination is made to look like an accident, or from natural causes."

"So, you're suspecting a judge might get hit somewhere in the Lower Peninsula?"

"This goes totally to conjecture," Jack replied. "I just don't think that these guys are in any way sympathetic to terrorism. But they might use it for misdirection … to cover up what they are actually up to."

"Which is killing federal judges."

"That's how it looks to me."

"Are you ready to lay this out to Roger?" Kate asked. "He could have some information that might add some light."

"You should head back up to the house and pack some stuff for the boys," Jack said. "Use your Tahoe to drive them over to the Fletchers'."

Kate kept a late-model white Tahoe in the garage for use on her visits.

"The boys need to be as far from here as possible until this all gets sorted out."

The Fletchers were the assistant caretakers at the resort, and frequent caregivers to the boys. Unlike the Lundgruns, who were the resident cooks and caretaker at the resort, the Fletchers lived off campus, and so were able to offer the boys the safety of distance from *ground zero*.

"And, Kate," Jack said just before she closed the door behind her, "stay with the boys until you hear from me."

She nodded and said, "Love ya, Dad. Take care of yourself."

There were a few reasons Jack had asked his daughter to leave while he placed his call to Roger. Plausible deniability was one of them. It could do Kate no good to hear Jack's conversation with Roger. He would later fill his daughter in on what she needed to know, but that would be it.

Second, both Jack and Kate recognized the fact that they were in violation of federal law just being in possession of a weapon of terror.

Finally, they were dealing with a bomb. And Jack was very much aware that bad things often happen when explosives are involved—particularly volatile explosives.

"Roger, I think I've got a problem."

Jack explained to Roger everything he knew about the two men who had attacked him, and told him about the contract on Judge Thompson. Jack also explained to Roger his dilemma with regard to the TATP device that was now in his possession.

"Do you have any information on this?" Jack asked. "Or recommendations?"

"Give me a few minutes to ask around," Roger said. "I'll call you back."

While he was waiting, Jack dusted the gold coins for fingerprints.

He was hoping to identify the woman who had given the coins to the shooter, but there was only one set of prints on them, and they were the same prints as he had pulled off the shooter's gun.

This is not going to have a very happy ending, Jack began to think. *There is no reasonable way for me to dispose of this bomb. And it will not be good for me to be found in possession of it.*

Thankfully, I did not leave my prints on it. Nor on any of the rest of their shit. But it is still in my possession. And, if the Feds run my Tahoe, or me, they will undoubtedly turn up some TATP.

What if I dropped all of it off out in the middle of the St. Mary's River? he asked himself. *But I can't do that. Disposing of a bomb of this type is too important to simply toss it in the river. This is one hell of a dilemma.*

Jack's phone vibrated.

"Yes, Roger."

"Jack, you've got a big problem."

"I'm aware of that," Jack said. "But you obviously know something I don't."

"Do I ever," Roger said. "That package you've got there, that's not just a bomb. It is that, for sure, but it's a lot more."

"I'm listening," Jack said.

Chapter 16

It might already be too late to get out," Roger warned.

"What do you mean?"

"The Feds are already aware of that bomb. They've received a tip. Apparently someone well up the ladder informed the FBI that there was a large bomb stolen from a vehicle on M-28, and that it was headed for Sugar Island. Not sure if your name came up, but when Sugar Island is mentioned, so does your name, eventually."

"I'm not sure I know what that means. Who could have warned them?"

"Whoever contracted those two guys to kill you. At least that's what I would guess. I'd say that the Feds are on the way to the island right now, and that they are going to make a beeline to your house."

"How much time do I have? I sure as hell don't want them to find the bomb on my property."

"Don't know exactly, but could be quite soon."

Jack thought for a moment, and then asked, "This is not a dirty bomb, right?

"No. It's pretty standard TATP. With the addition of shrapnel it'll do a lot of damage to everything within a short distance."

"And how did you find all that out? ... Never mind. I appreciate your help, and I'll be in touch when I get this all ironed out."

Jack ran as fast as a man with three broken ribs can run. "If this puppy starts, my plan just might work," he said as he jumped into the driver's seat of a 1982 ATV. He had earlier given Henry the project of restoring the Honda Big Red ATC 200E, but he did not know if his friend had finished it or not.

"It started!" Jack said out loud. "And it's got gas. This must be my lucky day."

He chuckled when he listened to himself. *How can a guy get shot three times, end up with a face full of glass, and still call it his lucky day?* he thought. He looked around until he located a short stack of red shop cloths. He snatched up two and stuck them in his pocket.

He drove Big Red back to his shop, scooped up everything he had removed from the shooters' vehicle, including the two suitcases, strapped the bundle down on the ATV, and set out through the woods.

Henry's not going to be very happy when he hears about Big Red, Jack calculated, *but it is the only vehicle at the resort for which there is no paperwork.*

It was on site when Jack and Kate took possession of the resort. At one time Jack did a search on the vehicle, and it came back as having been stolen. Apparently, long before Jack and Kate took possession of the resort, a guest had left the ATV and never returned to claim it.

"Kate," Jack said after dialing his daughter. "I need you to pick me up. Leave the boys at the Fletchers and meet me up on Brassar just north of Lecoy. Wait at the intersection until you see me. Can you be there in ten minutes?"

Jack headed out onto a trail that led into the forest. When he got close to Brassar, he stopped the three-wheeler and removed the gas cap.

He stuffed one of the shop cloths into the gas tank until it was saturated. He pulled most of it back out, leaving a corner of it in the tank.

He looked at his watch. "Nine minutes. That works."

He then touched a match to the gas-soaked cloth, and headed for his rendezvous with Kate.

"Dad!" she exclaimed. "Is that smoke?"

"Sure is," he said. "Isn't it beautiful?"

Kate did not know how to answer that question.

"Where should I go?"

"The boys are safe?"

"They're with Mrs. Fletcher."

"We should get off the island then," he said. "Before long this place is going to be crawling with the Feds."

"I suppose I should not know what you're talking about," Kate said.

"That's right," Jack agreed. "Better you don't know."

They had not traveled more than a few hundred yards when the Tahoe was shaken by a massive explosion.

"Wow! That was incredible!" Kate said. "All that power was compressed into that little suitcase! It's just amazing."

"I'm a little surprised it didn't explode when I was bouncing along on the trail out there."

"Never underestimate the power of a woman," Kate said through a smile.

"What does *that* mean?" Jack asked after thinking about her words.

"TATP," Kate replied. "The *mother* of Satan."

Both rode quietly for a few minutes, and then Jack's phone vibrated.

He took a look at it, and then at Kate.

"It's Roger. Crank your hearing aid down for a minute while I talk to him."

Chapter 17

"Whereabouts are you, right now?" Roger asked.

Jack knew that his friend was tracking him, and what Roger was really asking Jack was where he was headed.

"About to board the ferry and get off the island while I can. What do you have in mind?"

"That bomb. Had you not intercepted it, rumor is that it was to be detonated in some major location of importance … as soon as tomorrow. The plan was for the two hitmen to take you out, and then transport the bomb to Grand Rapids. Others were meeting them there, and the second group would be the ones to place the bomb at its target destination."

"If they're thinking airport, they would never make it past security," Jack said.

"They would not have even had to. The instant it was received, and the delivery man moved on, it was to be remotely detonated. That was a powerful bomb. It still would have killed or injured dozens. That's all they wanted. It was to be a distraction. To draw attention away from their real target."

"And let me guess, the delivery man, as you call him, would have looked like a Muslim. Right? Stereotypically."

"I don't have those details, but that would not surprise me."

"Who was to be the real target?" Jack asked. "And where was the hit to go down?"

"We've given it a lot of thought, and concluded that the most likely candidate would be Judge Milton Proctor of the Sixth District Court of Appeals. He is delivering an address at Grand Rapids University tomorrow evening."

"But we're not sure he's the target?"

"Not specifically, but that's our best guess."

"Roger, your *guesses* are generally actionable evidence."

"Well, if you have some time on your hands, you might think about observing Judge Proctor."

"The FBI knows about this?"

"Nothing official to know," Roger said. "Remember, it's just my gut feeling that he could be targeted."

"And who do you think is behind it?" Jack asked.

"That, my friend, would be nice to know. Maybe you can figure it out."

"Can I assume that you have an idea who it might be?"

"You know what they say about making assumptions."

Jack, remembering that one of the gunmen had told him that the woman who had hired him called herself *Dana*, then said, "I suspect the name Dana rings a bell for you."

"I think we both know the name that goes with it is Reynolds—AKA

Allison Fulbright. My boss, and your old friend. ... She seems to be working in very close association with another one of our old friends—Alexander Sipos. You recall our conversations about him?"

"I get the picture," Jack said. "It appears they are waging one hell of a pervasive attack on our judicial system. Wouldn't you agree?"

Roger thought for a moment.

Jack sensed his friend was about to deliver something profound, or at least humorous.

"Good day, Mr. Handler," Roger finally said. "Your mission, should you choose to accept it, involves the prevention of the assassination of a Federal judge, and the destruction of a sinister plot to subvert our entire judicial system. This message will self-destruct in five seconds. ... Or, maybe I'll just cut this conversation short before I say too much. ... In any event, Jack, you've got some decisions to make. This task could easily result in your death. These are very dangerous people."

Roger then did exactly as he had threatened—he terminated the call.

"How much of that conversation did you hear?" Jack asked.

"Enough to know we've got a big job ahead of us," Kate replied. "I guess we're headed to Grand Rapids."

As Jack and Kate drove off the ferry, they passed a line of vehicles waiting to get on. They included three SUVs with Homeland Security markings, and two black Ford SUVs with no markings at all.

"Wonder what that's all about," Jack said, with what looked to Kate like a sneer.

* * *

At the same time as Jack and his daughter sped down Portage toward I-75 South, two casually dressed men were approaching Jim and Mary Fletcher's front door. Mary had spotted them when they first drove up, so she cracked the door to greet them.

"Hello, gentlemen," she said.

Jim Fletcher had pulled the curtains aside to see who they were, and when he did not recognize them, he walked over to the door and opened it fully.

"We're looking for Jack and Kate Handler," the taller of the men said. He was lean and appeared to be the spokesman.

"They're not here," Jim Fletcher said. "And who might you be?"

"Me? Who might *I* be? I'm the guy you need to talk to. Now, I'll ask you one more time. Where are the Handlers?"

Jim Fletcher then pushed past his wife to more directly address the aggressive stranger.

"Young man, you need to go right back to your—"

That's all Jim Fletcher had a chance to say before his inquisitor smashed his larynx with a lightning-quick strike of his black steel nunchucks.

Grabbing his throat, Fletcher felt his knees buckle as he stumbled forward and fell to the ground.

The next strike caught Fletcher on the left side of his head. It crushed his skull.

Nunchucks then turned to Mary Fletcher. She had lunged to her husband's side and tried to cradle his head, but it was obvious to her that he was no longer there.

"Your turn," he said. "Where are the Handlers?"

She was unable to respond.

"You saw what happened to your husband. So talk to me. Where are the Handlers?"

"What did you do to Jim?" she cried. "I think you killed him. Jim. I think he's dead. Why did you do that?"

"Look, you stupid old lady. If you know what's good for you, you'll tell me what I want to know. Where are the Handlers?"

"Kate left here an hour ago. I don't know where she went. Jack was never here. Not today."

"How about those two boys. Where are they?"

"Haven't seen them today either," Mary Fletcher said. She was not accustomed to lying. Nunchucks could see it in her eyes, but he knew that she would not give him any information that might endanger the boys

"I think they all went in to visit Henry in the hospital. Jim and I are here by ourselves."

Again with lightning speed Nunchucks delivered two blows to Mary Fletcher's head. She slumped over on top of her husband.

"Check inside," Nunchucks barked. "See if the boys are here. I know she was lying about something."

Chapter 18

"I think it was more over here," Robby said, pointing into the woods. Red nodded his agreement and the boys altered their search.

The two boys had heard the explosion and driven out to investigate. Earlier they had asked for and received permission to use Jim Fletcher's brand new ATV to inspect the condition of one of the trails. Sometimes branches fall across the trails and have to be removed, so Jack had the boys assess each of the nearby trails weekly. If they found problems, they would correct them if they could. Otherwise, they would report them to Jack and he would send Jim Fletcher out with a chainsaw.

While the resort compensated the Fletchers for their efforts, to the boys it was just another adventure.

As it turned out, they were within a mile of the bomb when Jack detonated it. They heard the blast, and saw the plume of smoke. That was enough. Red was driving the ATV. He looked back at Robby, and then turned the three-wheeler toward the still visible column of black smoke and throttled the ATV into a ten-foot wheelie. Buddy alternately rode on the back of the vehicle, or ran behind.

By the time the boys reached the vicinity of the blast the smoke had disappeared. They shut off the ATV and began scouring the ground and the air for any telltale signs of a major event.

Red, because he had lived on his own in the woods for several years, possessed the more developed set of sensors. He walked around trying to catch scent of something he would not expect in the middle of the woods. But he smelled nothing.

Finally he pulled out his cell phone and motioned for Robby to read what he was texting.

"Smell nothng. Lts head dnwind."

They jumped back on the ATV and turned away from the stiff breeze.

After about fifty yards Red again switched off the ATV. But this time he remained seated on it.

After a few minutes Red let out a loud grunt. Robby knew that meant he should hang on.

Red sped ahead about twenty feet, and then he stopped again. He had spotted Jack's Honda tracks. He pointed down at them to show Robby, and then they set off following the path that Jack had made only minutes before.

A hundred yards later the boys crested a small hill. At the very top of it they stopped.

"This is it!" Robby shouted. "You found it. Good work."

It was obvious to them that something momentous had just taken place. The leaves on every tree within a one hundred foot radius were gone. Only the pine trees remained intact, and even those that were close to the center of the circle were stripped of their needles.

The boys got off the ATV in order to examine the site more closely.

Red was the first to pick up a piece of the Honda. It was the seat. He examined it closely and handed it to Robby.

At first glance, Robby did not understand the significance Red saw in the seat. But the longer he examined it, the more he realized what he might be looking at.

It was not until Robby found the ignition switch, with the key still in it, that they both had their worst fears confirmed.

"This is the Honda Henry was working on," he said. "Look, it still has the keychain that Henry used."

The key had become stuck in the ignition, and so had been left in the old machine. Jack couldn't get it out either.

Robby broke the key off and stuck it in his pocket. He feared that if the authorities investigated the explosion, the old keychain might lead them back to Jack and Henry.

"Do you think Jack's okay?" Robby asked.

Red immediately nodded.

Even though Robby anticipated that answer from his friend, he still found it heartening.

The boys made their way to the outer fringes of the blast site and searched for Jack's escape route.

Both of the boys knew what they were looking for. Robby was the first to spot it.

"Here!" he shouted. "This is where he left. Looks like he was running."

That was all they needed to know—*Jack made it out okay.*

Red then grabbed Robby's arm and signaled toward the ATV. They jumped on it and headed in the direction that Jack had left in, driving over his tracks to obscure them.

They then both had the same thought; *Maybe if we obscure the origi-*

nal tracks it will take the authorities a little longer to trace the old Honda back to Jack.

They soon discovered that Jack had also taken evasive action. When the original tracks hit Brassar, which was paved with asphalt, they looked for Jack's tracks in the gravel on the other side but couldn't find them.

"Looks like Uncle Jack drove down Brassar to throw off a search," Robby said. "Why don't we rip up some dirt and see if we can make it look like Uncle Jack came up directly from the other side."

So, that's what they did. After having made half a dozen wheel-spinning passes across Brassar, they pulled back on the paved road and headed back toward the Fletchers' house.

Chapter 19

Jack and Kate had just crossed the Mackinac Bridge heading south. Mostly they said nothing. Roger's warning was, indeed, ominous. And they both knew it.

What will fate thrust upon those two boys? Jack wondered. Throughout his life Jack had faced death so many times that he no longer gave it much thought. His view regarding it was that he would do everything in his power to defeat it, but never would he let it unduly influence his decisions, much less control his actions.

But now, it was different. *I have those two boys to think about.*

Practically speaking, Jim and Mary Fletcher had always been there to step in when the boys needed a place to stay—that is, when the heat was on Jack.

That's where they went when Jack was sent to the prison camp earlier in the year. And, more recently, that's where Jack had them go when he discovered he was dealing with a very dangerous bomb.

Those, however, were temporary events. Death is anything but temporary. Were he to die, the boys would go to live with Kate in New York.

He and his daughter had discussed it, and to both of them that seemed a no-brainer.

But, what if they *both* got killed? Then where would the boys go? And that could easily happen. After all, it was exactly that sort of danger that Roger was warning them about this time around. Even though he did not come out and say it, Roger certainly implied that the only way to put an end to the threat against federal judges would be to terminate the efforts of woman behind it—his boss, former First Lady Allison Fulbright. Jack knew that Allison would not go down easily. Add to that the fact that Alexander Sipos, the shady and always dangerous billionaire, was also a player, and the danger quotient rose substantially.

Both Jack and Kate were keenly aware of their predicament, and of their vulnerabilities. They could die, and they knew it.

Nevertheless, someone has to destroy this conspiracy, he determined. *We cannot count on the FBI doing their job because the Bureau has become too incredibly politicized of late. I believe that the only way this will be solved is if Kate and I do it ourselves. ... But, damn, I hate gambling with the futures of those boys. I just guess she and I will have to do the job perfectly, so we will come out okay in the end. Too bad there are no guarantees in life. And, I suppose if it all goes south the boys will be smart and resilient enough to make it without us.*

"You know, Dad," Kate said, interrupting his thoughts, "some things in life are just worth fighting for. And this job is one of them. Don't you think?"

"Where the hell did that come from?" Jack said, flashing a thoughtful smile in her direction.

"I can read you like a book. You're concerned about me and the boys. I heard what Roger said, and I know he meant it. If you walk away from this, he would understand. ... And so would I. But I know you pretty well. There are some things in life that simply have to be done. Or at least attempted. And we both know this is one of them. … If our court system crumbles, so does our freedom. Too much is riding on this for us to walk away. Isn't that just about what you were thinking?"

Jack didn't answer her, not because he thought she was wrong. His phone had vibrated.

"Robby. What's up?"

"They're dead! Uncle Jack! The Fletchers! They're dead! We came back! And they're dead! Both of them! Dead!"

"Slow down! *Who's* dead?!"

"Mr. and Mrs. Fletcher! Both of them! Right on the ground outside their front door."

"How do you know?"

"They're not moving. They don't answer when I talk to them. There's a *lot* of blood. Especially on Mr. Fletcher. He has a huge cut on his head. And so does Mrs. Fletcher. Her head is cut too. They're not moving. I tried to talk to both of them. I think they might be dead."

"Check for a pulse."

"I did, and so did Red."

Robby began crying uncontrollably.

Jack did not want to interrupt, but he needed to.

"You could not feel a pulse, not on their neck, or their wrist?"

"Their eyes are open, but they can't see us. … Uncle Jack, what should we do? Should we carry them in the house?"

"No. If they're dead, you can't help them. If they're still alive, you still shouldn't move them. I'll call an ambulance, just in case. But don't try to move them. We've got to figure out how to get you boys out of there quickly."

"We could take their Gator and go back to the house."

"Okay," Jack said as he directed Kate to pull off at a rest stop, "That's a possibility. But I think we've got to get you guys out of there right away. Damn, I wish Henry was out of the hospital."

"Could we have Scott Lundgrun pick them up?" Kate suggested. Scott and Mary Lundgrun were cooks at the resort, as well as serving as the on-campus caretakers.

"We could," Jack said, placing his hand over the mic so the boys could not hear. "But we've already got the Fletchers killed. And where would Scott take them? He lives at the resort. … Let's think about this."

"Check the garage," Jack finally said to the boys. "Is their Buick in the garage? Go check right now."

"I can see it from here," Robby said. "What do you want us to do?"

"Hold on," Jack said.

He then turned to Kate and said, "Give Millie Star a call and see if she's home. If she is, have her drive the boys down to Grand Rapids. To the river house. We could meet them there."

Millie Star was a good friend of Kate's, plus, she lived on the mainland virtually across the street from where the ferry docked.

"Do you boys have any cash?"

"Uncle Jack," Robby said, "we never have any cash. But we do know where some is. Mrs. Fletcher always keeps some cash in the kitchen cupboard. She said that's her emergency money. She did tell Red and me that if we ever needed any of it, we should just take it, and we could pay her back later."

"Take the money," Jack said. "All of it. Grab Buddy and drive over to Millie's and Angel's house. Kate is calling them right now."

"Will they let us on the ferry?"

"They'll let you on, but they might ask you where you're going. Tell them I am sending you over to Millie's house. Remember, they won't charge you to leave the island because they charge only in the other direction. Just watch where they tell you to park, and don't hit another vehicle. You've driven before. You won't have any problem."

Jack, noticing that Kate was trying to get his attention, said, "Hang on again. Kate's talking to me."

Jack again covered the mic.

"Millie's not picking up. She still might be home, but she's not answering."

Jack turned his attention back to the boys.

"Millie and Angel might not be home. But go there anyway. Drive the car around to the back of the house and park it there."

Angel, Millie's fourteen-year-old daughter, was almost like a sister to the boys.

"I want you to stay on the phone with me until you get off the ferry," Jack said. "Red needs to drive, and you need to handle the phone."

Again placing his hand over his cell, Jack asked Kate to call the Lundgruns. "We need to warn them to get off the island. Try not to alarm them. Don't mention the Fletchers."

Then addressing the boys, Jack said, "Take Brassar up to Ferry Road. Don't waste any time. I want you off the property ASAP."

"Scott's not answering," Kate reported. "I'll try Mary."

"Where are you right now?" Jack asked.

"Just leaving the Fletchers'."

"I don't get it," Kate said. "Mary picked up, but she hasn't said a word."

"Mary, can you hear me? Mary?"

"Kate Handler?"

The deep male voice coming out of her phone was not what Kate expected.

Jack's ears were tuned to both phones. His eyes flashed to meet Kate's.

"Who are you? And where's Mary Lundgrun?"

"Mary's right here with us. But she doesn't feel like talking to you."

"What have you done to her?"

"You ask too many questions. ... Where are you and your father, by the way? We would really like to meet with you. Get some matters ironed out. ... The sooner the better, I would say. And so would the Lundgruns. You need to talk to us before you run yourself out of friends."

Kate looked over at Jack. He had heard every word.

He held his finger over his mouth and shook his head.

Kate understood that he wanted her to let the man continue to talk.

"You there?" he finally asked.

"Yes."

"We'd like to talk to your boys, too. Where are they?"

Jack began nodding his head and pointing toward the back seat of their Tahoe.

"The boys are with us."

"And where would that be? As soon as you meet with me, we'll start leaving your friends alone. My boss says Jack is a reasonable person. In fact, she says she still has high regards for him. ... But the two of you are beginning to make a nuisance of yourselves. Those are not my words. That's what *she* says. Personally, I think you two are worthless bags of shit just waiting to get flushed. But, that's just me. She wants to talk to Jack. If he will contact her, she will call us off. Personally, I hope your sonofabitch father *doesn't* call her. I'd rather take care of him myself."

Jack had listened for as long as he could bear it. He handed his cell to Kate and grabbed hers. But before he would talk, he got out of the Tahoe.

"Exactly who is it I'm supposed to talk to?"

"Dana Reynolds. I suppose that's not her real name, but I don't know. Don't need to know, either. She said you would know how to get in contact with her. She said to tell you that she takes no pleasure in hurting your friends. And she really does not wish harm to you or your family. But you *must* stay out of her affairs. … She said that if you call her, she will explain everything, and that you will completely understand."

"Fair enough," Jack said. "Now, if you would be so kind as to leave the Lundgruns alone. Just walk away from them. I will give … *Dana* a call. And then, if it seems beneficial, you and I can get together. But we're done talking for now."

Jack knew that the Fletchers were dead, and he strongly suspected that the Lundgruns had met the same fate. But he did not want to let on what he thought, because to do that would be to tip the killers off that the Fletchers' bodies had already been discovered. That would suggest that the boys had returned to the house and found the bodies. Jack was reasonably confident that the killer had bought the story that the boys were with him, and that he was going to make the call to Dana Reynolds.

Jack got back in the Tahoe and switched the phones back with Kate.

"Where are you now?" he asked.

"We're just getting off the ferry," Robby said.

"Change of plans. Instead of going over to the Star house, I want you to turn right on Portage and take it all the way around until you reach the on ramp for I-75 South. Be careful not to go the wrong way on I-75. That would take you toward Canada. *Don't* do that."

"You want Red to drive on the Interstate?" Robby asked.

"Yes. It's much easier than city driving. And I will need you on the phone. When you get on it, accelerate to seventy-two miles per hour, and hit cruise. That's it. … How full is the tank?"

Robby leaned over and checked the fuel gauge.

"Three-quarters, maybe a little more."

"That'll get you to where we are. The first rest stop south of the bridge."

"How do we get across the Mackinac Bridge? Won't they get suspicious about a kid driving?"

"Check around," Jack said. "Maybe in the visor. For a Quick Pass card. I'm pretty sure Jim bought one. Can you find it?"

Robby started looking. Finally he found it in the ashtray.

"Yes. Got it."

"Great. All you have to do is drive close enough to swipe it on the reader. Do not go through the green gates. That's for those who are going to pay in cash. There is always one of the automated gates open. Usually more than one. Be careful not to cut anyone off in the queue. And try to stay in your lane on the bridge. Don't pass on the bridge. You'll be fine."

"Why don't you want us to go to Angel's house? That would be much easier."

"We just think that it would be better for you to meet us down here at the rest stop, and we will go to the river house together. We'll have a great time."

"We don't feel very great right now. Mr. and Mrs. Fletcher getting killed, and everything."

"Kate and I are very sad about that as well. We just want to get you down here with us. You can do it. I know it's hard, but you guys are tough."

Jack could tell that Robby was beginning to cry again.

The boys did not articulate it, but they couldn't help reliving in their minds all the great times they had had with the Fletchers—the fishing, exploring, and mechanical repairs with Jim Fletcher; the fresh blueberry pies, homemade bread, hot soups, donuts and peanut butter cookies with Mary. It all played fresh in the boys' minds. By any measure, the Fletchers were the perfect adopted grandparents. And Jack, on the other end of a silent phone, knew exactly what was happening.

"Hey, son," Jack said. "I just want you to know that Kate and I love you two guys with all our hearts. I know how this hurts you. It hurts us too. But we have to get through this together. We *have* to. ... I am going to disconnect this call for now. I want you to save your battery. But, if anything comes up, call us immediately. We will be waiting here at the rest stop. First one south of the bridge. It's about ten miles, after you get off the bridge. Watch for signs. In fact, call me as soon as you get across."

Kate was struggling to make sense of the whole ordeal.

Blotting her tear-filled eyes, she said, "The Fletchers are dead. That we know. We can be fairly confident that the Lundgruns are hurting, if not dead. And Millie doesn't pick up her phone. Do you think they got to her?"

"I don't know. We have to deal with what we know," Jack replied more tersely than he intended. His anger was beginning to overwhelm him.

"We need to get the police over to Millie's and the Lundgruns.'"

"I'll have Roger do it," Jack said. "Otherwise the call will be traced back to me, and I'll have too much explaining to do. We don't have the time to deal with the police right now."

* * *

The boys did not try to communicate once they reached the Interstate. While it was never easy for Red to convey his thoughts to Robby under normal circumstances, he always managed. But neither one of them had anything to say. Red was preoccupied with his driving, and both of them were overcome with grief. So total was their oblivion to their surroundings, neither one of them noticed the black Ford SUV that had slid in behind them just before they had reached the Mackinac Bridge.

"That's it," the big man who was driving said. "That's the Fletchers' car. The tag matches what Nunchucks gave us. And I'm sure that's our two boys inside. … They are going to take us right to the Handlers."

Chapter 20

At a repair shop just outside Detroit, a crew of three men were feverishly working on a brand new Type-D extended-length school bus.

They had earlier stripped out all thirty seats, and then cut the legs off of them. The legless seats were then haphazardly stacked alongside the bus.

A major conversion was going on inside the big yellow vehicle. Its entire floor, from front to back, had been exposed. And on top of it the workmen had laid a floor of one-quarter inch steel plating. They had precision welded every seam.

They then welded sides on the floor plates, again using one quarter-inch steel plates. This created a steel box nearly thirty feet in length, and two feet three inches high.

Inside that box they had placed plastic barrels custom made to fit it. Inside those barrels was a carefully measured mixture of diesel fuel and fertilizer.

The entire box was filled with the barrels, except for a space left empty in the middle.

Once all the barrels were in place and inspected, they began placing two-foot wide strips of plate steel across the top of the barrels. It extended from sidewall to sidewall, but it was not welded to the sides. Instead, it was designed to fit like a lid, with a piece of angle iron pre-welded to the edges. It slid over the top of the sides. It was supported in the middle by the tops of the barrels.

When the workers reached the middle of the steel box, the place where they had left an open area, they slipped in that space a suitcase exactly like the one that contained the TATP bomb that Jack had commandeered and exploded earlier.

However, instead of TATP, this suitcase contained dynamite, along with a remotely activated detonating device.

Once the top of the steel box was totally secured, they placed each of the legless seats on top of the lid, affixing them using a heavy-duty polyurethane adhesive.

In the seats, using Velcro, they attached the upper torsos of child-sized mannequins. From the side, a casual view of this bus gave the appearance that it was fully loaded with middle-school children.

The workmen walked around the outside of their masterpiece several times verbally applauding the quality of their work.

"All we need now is the driver," said the workman who appeared to be the oldest. Not only did he seem senior to the other two men, whenever directions were given, he was the one delivering them.

His name was printed on the front of his navy blue jumpsuit: *Jim Martz, Plant Manager.*

It was obvious to any observer that the jumpsuit was a holdover from a previous job, probably one that Martz had lost during the recession.

Men like Martz were plentiful in the eastern part of Michigan after the collapse of Detroit's auto industry.

His two helpers were former autoworkers as well. But, since neither of them were plant managers, they had no nametags on their jumpsuits.

"When do we get the driver?" one of the other two asked.

"I'll be damned if I'm gonna ask any more questions," Martz said. "Mr. Alexander is still hotter than a pistol about losing that other detonator—that suitcase that got stolen in the U.P. I'm sure that he'll get the driver set up when he is damn good and ready."

Just as the three men broke out a six-pack of beer, a dark Ford SUV pulled into the shop. Alexander Sipos was sitting in the front passenger seat. He got out but did not say a word. At least not at first.

Instead, he simply walked around the bus, viewing it from every angle. And then he stepped inside of it.

Finally, he walked up to Martz and asked, "Is it all set and ready to go?"

"Yes, sir. We just need the driver."

"Wonderful, wonderful," Sipos said. "That will please Dana, I am sure. She sent a bonus for you boys. It's her way of thanking you for a job well done."

Sipos then turned to face the black SUV, and said loudly, "Andre, give these boys their present from Dana."

A dusky man wearing a cheap-looking black suit emerged from the back seat. He was carrying a black leather briefcase. He walked up to where the men were seated with their beers.

"Hope you boys like her little present," he said. "She picked it out herself."

He set the briefcase down on the oil-stained concrete floor, and opened it. Looking up at the men and smiling, he said rhetorically, "Hope you're ready for this."

He then pulled out an Uzi submachine gun and sprayed at least twenty rounds into them.

After the initial volley, he walked up to each of the victims and fired a single shot into the head.

"They're all very dead," he announced with a smile as he returned the Uzi to the briefcase. He then got back into the SUV.

Chapter 21

As Red approached the gate at the bridge he raised his right palm up to get Robby's attention, and then pointed to the red LED sign over one of the gates on the left.

"Yeah," Robby said. "That's cool. The green ones have an attendant and collect money."

Robby handed the plastic Quick Pass card to Red and said, "Watch the car ahead of us and see how he does it. I think you just swipe the card on the reader, and the gate opens."

The black SUV that was following them pulled into the longest green sign lane. "We don't want to come out ahead of the kids," the driver said. "As slow as they're going it'd take us forever to let them catch up."

Just as the boys passed the first bridge tower, Robby's phone rang.

"How much battery do you have left?" Jack asked.

"My phone's at forty percent, but I'm sure Red's is more charged."

"Forty is fine. Where are you right now?"

"Almost halfway across the bridge."

"Good. You're only ten minutes away. Once you're off the bridge, hold your speed to seventy-two, but try to avoid passing anyone. And watch for the rest stop sign. … How's the fuel holding up?"

Robby leaned over and checked the gauge.

"Still have a quarter tank."

"That'll be fine. We'll worry about gas after you get here. … Speaking of when you get here. When you pull in, there will be a sign saying 'Trucks, Cars with Trailers,' and another one saying 'Cars.' Even though you're not pulling a trailer, I want you to pull into the parking area reserved for trucks and trailers. You'll see Kate's car—her white Tahoe. Pull in behind it."

"Okay, Uncle Jack," Robby said.

"Red's driving?"

"Yup."

"Did he hear what I just said?"

Red nodded his head.

"He heard. I have the speaker on."

"Pull in directly behind Kate's car, but do not get out right away. The parking places are large enough for semi trucks—there'll be plenty of room for you behind her car. Just wait until we come and get you."

* * *

The black Ford SUV had pulled away from the gate four vehicles behind the boys. The big man did not want to follow too closely because he feared the boys might spot them and report to Jack. So, he dropped back a full two hundred yards. This allowed them to maintain three or four vehicles between them and the boys, while still able to keep an eye on the Buick.

"We got gas?" asked the big man's quiet partner.

"Almost half a tank. But with our extended fuel capacity, we're good for another three hundred miles. We should have more gas than that Buick."

"How're we gonna do this?" the partner asked.

"As soon as we know exactly where we are going, and can see the lay of the land, I'll know more. For right now, make sure we have adequate firepower. I want to get in as close as possible. No long range shit. I'm thinking we each take an Uzi with a second magazine. We'll take forty-five semi autos as backup. Two spare magazines each for them. That's what Nunchucks packed, and I think we should stick with his plan.

"We get in close. Our body armor, along with the element of surprise, will give us the advantage. Hit the kids too—no one lives.

"As soon as we figure out where we're goin', we'll be better able to plan our attack. If it looks bad, we'll just pull back and devise a new plan. The worst case, we will at least find out where the Handlers are."

* * *

"Rest area one mile," Robby said, reading the blue sign. They were both happy to be meeting up with Jack and Kate.

"Remember to park behind Kate," Robby said, "in the part where the trucks and trailers park."

Red was very nervous. He had never driven a real car that far before. Sometimes Jack or Henry would allow him to move vehicles around the resort, or to act as a valet and fetch a patron's car for him. But never had he driven off the island, and never on the expressway.

Red's approach to the rest stop exit was not perfect. He had begun to slow down long before he reached the exit lane. Drivers behind him blew their horns and swerved around to miss his rear bumper.

"Pull over!" Robby shouted. "You're beginning to block traffic!"

And, Red was probably the only driver who ever took seriously the fifteen MPH exit speed.

But it all worked out. The boys managed to avoid catastrophe and find the proper parking area.

"There," Robby said. "That's Kate's car. Just pull in behind it. … Jack said to wait in the car until he comes and gets us."

Pulling into the rest area behind the boys was the Black Ford SUV. The driver stopped well back—fifty yards behind the boys—and there the two men waited and watched.

The boys, however, were totally unaware that the men had ever been behind them.

Finally, the big man began to creep slowly ahead. He drove up to the parking place where the boys had pulled in, but did not commit to it. He and his quiet partner just continued looking for Jack and Kate.

Jack, who was still on the cell with Robby, said firmly, "Both of you hit the floor right now! And stay there until I come for you! Make sure you take Buddy down too."

And then it happened. Two suppressed rounds almost simultaneously rang out from .22 caliber rifles. One of the rounds shattered the Ford's side window and struck the big man in the left temple killing him instantly. That bullet was fired by Jack.

Kate's shot passed behind the driver, striking the quiet partner in the forehead. He died instantly as well. Her aim had been for his temple, but he had turned to face the big man just before she fired.

"Grab this!" Jack quietly commanded, as he shoved his rifle toward Kate. "That vehicle is still in gear."

Jack bolted to the driver's door. By then the driver's body had relaxed and, just as Jack expected would happen, the SUV had begun to roll forward.

Jack reached in through what remained of the shattered window and shoved the shifter into neutral.

He then opened the door and forcefully shoved the dead driver onto the center console. Sitting on the edge of the seat, he steered the vehicle on past several other trucks and cars until he reached an open parking place. He pulled into it, but not all the way to the front. Instead he just made sure the rear of the SUV was out of the way, and there he stopped.

He parked in that fashion so that other drivers would not be tempted to casually peer in one of the SUV's windows as they walked to the restroom.

Jack then unceremoniously muscled the big man all the way into the rear seat, and there adjusted his body to look like he was sleeping.

The quiet partner had slumped forward, so Jack straightened him up on his seat and turned his face toward the center.

"They both look like they're sleeping to me," he said aloud.

He then tossed the keys in the back and got out, locking the door behind him.

Once Kate removed and secured the bolts from the two rifles they had just used, she then discarded the rifles in the grass behind her and headed toward the Buick where the boys were hiding. Buddy greeted her as she walked up.

"False alarm," she said as she opened the car door. "We thought someone might have followed you here, but it's all clear."

Red and Robby both sat up and looked around.

Kate leaned over and kissed Red on the head and tousled his hair.

"That's *totally* disgusting!" Robby said, scrunching up his face to emphasize his words. "Don't think you can do that to *me*."

Chapter 22

It was four in the afternoon. Zero hour had arrived to carry out Alexander Sipos's scheme. Two of his operatives had put the finishing touches to the school bus, and the driver was seated behind the steering wheel.

Rush hour had already begun in Detroit, so driving the big school bus to Detroit Metropolitan Airport, generally referred to as Detroit Metro, would take a while. But time was not likely to be an issue. All that was necessary would be to arrive on schedule. Once the bus was in place, they could easily stall.

The bus pulled into the drive that provided curbside drop off for Concourse A, also known as the "Edward H. McNamara Terminal."

Traffic was heavy, however, so the driver had to perform a rather awkward approach, running the bus's front wheel up onto the curb and then back off after about twenty feet. The result was that he was able to bring the bus fairly close to the curb, but not without attracting the attention of two uniformed protective service personnel.

The first security guard strode up to the door of the bus and pounded loudly on it with an open right hand.

"You're not supposed to bring that bus in here. What's wrong with you? And you sure as hell can't be driving on the sidewalk. Where the hell did you get your license to drive one of these things? Open this door up right now!"

The driver just looked over at the fuming guard and smiled.

By then the second uniform arrived on the scene. "What's going on here?" he said. "Did this idiot actually drive that bus on the sidewalk?"

"He sure did, and now he won't open up the door. ... Get on the radio and get a supervisor over here."

While the second guard made the call, the first one tried shoving his night stick through the rubber seal between the two sections of the bus's door. "Maybe I can force this damn thing open. That bus is still running. ... And take a look at this door. He's got a chain through it. A big chain. We're gonna need a key for that padlock, or a torch. You ever seen anything like this? This is crazy."

"Shut it down and open this door!" he shouted at the driver.

The driver acknowledged the command by nodding his head and smiling, but he did not open the door.

A few minutes later the supervisor arrived. "What the hell do you have here? Doesn't he know that he's not supposed to bring a bus up here?"

"He won't talk to us. And he's got the door chained shut," the guard said. It appears that he's got a full load of students. They look like middle-schoolers."

"Hey, buddy," the nattily dressed supervisor said. "Please open this door before we have a situation, and you end up in some really *serious* trouble. If you make us break this door in, you will go straight to lockup.

I promise you that."

"Boss, maybe I can get one of the kids to open the rear emergency door."

"It's worth a try, see what you can do."

The windows on the bus were not only too high for the guard to get a good look at any of the students, they were unusually tinted as well. So, he dragged a luggage cart over and turned it up on its side. He then climbed up on top of it, leaning against the bus for balance.

"Holy shit! Boss, you're not gonna believe this! Those are not real kids. They look like store mannequins, or something. What the hell is going on here?"

Sitting in his car on the topmost level of the parking ramp for the North Terminal was a man with a joystick and a computer screen. Sitting behind him in their black Ford SUV was Alexander Sipos.

They both could hear everything the two guards and their supervisor were saying.

Sipos scrutinized his watch, and then made a call.

After receiving the confirmation he was seeking, he said, "I think the time has come for some fireworks."

The technician smiled.

"Here we go."

He then, using his joystick, directed the robotic driver to smile and flash the guards his middle finger. After the technician was sure the guards fully appreciated the gesture, he hit the *execute* button. The screen went blank. At the same time the whole structure of the parking ramp where he and Sipos were parked quaked, even though it was located nearly a mile away.

"Not perfect, but good enough," Sipos said. "Not happy at all about using dynamite for the detonator, but, all told, it got the job done. And it will still be chalked up to terrorism."

"The bomb was textbook homemade," the technician said. "Aside from the dynamite. It was basically the same bomb as was used in the Oklahoma City bombing. The dynamite won't matter. … And, the video of that bus pulling up. The name we had painted on the side of it, that's all the press will be thinking about. By the time the dynamite gets traced, the terrorism narrative will be out there and irrefutable."

The lettering on the side of the bus that the technician was referring to consisted of two words: "Allahu Akbar."

Chapter 23

Jack," Roger said, "did you hear what just went down in Detroit?"

"No, but I bet I could guess."

"Detroit Metro. Virtually destroyed."

"That big! A bomb like the one I disposed of, that would not have accomplished that much damage. Are you sure about your report?"

"Oh, yes," Roger said. "Concourse A is no more. Totally down."

"How could that be?" Jack asked. "The bomb I had could have done some superficial damage, and probably killed a number of people, but it would not bring a whole building down."

"This is how I see it," Roger said. "We have no solid info yet, but I think your bomb was merely the detonation device. The bombers wanted the bombing to look like a terrorist attack, and the TATP device would have strongly suggested terrorism—homemade terrorism.

"I'll bet the bomb used at the airport was constructed out of fertilizer and diesel fuel—easy to come by components. If you had not lifted the TATP detonator, their subterfuge would have been complete. But I'll grant you that they had to come up with some other explosive to set the fertilizer off, and that was probably dynamite. If so, that stuff is pretty easy to trace."

"That means that we are on here," Jack said. "They are really coming after this judge tonight."

"I'd say so. Who you got with you? I assume you are in position at the university's auditorium."

"Kate and I are here, and we've got our boys. And Buddy."

"Are you kidding me?" Roger asked with an incredulous tone. "You've got Red and Robby there with you?"

"Safer with us than anywhere else," Jack retorted. "Lately, every time we have someone take care of them, people get killed."

"Far be it from me to question your motives," Roger said. "Or your parenting style. It was tragic, what happened to your friends, the Fletchers. And your cooks—Scott Lundgrun and his wife."

"I suspect that the same thing would have happened to Millie and her daughter had they been home. We just can't gamble with the lives of our friends. This whole business with the judges, and the people responsible for these killings, we have to put an end to it. There are bad people in this world. And they just seem to keep coming back. I should have dealt with … Dana Reynolds, or whatever she calls herself, back when I first realized just how evil she was. A lot of good people would be alive today had I listened to my conscience. Some people are just irredeemable, and I'm afraid she is one of them."

"Do I detect a veiled threat?"

"Roger, I never make threats. You know that."

"I just hope you understand that I have a job to do, and protecting Allison is it. So, you'd be wise not to test my dedication in that regard. You are an old friend, but I have a job to do."

"Were we talking about Allison?" Jack asked. "I mentioned only Dana Reynolds."

Roger did not respond.

"We've got a judge to save, my friend," Jack said. "We need to get on with it."

"Agreed."

"What do we know?" Jack asked.

"The bombing strongly suggests that our information was correct. The plan was to do significant damage to Detroit Metro, making it look like terrorism. And then to kill Judge Proctor. How he is to be killed, we don't have a clue. My only guess is that it will be made to look like something else—an accident, or suicide."

"These are the guys who killed Associate Justice Pelosi. And they made that look like natural causes. Maybe more of the same?"

"Holy shit, Jack. I just received a message. … How the hell could we have missed this?"

"Missed what?" Jack asked.

"Judge Proctor. He's just been named among the missing at Detroit Metro. … The bomb was more than subterfuge. It was the instrument of his assassination!"

"Ladies and gentleman," came a shaky male voice over the auditorium's sound system. "We regret to inform you that there has been a major event at Detroit Metropolitan Airport, and our speaker, Judge Proctor, has been delayed. He will not be addressing us tonight. We will provide more information when it becomes available. We apologize for the inconvenience."

"Roger," Jack said. "I take full responsibility for letting them get to Proctor."

"It's not your fault, Jack. You, me, the FBI, even Judge Proctor, we all expected the attempt to go down while he was speaking—not en route. We were thinking suitcase bomb, with limited destructive capability, while they were planning something like Oklahoma City. There were a dozen agents in the auditorium. … We *all* missed it."

"That leaves Judge Lawrence Thompson," Jack said. "I take it you've warned him?"

"The FBI has issued a warning to all federal judges, Thompson included. But he has not been told that a credible threat has specifically been made on his life."

"Has he been issued protection?"

"It's out of my hands. When the FBI gets a case, they slam the door in my face."

"I know that feeling. But, given all that has been transpiring, wouldn't it be pretty safe to say that they have him under twenty-four-hour surveillance?"

"I'm confident that they're doing their job."

"Like they did it for Proctor?" Jack said. "We're headed out—all of us."

"To California? All four of you?"

"To San Francisco. All *five* of us."

"You're putting Buddy on a plane?"

"Wouldn't do that. We'll contract a pet transportation service. Only humane way to do it."

"Who's picking up the tab for this? You don't have a client, do you?"

"I think I'll get Dana Reynolds to pay for it. She's got the money, I'm sure about that."

Roger laughed out loud. "Have you discussed the arrangement with her yet?"

"If she's not good for it, then I'll collect it from Sipos."

"Now that would be something I'd pay to see."

"Stick around. It's going to happen. And I won't charge you a penny."

Chapter 24

Don't speed," Sipos told the technician. "There is absolutely no need to hurry. The last thing we need is to get stopped. That's where stupid people make their mistake. Overconfidence and impatience. They're killers. Or at least destroyers of perfection. What we did was perfect. Don't spoil it now."

The two men were in for a long drive, and Sipos did not want his assistant to get careless.

"Cruise at exactly two miles over," Sipos said. "Won't do to speed, or to drive too slow."

They had rehearsed the route a dozen times. They would hit I-94 West to I-275 North. From there they would exit onto I-96 West toward Lansing.

When they reached Williamson, just east of Lansing, Sipos had them pull off the highway.

"What's this about?" the technician asked. "I thought we were headed straight to Lansing International Airport."

"We're going to switch cars. Who knows how many cameras have captured this one," Sipos said. "Just being careful."

"Turn in there," Sipos said, pointing at a Park and Ride parking lot just south of the highway. "Pull in beside that black Ford SUV. That's our new ride."

The technician parked as ordered, and shut off the engine.

Sipos, who had remained in the back seat for the entire trip, removed from his pocket what appeared to be a pen. It was, however, nothing like one. The device, manufactured by RJ Raverman, was actually a .22 caliber pistol. The barrel was threaded to accommodate a small Gentech suppressor. It took him only a few seconds to convert it from a straight pen-appearing object into a pistol, and only another second to fire a .22 long round into the back of the technician's head.

Death was immediate.

Sipos then took a brick-sized device from his briefcase and set a digital timer for five minutes.

He lowered two windows halfway, got out of the car, locked it, and entered his escape vehicle.

By the time he had driven back to I-96 West, the car containing the technician had caught on fire.

Instead of heading to Lansing International, he instead took I-69 South to I-94, and then on to O'Hare International Airport. From there he caught a direct flight to San Francisco. He chose such a circuitous route because he thought it possible that someone might have been tracking the technician's cell phone.

The Handlers' San Francisco flight, while originating in Grand Rapids, made its connection in Chicago. And, as fate would have it, the plane they switched to was the same one that Sipos had boarded.

Sipos had entered the plane first. And, as was his custom, he requested and received a seat in the very back of the plane. He had read that in a crash those passengers riding closest to the tail of the plane had the highest rate of survival.

Jack, Kate and the boys boarded the plane later, and were seated near the front of the first class section.

Neither Sipos, nor Jack, were aware that the other was on the plane with him, at least not at first.

However, even had Jack bumped into Sipos, he most likely would not have recognized him. The Hungarian businessman was wearing a fake beard and was disguised as a Hasidic Jew.

Half way through the flight Sipos did catch a glimpse of Jack when he stood to use the restroom.

Chapter 25

Henry was recovering as well as could be hoped for. While he had lost a lot of blood, no vital organs had been damaged, nor had any bones been shattered. The round passed through his shoulder cleanly.

That does not suggest, however, that Henry was not in a lot of discomfort. High velocity rounds have a way of impacting the tissue some distance from the actual wound. Henry was pleased that the prognosis was positive, but he found it difficult to deal with the constant throbbing.

It might have been much easier for him had he been willing to take the painkillers the doctors tried to give him. But he would have none of it. He was half convinced that the men who had shot him would try to finish the job.

While he never engaged in contract killing, he knew that a botched hit was just about the worst thing that could happen to a hitman. And, even though Henry was convinced that the attack on his life was not actually a hit, he was concerned that the man who shot him might not be of the same mindset, and that he could decide to come back and finish the job. *If that happens,* he thought, *I don't want to be all drugged up.*

So, he refused all medications other than antibiotics.

Henry quickly grew impatient. Even though he had been admitted only three days earlier, he decided he wanted to go home. While under any normal circumstances release from the hospital would not be considered, because he had been admitted as a "special case patient," at Roger's request, his release rested solely on his own determination. As long as he could walk out of the hospital under his own power, no one had the authority to stop him.

So that's exactly what he did.

Jack assumed that his friend would remain hospitalized for at least ten days, given the severity of his wounds. So he did not tell Henry that he was headed out to San Francisco to try to save another judge.

The first thing Henry attempted once outside was to phone Jack. His call caught Jack while his plane was still on the tarmac at O'Hare.

"Henry, sorry about not visiting today," Jack said. "A lot's been going on. I suppose you heard about the bombing in Detroit?"

"Just bits and pieces. What's that all about?"

"This business with the judges. It's all part of that. And so far, we're still running a little behind. … Kate and I, and the boys, are headed to San Francisco. We've got another judge in trouble. Hope we can save this one. I'll stay in touch. How are you feeling?"

"I just checked myself out. I felt like a sitting duck in that hospital."

"The doctor released you?"

"I suppose you could say that. I sort of just walked out. I wasn't officially checked in, you know, so there was nothing they could do to stop me."

"Don't go back to the resort. It's not safe there. Check into a hotel. But don't do it under your name. They might be looking for you."

"I'll use my Hopi name—my *real* name. I don't think anyone in this area knows me by it."

Henry's real name was Chuchip Kalyesveh, but because it always got butchered in prison camp he had assumed the first name of Walt Longmire's best friend on the popular TV crime drama—Henry Standing Bear. Most people knew him as just Henry.

"I'll spend the night in Marquette, and then catch a flight to Frisco."

"Henry," Jack said, "you need to get rest."

"Are you kidding me?" Henry asked rhetorically. "You *need* me. … I'm better with one good arm, than most men with two. Besides, you just said it would not be safe for me to stick around the U.P. … Didn't you just say that?"

"Give me a call when you get in. I'll reserve you a room."

"No need. I have friends and family in Frisco. I'm not sure that I told you, I used to fight out of San Francisco."

Before Henry got in trouble with the Feds he had made his living as a bodyguard, and by MMA fighting, along with some other odd jobs that he never cared to talk about.

"Call me when you get settled," Jack said. "We'll discuss accommodations later. Got to go now, the flight attendant is about to mug me."

Chapter 26

Dana Reynolds walked into the room. As was always her practice, she was wearing a Margaret Thatcher mask. Because of the mask, no one wanted to make direct eye contact with her.

"Do any of you have any question as to why I've called this meeting?" she asked.

Not one of the ten assembled leaders of "The Group" so much as looked up.

"Good," she said. "Then I'll get right into it."

The Group was the most used name for a secret society that had chapters on every Ivy League campus, as well as at several other well-known institutions.

Unlike other so-called *secret societies*, such as Skull and Bones or Scroll and Key, The Group was truly secret. If a member wanted out, he or she would be killed. While on the surface, physical elimination might seem a bit harsh, no one was ever invited to join who did not know up front that leaving The Group was never an option.

And besides that, possibly an even greater incentive was the fact that the rewards associated with being a member of The Group were more than substantial.

For example, once a student was recruited, never during his entire life would he ever be faced with a career decision. The entire path of his life was laid out for him.

And, as an added benefit, every legitimate cost he might incur for the rest of his life would be expensed out and paid for by The Group. That included tuition and student loans, apartments, homes, cars and other modes of transportation, food, clothing, entertainment—everything.

While matriculating, members received automatic membership into all of the elite organizations. They never had to worry about grades. Their classes and classmates were selected for them by The Group, and their grades were foreordained.

After graduation, The Group placed the students in a top tier-one law school. Their positions of leadership on their respective university's law review was also a foregone conclusion. Because The Group had members on the faculty and in the administrations at every major university in the country, the success of the upcoming members was guaranteed.

If, however, the member were to lose interest, or succumb to alcohol, drugs, mental illness, or any other debilitating malady, that member would be physically terminated.

As they worked their way through law school, members were closely mentored by The Group's representative on the campus where they studied. The candidates recruited by The Group were required to write academic papers reflecting a constitutionalist view of the U.S. Constitution. In other words, they were required by The Group to be conservative, both legally and politically.

The members of The Group were expected to govern every aspect of their lives by biblical principles, and to take legal positions in accordance with those espoused by the Church. Politically, they had to contribute only to the Conservative Party, and to vote conservative. To do anything other than that would be to commit suicide—literal suicide.

The Group's influence was pervasive. Members of The Group had worked their way into positions of leadership at several of the most prestigious institutions of higher learning—four of them serving as presidents of these schools.

But the objective of The Group was not to run universities. Educational management and teaching were merely the means to the end. The real objective was to acquire as many appointments to the federal courts as possible—by the *opposition* party.

While it might seem incongruous for a progressive such as Dana Reynolds to seek to further conservative principles in such a fashion, one has to understand that the whole purpose of The Group was one of subterfuge. The entire purpose for The Group's existence was to find bright but flexible students, nurture them in the ways of conservatism, promote their careers, and groom them to become the choice of conservative presidents and conservative senators for appointment to the federal courts.

Once appointed by the president, and approved by the Senate, these judges would then slowly convert to the progressive ideology of judicial activism. The Group's plan was far from perfect. Two-thirds of the candidates groomed were never appointed. But that was viewed as an acceptable percentage. All they needed to be successful was to get a handful of appointments to a federal court every year.

For instance, Ronald Reagan appointed three justices to the U.S. Supreme Court, and eighty-three judges to the various Federal Courts of Appeal. Because all of those appointments were for life, all The Group needed to do was to sneak one associate justice, and twenty-five federal judges past *Ronaldus Magnus*, and their purpose would be successfully realized.

Given the likelihood that half of the presidents would be fairly progressive, and therefore appoint knowingly progressive judges and justices, any number of judicial Trojan Horses would be highly beneficial.

For several decades the program was exceedingly successful. But, somewhere along the way, either through poor selections, or conservative infiltration, one after another of The Group's placements failed to switch sides when commanded to do so by The Group's leadership.

As a result, other judges, even those not turned by the conservatives, began refusing to toe the progressive line, and continued to render decisions along more conservative lines.

By the time the leaders of The Group realized the pervasiveness of the problem, two of their recruits were failing them on the Supreme Court, and dozens were beginning to present problems on the Appeals Courts.

Something had to be done.

While Alexander Sipos was not involved with the founding of The Group, his endless infusion of money had kept it going for the past twenty years. And, now that there were obvious problems beginning to emerge with the organization, he had decided to take a hands-on approach to fixing them.

Dana Reynolds, AKA former First Lady Allison Fulbright, found herself in a similar position. Like Sipos, she was not associated with The Group during her early years. In fact, even though her husband's agenda was the beneficiary of strategically placed counterfeit conservative judges and justices, it was not until after her failed run for the presidency that she even learned how the Trojan Horses came to be there.

She was informed of The Group's existence by Sipos himself, as he had totally taken over the group and was running it from an office he maintained in the Upper West Side of Manhattan.

It had become clear to him that while he controlled the Federal Courts, he was not able to make full use of his power because he lacked political expertise. He saw in Allison someone who could provide the aspect of his kingdom that was yet missing—acquiring political operatives who would help him recruit the strongest candidates. He believed she could be his *rainmaker*.

"Some of you think you know who I really am. Well, you don't have to sit there staring at your crotches. You might be right. You might be wrong. It's okay to look at me and speculate. But you'd damn well better not ever refer to me by any name except Dana Reynolds. I will kill you myself, on the spot. Is that clear?"

No one responded.

"That was a question that requires an answer. … Hold up a hand if you're too stupid to talk. I'll do this again. As far as you are concerned, my name is and always will be Dana Reynolds. Is that *totally* clear?"

Every man in the room responded at the same time with a collective *yes*.

"That's better."

"Now, I'm sure you all know why you are here today. Right?"

The ten men all nodded their heads and mumbled *yes*.

Dana did not say anything for a few moments. Instead, she just looked at each of the men until they were forced to look away.

Finally, she said, "How much do we pay you to do your job?"

No one wanted to respond.

"It's no secret. You all earn the same. How much is it?"

"About five hundred, with benefits," one of the men said.

"That's about right. Only it's closer to seven fifty. … You assholes don't even know how much we pay you."

Again, silence. And again, she stared each of the men down.

"I want to show you something. I want to teach you an important lesson. And to do that, I have a little show-and-tell."

She then reached inside of her designer purse and removed a Glock 17 semi-automatic pistol.

Chapter 27

Do you really think this is necessary?" Judge Lawrence Thompson said, as he invited two special agents into his home. The judge was just completing his eighth year on the Ninth Circuit Court of Appeals.

"I'm only one voice out of twenty-nine judges on that court. I'm a nobody. Only three have less seniority. And there are no major cases before us. Who would want to harm *me*?"

"All I can tell you," Special Agent William Luskin said, "is that the FBI has received credible evidence that your life is in danger. That's why we're here."

"Well, I'm sure it's totally unnecessary. … Are you planning to spend the night in my house? That will be awkward, I think."

"We don't have to be in your house, unless there is a problem. You do have an alarm system, right?"

"Yes, of course."

"You should arm it," Special Agent Luskin said. "If you need help, we'll be right outside. … By the way, do you own a gun?"

"Yes."

"Would you mind getting it for me?"

"Why?"

"You don't have to, but I would like you to."

Judge Thompson disappeared for a few minutes while he retrieved a Walther .380 and a 9mm Glock. He set them down on the kitchen counter.

"Are they loaded?" Luskin asked.

"Yes, of course."

"Do you have a gun safe?"

"Yes."

"Would you mind locking these up in that gun safe while we are stationed outside?"

"That's where they were in the first place. I'll put them back in it."

"Thank you."

"I don't want me or my partner to get shot if we have to come into your house for some reason."

"No problem."

As the judge walked back to the bedroom to return his firearms, he passed his wife who was standing in the hall with her arms wrapped around their two young children. He smiled and raised his eyebrows when their eyes met.

"Don't ask me," he said to her, "I think it's all a bunch of bullshit."

"When Luskin heard his comment, he turned to his partner with a sarcastic smile and said, "Definitely, I think we should set up surveillance *outside*.

"Call us if you need us, or have any questions," Luskin said as the two agents walked out of the door. "Remember to lock the door behind us, and to arm the system."

The judge did lock the door, but he did not engage the alarm system.

"What did that agent mean?" Dorris, the judge's wife, asked. "That there was *credible evidence*?"

"Nothing. Absolutely nothing. There have been some judges, and a Supreme Court Justice, die recently, and they are just being careful. I'm sure every member of the Ninth is getting the same treatment. We have nothing to worry about."

Judge Thompson had been recruited by The Group during his sophomore year of college. At first he was not interested in what The Group had to offer, until the subject of his student loans came up.

Even though his grades in high school were exemplary, he was not able to secure a good scholarship. And because he came from a single-parent home, he did not receive much support from his family. That meant that he was forced to borrow heavily to pay his tuition for his Ivy League education.

And then the prospect of law school bills would only add more pressure. As was the case with most candidates for The Group, his recruitment occurred while an undergraduate. One of Thompson's professors, who happened to have been placed at the university by The Group, saw his plight, and thought him to be a viable candidate for the secret society.

After the third recruitment meeting, Thompson gave in and accepted The Group's offer. Curiously, had he rejected that final time, enforcers for the organization would have had him killed. He never realized just how close he had come to death.

Unfortunately for the judge, he also did not realize the significance of his acceptance—not at that time, and certainly not now.

Once The Group had made all of his student loans go away, and secured him his seat on the bench of the Ninth Circuit, he began to regard his monthly stipend, and other benefits, as no-strings-attached entitlements.

When the secret society's representative gave him instructions as to how he needed to vote on specific matters, he regarded the directives only as suggestions to be considered when rendering a decision, not as orders handed down by an authority.

Usually, he voted as instructed, but sometimes he based his decisions on precedent, and at other times on personal preference. In his mind, he was *just doing the right thing*. Once, when he was confronted by his controller for going against orders, he argued that he would have followed instructions had there been even a shred of evidence or precedence to support the suggested position.

"If I voted as told," he said, "I could have been impeached."

He was displeased that The Group "did not give a damn" about his reputation, and he seemed not to appreciate the fact that his total compliance was a do or die matter to them.

The *jury* had returned with its verdict on Judge Lawrence Thompson, and he was found guilty of a capital offense.

Chapter 28

With the Glock 17 resting at her fingertips, Dana asked the ten men another question.

"Do you boys know what this is?"

"It's a semi-automatic pistol," the man to her left said. "I think it might be a Glock."

"Right and right," she said. "Very good. It is a Glock. A Glock 17, to be more precise. Now, an interesting thing about Glocks, at least most of the Glocks sold in the U.S., they don't come with a thumb safety like most semi-autos that you see in movies. With this weapon there is something like a second trigger. When you want to shoot it, you squeeze the trigger until your finger comes in contact with the safety, this second trigger, and then you just squeeze a little harder. And the gun fires. … No thumb safety.

"It works like this," she continued as she raised the pistol, pointed it at the head of the man to her right, and squeezed the trigger.

Click.

He was terrified. So much so, in fact, that he wet his pants. And not just a little. He soaked the foam of the chair he was sitting in.

"Damn you!" he said as he stood to leave.

"Sit your ass down!" she shouted with authority.

"I … I need to do something," he said.

"You need to sit your ass down until I tell you otherwise. Now sit down!"

He did.

She then pulled the slide back and allowed a round to flow into the chamber.

"There, this dog can now bite. Anyone who tries to leave before I tell them to will discover just how vicious this little bitch can be."

She set the Glock down in front of her and signaled for two men, each armed with an automatic weapon, to walk in the door and take positions, one at either side.

"I trust I now have everyone's full attention. In about thirty minutes, maybe less, if this meeting goes the way I hope it does, each of you will be allowed to leave this table and to continue with the tasks at hand. If it doesn't go the way I want it to, one, two, maybe all of you, will be dead. Everybody follow?"

All ten men indicated that they understood what she was saying.

"Okay, then, here's the deal. I do not think any one of you have betrayed me. At least, not intentionally. But some of you have let me down. And in so doing, you have let The Group down. That … must … end.

"*How* did you fail me? By failing to keep the recruits under you in line. I don't give a shit if it is a veteran associate justice of the Supreme Court, if he stops toeing the line, he gets one warning, and then he's dead. You have issued warning after warning, and they do not take you seriously at this point. The Group has become a joke to some of them.

"You have begun to think that your job ends once your charges have been appointed to the bench. But, that's only half of your job. Those justices and judges are worthless to The Group unless they produce the decisions we require. And they're not always doing that.

"In fact, Alexander believes that in some instances The Group has been played. That some of our recruits know exactly what they're doing, and have been placed with us to use up our resources, and destroy our organization. To me that sounds like a far-fetched conspiracy theory. But we do have a serious problem.

"Alexander, I'm afraid, is ready to give up on all of you … to start over with fresh blood.

"To help drive this point home, I want to introduce you to someone."

Dana then looked toward the guards behind her. They caught her signal and turned to face the door. The one on the left opened and held it.

A few seconds later a tall, very shapely woman stepped into the room. She was carrying an Uzi.

"Boys," Dana said. "This is Emma. If any of you fail me again, you will be dealing directly with her. Don't let her looks fool you. She can and will kill any one of you in a second. Don't doubt me on that.

"I don't agree with Alexander about you boys. He's prepared to take drastic action right now. I'm not quite ready to admit that level of failure where you are concerned. The way I look at it, you've performed well in the past, and I think at least some of you can in the future. But just know that there will be no further warnings. Fail me again, and the last sound you will ever hear will be that of an Uzi exposing your entrails. … Do you have any idea what it might be like to get shot up by one of those things? I've heard that some of them are capable of thirty rounds a second.

"You boys all know who you are responsible for. If you've got someone in the pipeline that you don't think is going to perform properly, take care of it. Work with him if he can be worked with. Or give me the names, and I'll have Emma take care of it.

"But, as far as those already serving on the courts, those who are currently screwing up, they will all be dealt with in the very near future.

"Any questions?"

After an uncomfortably long pause, she continued, "I didn't think there would be."

The men all looked at each other as though communicating a collective sigh of relief that the meeting was over.

"Now get your lazy asses out of my sight. … Now! Move!"

Chapter 29

Just how serious is the FBI taking this threat?" Jack said to Roger. Jack and family were in a taxi on the way to the Plaza Hotel.

"I'd like to think that they are fully involved at this point," Roger said. "Especially in light of this business with the airport bombing—that's the single biggest terror attack since 9/11. In this country or abroad. You and I may suspect that it was an act of domestic violence, rather than an act of terror perpetrated by some foreign entity, but the American public is convinced it was the work of ISIS.

"I'm afraid that the FBI will be forced to devote the lion's share of its resources to investigating the bombing. And it doesn't help that one of the first calls came from someone identifying themselves as ISIS, and claiming credit."

"That was probably one of Sipos's people—just more misdirection," Jack said.

"Could have been."

"Put a bug in their ear to examine the primer," Jack suggested. "They'd hoped to use homemade TATP, but that didn't work out so well for them. FBI ought to be able to trace any commercially-produced explosive. I would assume that they ended up using a more conventional compound—one like dynamite. It should be relatively easy to trace."

"Don't think that strategy will work this time," Roger said. "The night before the bombing there was a robbery at a mining operation in Ohio. Two security guards were killed. And a significant quantity of dynamite was stolen—not sure exactly how much, because the storage building itself was blown up afterward. But, it would have been enough to do that job, and probably even a few more. Almost certainly the detonator will lead them back to that robbery."

"Damn it, Roger," Jack complained. "They are one step ahead of us at every turn."

"Sure seems like it."

"Can't you do *anything* about Allison?" Jack asked. "We both know that she's behind this. ... and the contract on my life. She's behind that as well."

"You can speculate all you want, but there's no admissible evidence to prove it, and you know it. ... Until I receive orders to the contrary, my sole job in life is *protecting* her. That's what I've been assigned to do, and that's exactly what I will continue doing."

For the first time in their professional careers, Jack and Roger seemed to be emerging on opposite sides of a conflict.

It was clear to Jack that Allison was most certainly the Dana Reynolds who was spearheading the attack on Federal judges, as well as funding the contract on him and his family. It was also easy, and correct, for Jack to assume that Roger fully understood the role his protectee was playing.

While Jack had enjoyed a cordial relationship with Allison during her stay in the White House, after she moved out, his relationship with her cooled. This was especially obvious during her failed assassination conspiracy against a sitting president. During that debacle Allison had hired Jack to aid in the scheme; however, he covertly worked against her to thwart the plot. She never forgave him for that.

And now, with Allison contracting the hit on Jack, and especially with the collateral murder of the Lundgruns and the Fletchers, in Jack's mind the rift had become irreversible.

So much so, in fact, Jack could no longer imagine a scenario whereby he could allow Allison to remain alive. That thought was particularly bothersome to Jack because it threatened his relationship with Roger.

If I go too fast and hard after Allison, Jack thought after ending his conversation with Roger, *I could easily put myself in the position where I might have to terminate one of my best and most trusted friends. And, if I'm not extremely careful, I could force his hand and he just might kill me. This is not a good situation, but I have to do everything possible to protect those judges. Just don't know how this is going to turn out.*

"Where to first?" Kate asked. "After we check in at the hotel."

"I'm going to look up that judge, Judge Thompson. Seems like I'm just a little late with everything. I'm not going to wait around on this."

"And me?" Kate asked.

Jack thought for a minute, and then said, "One of us is going to have to take care of the boys. They have come too close to getting hurt on this job already. We've got to do a better job with them.

"Henry will be here tomorrow," Jack said. "At least those were the plans he shared with me. … Unless something comes up, we can count on him."

"He's got to be in a lot of pain."

"And he refuses all painkillers."

"If that was me," Kate said. "I would be as crabby as that proverbial bear."

"It'll be interesting," Jack said. "He's a tough guy. A fighter. He's had a lot of pain in his life. Somehow I can't see him giving in to it. And, like he said, he's a better man with one good arm than most men are with two."

"Uncle Jack," Robby said. "Red and I were wondering, when will Buddy get here?"

"It's normally a four-day trip. But the drivers are a husband and wife team. And they take turns. So, between periodic exercise walks, I'm told they can make the trip in a little over two days. That would get them here sometime on the day after tomorrow—give or take."

Chapter 30

"Have you heard anything from your brother?" Eddie said.

"No, but that doesn't mean anything," Harvey replied. "When Jimmy's deep undercover, he can stay down for weeks at a time."

The two men had snuck up to the Thompson house and were disabling the phone lines. First they cut all the phone cables entering the home, and then they powered up a cell phone-jamming device.

"You make it sound like your brother's a cop, not a contract killer."

"He *used* to be a cop. Spent eighteen years tracking down criminals. Till he got fired. Worked narcotics. A lot of it undercover."

"No shit! You never told me that."

"There's a lot of stuff I haven't told you. And I probably shouldn't have told you that he was an ex-cop. ... Just forget it. We've got a job to do here."

Harvey Fuhrman was the older brother of Jimmy Ray Fuhrman, the man who Jack shot after he had drained him of information, and his suitcase full of homemade explosives. It was Jimmy who had received the original contracts from Dana Reynolds to kill Associate Justice Pelosi and Judge Lawrence Thompson.

Initially, Jimmy was supposed to catch a flight to San Francisco immediately after the Pelosi hit, but once Jack had become involved, Dana signed off on having Jimmy assign the contract on Judge Thompson to his brother, so that Jimmy could take care of Jack.

Jimmy and Harvey had worked together ever since Jimmy was terminated from the Houston Police Department for his involvement in the misappropriation of confiscated narcotics. He was highly resentful of the way the union failed to protect him, especially since he was only two years away from a pension.

Right up until the day he got fired, if you were to have asked Jimmy if he could ever envision himself as a triggerman for wealthy, powerful people, he would have laughed at you, or punched your lights out.

He fully intended to toe the line until he retired—and he was counting the days, and the dollars. At eighteen years on the job he was pulling in an annual salary of just under one hundred thousand dollars. His pension would have paid him up to eighty percent, or a maximum of seventy-seven thousand per year. Of course, his divorce settlement would have turned over nearly fifty percent of that retirement to his ex-wife. But that still would have left him with about forty thousand. *I can do a lot of fishing with forty thousand,* he reckoned.

But then he got himself jerked up in a nasty situation. His partner had been stealing and selling drugs. Jimmy was clean, except that he knew what his partner was up to but did nothing. That was all it took. His partner went to jail, and was subsequently killed by an inmate, and Jimmy got terminated with no pension.

Jimmy was a very bitter man, and he never spared sharing his grievances with anyone who would listen.

It was as a result of his whining about his bad luck in a bar six years ago that he was offered his first contract hit. An old buddy of his, also a defrocked law enforcement officer, told Jimmy that he occasionally took jobs from a friend of his who had political connections, and that he knew people who were in the market for guys with his exact skill set, and that they were willing to handsomely reward a good man.

After a few years knocking around and working as a bodyguard, Jimmy got his big chance. He received a phone call from a woman named Emma. She offered to pay him thirty thousand dollars to do a job for her boss. The target was the girlfriend of her boss's husband.

Jimmy never before imagined killing a woman, but he was desperate.

The job was easy. He followed the young lady when she got out of work. When she stopped at a traffic light, he got out of his car, walked up to her and motioned for her to roll her window down. When she did, he popped her two times in the head. He then reached in, placed the vehicle in park, and casually returned to his car.

Jimmy was ecstatic. His earnings that night equaled half a year's pension. Plus, it was tax-free.

He loved his new job.

So, when Emma, acting on Dana's behalf, offered him a contract in Michigan's Upper Peninsula, and another one in San Francisco, he took them both.

He had made a deal with his brother, Harvey, to kill Judge Thompson—that was the San Francisco hit. He told his brother that he could hire a partner, but that after the job had been completed, he had to kill that partner. For the entire job, Jimmy would pay his brother twenty-five thousand dollars. There was a total of fifty thousand dollars connected to that contract, so Jimmy was to make a total of twenty-five thousand for what amounted to nothing more than *administrative fees.*

Because the Upper Peninsula hit on Associate Justice Pelosi was very involved, Dana had authorized Emma to pay Jimmy a flat fee of two hundred thousand, plus another twenty thousand in expenses. That was the biggest payday of his life. It allowed him enough to hire two additional accomplices.

The hit on Jack and Kate came about as an afterthought. And, had he been able to pull it off, it would have earned him another million dollars. Unfortunately for Jimmy, he did not have time to do his homework on Jack Handler, and therefore underestimated the daunting difficulty of the task.

Now, unbeknownst to older brother Harvey, he was about to tangle with the very man who had just blown his brother's feet off, and then left a calling card in his brain.

* * *

Jack suspected that the hitman hired to kill Judge Thompson would be eager to act swiftly. And he was right. By the time Jack had settled his family into the hotel, Harvey and his partner were scouting out the Thompson home.

"Looks like we've got a couple agents babysitting the judge," Harvey's partner said.

"Must be the judge kicked them out of the house," Harvey said. "We take the agents out, and the rest should be easy."

"Maybe there's more inside," the partner said. "How will we know?"

"Nothing's for sure. Ever. … Here, take this radio. If a car, if *anything*, approaches, call me. But do not bother me unless something is happening. Got it?"

"Yeah. Sure."

"And pay attention to your radio. I'll key it if I need you."

This was the first time Harvey had ever worked with Eddie Miles.

What the hell are these guys doin'? Harvey wondered. *Are they playing cards? They are. I don't believe it.*

The two agents never noticed Harvey sneaking up from behind while they were playing cards. They had the dome light on, and they were totally absorbed in a game of penny ante poker.

Harvey ducked below the view of the review mirror until he was even with the passenger's window. He then slipped on a pair of protective goggles, stood to his feet, and fired a total of four shots from a .22 caliber suppressed revolver, killing the agents in the middle of their game.

He opened the passenger's door and ripped the jacket off the closest dead agent, and then wrested the agent's FBI credentials from his pocket.

Walking around to the other side of the car, he snatched the other agent's jacket and credentials.

He then keyed his radio.

Two minutes later Eddie appeared. "Did you kill them?" he asked.

"Put this on," Harvey said, handing his partner one of the jackets.

"Damn, this's got blood all over it!"

"Wipe it off," Harvey barked, but barely audibly. "It won't hurt you."

Harvey had intentionally given Eddie the driver's jacket, knowing that it had the blood spatter and brain matter from the passenger's through and through head wound.

"Put it on and shut up."

"There's more than just blood on this coat," Eddie continued to complain. "There's little pieces of bone, and other shit. … I ain't wearing this, I don't give a damn *what* you say. This has got brain shit on it!"

Harvey glanced up and over Eddie's shoulder just in time to spot Mrs. Thompson jerking the curtains closed. After a moment the lights started going out one by one.

"They spotted us," Harvey said. "All your horsing around let them know we were here, now it's going to make our job *very* difficult. You're worthless. I'll never use you on another job. Now, get your ass around back and don't let them escape. Shoot anyone who sticks his head out."

Just then a light came on. It was in a second-floor room. Harvey correctly assumed that it was the master bedroom, so he wasted no time. He bounded up a set of steps that led to a small balcony just off that room, and then smashed out a glass panel in a door.

Lawrence Thompson, who was in the closet at the time trying to open his gun safe, heard the commotion and ran out of the bedroom still unarmed. He was able to turn the light out on his way.

Harvey managed to reach through the broken glass and unlock the door.

By the time he entered the dark room, the judge was nowhere to be found.

Harvey carefully walked over to the closet and shone his flashlight on the gun safe.

"Damn it," he muttered, "A gun safe—the SOB might be armed."

"FBI!" Harvey shouted. "We heard some noise in here. Are you okay?"

No one responded, so Harvey shouted a second time.

"Judge Thompson, this is Special Agent William Luskin. We met earlier. Please let me know if you are okay. My partner said he saw something going on in your house, and we came in to check. Are you okay?"

Finally, Mrs. Thompson answered, "I ... I saw two men ... slumped over in that car. I thought they were the agents."

"They are agents, too. There are four of us assigned to you. Two of us sleep, while two of us stand guard. We take turns. That's how we do it."

"You don't really sound like Agent Luskin," she said.

Harvey began walking toward Mrs. Thompson's voice as he talked. "Check me out. Turn the light on. I just want to be sure you're okay."

"Okay," she said. "Stand in the hall and I'll turn the light on. I'm just being careful."

"I understand," Harvey said, taking four steps toward her until he was in the middle of the hall.

Mrs. Thompson reached around the corner and flipped on the light switch. When she did, Jack stepped into the hall with him.

"What the hell! Who are you?" Harvey said.

"I'm the guy who just killed your brother. My name's Jack Handler. But don't bother remembering it."

Jack then fired four shots, all of which struck the hired gun.

"I think there's two of them!" Mrs. Thompson said. "I saw two of them out front. I think they might have killed the real agents."

"I met his buddy, Eddie, out back. He told me all about this guy. … By the way, where's your husband? The judge."

"I think he took the children into the safe room," she said. "But I'm not positive."

"Show me where the safe room is," Jack said. "We need to get you folks out of here and into a safer place."

"This way," Mrs. Thompson said. "There's a secret door at the back of this closet. … Where's that second man? I saw two men."

"Not to worry," Jack said. "He and I had a long talk. He's just hanging around by the back door until the FBI gets some more men on the scene. Now, you think your husband is in that safe room? Can you open it?"

Mrs. Thompson continued to lead the way to where the judge was hiding. As they passed by the rear entry door, Jack pointed over to it and said, "I think that's the man you were talking about. His name is Eddie."

There, still unconscious from Jack's heavy hand to the side of his head, Harvey's inept partner hung by his hands over the top of the rear entry door. His hands were cuffed behind him.

Before they reached the safe room, the judge and his two children emerged unharmed. Mrs. Thompson rushed to them and said, "Thank God, you're okay."

"Don't mean to break this up, folks," Jack said. "But we've got to get out of here right now. We're going to have to drive your car. I came by taxi."

Just as they reached the garage, four more guns broke through the front door. They were armed with automatic rifles, and they were not FBI.

A fifth man remained in a car out front. He was on his cell. He was dressed like a Hasidic Jew.

Chapter 31

As soon as they were all in the judge's car, Jack barked, "Everyone down on the floor! Now!"

Had he not sensed the urgency to hustle the judge and his family out of danger, Jack would have stuck around and attempted to chip away at the numerical advantage enjoyed by his adversary—especially when he caught a glimpse of the shadowy bearded silhouette seated in the back seat of a dark SUV sitting in the street in front the judge's house.

Judge Thompson's house was located on a corner lot, with a driveway that entered from the street in front of the house, but ran around to the side, and then onto the side street. The entrance to the garage was from the side, with the house extending two stories above the garage. This unusual design gave Jack the opportunity to sneak out to the side street without alerting the occupant of the SUV parked in front.

No one argued with Jack's command.

"Roger, looks like I got to Judge Thompson's house just in time. All are safe. We're on the way to my hotel."

"That's the right move," Roger said. "Apparently the FBI didn't do such a great job protecting the judge? Did they not have agents assigned to guard him?"

"They did. There were two of them."

"*Were*?" Roger asked. "Past tense?"

"Afraid so."

"They're dead?"

"They were shot in their car. Two rounds to the head … each of them … at least that's what I was told. I briefly interviewed one of the perps."

"Sounds professional."

"I'm not so sure about that," Jack said. "There were two killers. One of them was the brother of Jimmy Ray Fuhrman, the hitman responsible for taking out Pelosi."

"How did you come by that info?" Roger asked.

"I had a fairly long talk with Jimmy Ray, back in the U.P. He told me he had set this hit up as well. And the partner on the Thompson job, he gave up his boss's name—Harvey Fuhrman. … He, Harvey, seemed *fairly* competent. But it might have been that Jimmy Ray had given his brother detailed instructions as to how he wanted this done. … But their operation was anything but professional, aside from their success with the two agents."

"How'd they manage to get the drop on two seasoned FBI agents?" Roger asked.

"Apparently these two *seasoned* agents were totally engrossed in a game of penny ante poker, and Fuhrman was able to sneak up and pop them. Seems to me that there might have been an element of luck involved."

"Well, it's pretty safe to say that the *agents* weren't very lucky," Roger said. "… Tell me, Jack, by any chance was one of them holding two pair—aces and eights?"

"Bad joke, Roger," Jack replied.

* * *

"Boss," Emma said, using an earpiece and mic. "It's all clear in here. Your two guys failed their assignment. One of them was dead when we entered. They're both dead now."

"Are you sure the judge isn't just hiding in the house somewhere? It's a big house. Probably has a safe room."

"It does have a safe room, but it's empty. We checked the garage. The door is open and one of their cars is missing. The judge got away."

"How'd he pull it off?"

"*He* didn't. At least, not by himself. He had help."

"Help?"

"I talked to one of the guys. He was still alive at the time. The judge's knight in shining armor had left him with his hands cuffed behind him. He had been knocked unconscious, lifted and hung backward from the top of a door."

"That's crazy! Who the hell rescued the judge? Was it the FBI?"

"I'm not so sure how that could be. The person he described sounded a lot like that guy from Michigan—from the U.P. … Dana's old friend."

"Are you talking about Jack Handler?"

"He sounds like the one who could of pulled it off."

"Handler *is* in the city," Sipos said. "But I can't see how he could possibly have got here so quickly. … We were on the same flight, for God's sake! … Let's assume you're right. That it was Handler. How in hell did he get that judge's name? Only you, me, Dana, and the Fuhrman brothers—we're the only ones who should have known who we were after here."

"Are you suggesting that Dana is talking?" Emma asked.

"I'm not suggesting anything. I'm just saying that neither the FBI, nor Handler, should have known anything about the hit on Judge Thompson."

"Maybe it was one of the Fuhrmans, or this asshole that I just killed."

"I doubt that," the boss said. "It has to be from the inside. ... The Handlers were right on our heels with Pelosi. And then that Sixth Circuit Court judge, Proctor. I have it on good authority that Handler had set up shop at the university. That's where he thought the hit was going down. And now this. I've heard from Dana that Handler is *very* good, but no one is *that* good. He must be getting his info from someone close to Dana. ... You'd better round up your guys and get out of there."

"I'll be right out. But do we have any more business we can do in San Francisco?"

"We do have one more judge in the Ninth Circuit that has strayed badly. I'll elaborate later."

"You must be referring to Elizabeth Cohen," Emma said. "She was not on the hit list. Something change your mind to move her up?"

"Yes, I'm working on a plan. ... How did you know about her?"

"Dana had her name on a list, but had crossed it off."

That seems a little careless of Dana, Sipos thought.

"I'll discuss this with you in detail later. Let's get the hell out of here."

Chapter 32

The following morning Jack, Kate, and the boys were having breakfast in the hotel's restaurant when Kate's phone vibrated.

"It's a 906 area code," she said to Jack, "But I don't recognize the number."

She could tell by the area code that the call originated in Michigan's Upper Peninsula.

"Kate Handler?"

"This is she. And who is calling?"

"My name is Christina Baldwin, Chippewa County Child Protective Services. I'm calling because my office received an anonymous complaint regarding the two boys under your care—Robby Martin and Red. We don't have a last name for Red."

"A *complaint*? *Who* complained?"

Jack overheard enough of the conversation to know that the boys ought not to be privy to it.

"Red, Robby," he said. "See that brochure rack over there? I want each of you to pick out five of them. Kate and I will then go through them and we'll all decide what we want to see while we're here. Okay?

Skedaddle."

"I'm not at liberty to divulge the source of the complaint," Mrs. Baldwin said. "Only to inform you that CPS has opened up an investigation into the care being provided to the boys by you and your father. I would like to meet you at your home this afternoon. Will two p.m. work for you? We would like all four of you to be present for this first meeting."

"That would be just fine," Kate said, "*if* we were in Michigan. But we are all in San Francisco for a family vacation. How about when we get back?"

"And when will that be?"

"This is not going to be a long vacation," Kate said, looking to her father for some direction.

Jack held up five fingers, and then six.

"Five or six days, I'd guess."

"Call me as soon as you get back to Sugar Island, and we will set something up. I have to warn you, we cannot put this off. When a serious complaint comes in, my boss expects me to get right on it. Otherwise, it will look like you're dodging us, and we will have to pick up the children."

"Yes, of course," Kate responded. "You characterized this as a *serious* complaint. Could you at least explain that? What makes it a serious complaint?"

"I believe you were acquainted with the late James and Mary Fletcher. In fact, you have listed them both as employees of the resort you and your father own, and as frequent caregivers for the two boys. Of course, I'm sure you're aware that they were recently found lying outside their home bludgeoned to death.

"And then there were the Lundgruns, Scott and Mary, they were also murdered two days ago. I believe they worked for you as well.

"My boss called me into his office this morning to discuss the merits of the complaint. While there have never been any prior complaints or investigations, I'm sure you understand that our first responsibility is to the children. And, given the level of violence that seems to have encircled you and your father of late, we have to consider the safety of the children."

"I understand. But you said there was a complaint. Can you tell me what that was about?"

"I'm really not at liberty to discuss that. No one would ever let us know when there are problems in one of our placements if we didn't honor their confidence."

Kate was beginning to steam, so she measured her words.

"Ms. Baldwin, like I said, we are on vacation right now. I promise you I will call you the day we get back."

"Where are you staying in San Francisco?"

Kate thought for a moment as to how she should answer that question. Should she tell this worker where they were staying? Or where they were officially registered? For security reasons, they never stayed at a hotel registered under their real names.

Jack, understanding what was happening, wrote this on a napkin and slid it over to Kate: *Holiday Vista Hotel, 415.555.1368.*

"We're out and about a lot, but you can leave a message at 415.555.1368. That's the Holiday Vista Hotel."

"Okay, Ms. Handler," Christina Baldwin said, "That will do for today. But I do expect you to call me as soon as you get back to Michigan. Are we understood about that?"

"Yes, perfectly," Kate replied, and then disconnected.

"*Are we understood about that*," Kate repeated. "What sort of person actually talks like that?"

"Social workers," Jack said with a sarcastic smile.

"I guess," Kate said, matching Jack's smile. "Maybe a social worker with an inferiority complex."

"She's just doing her job," Jack said, clearly taking it seriously. "Really. If she did not do her due diligence on behalf of those boys, and something bad were to happen, she'd lose her job. Hell, they'd *all* lose their jobs. We'll just have to comply with her wishes. Let her write up a report. And, with a little luck, maybe we can move on."

"Then you think all that was legitimate? Or could it be a set up to find out where we are?"

"Oh, I have no doubt that she's legit," Jack said. "However, someone did file a complaint. I'm sure no one we know would have done that. So there could be something shady going on there. Maybe some money changed hands in an effort to locate us. Or, possibly her phone was tapped in order to learn our location. I think that's actually quite likely. ... As far as this worker wanting to set up a meeting—I have no doubt that's for real. But, this other stuff. I think the timing might be suspect. ... I'm going to head over to the Holiday Vista and see if anyone shows up, just in case my suspicions are correct."

Whenever Jack checked into a hotel on business, he would always do so under an assumed name, and then he would book a room at a second hotel under his real name. He would then check in periodically for phone messages.

In this case, he was not sure if the call Kate just fielded was totally legitimate. If it was a set up, he would like to find out as much as possible about who was stalking him.

"What about the brochures the boys pick out?" Kate asked.

"Go through them and find us some fun places. As soon as I check out the Holiday Vista, I'll come back and we'll do some sightseeing."

* * *

The Holiday Vista was only a few blocks away, so Jack was able to walk over quickly, and take a seat in the lobby. He had full view of the front desk, and of the main entrance, but could not surveil very much of what was behind him. He was in full disguise. He was wearing a blue workman's jumpsuit with a company logo sewn above the pocket. It read, *AAA Mobile Computer Service.* A tight-fitting baseball style cap bore the same insignia, as did his thoroughly beat up toolbox. Thick-soled black shoes added an inch to his height. And, as a finishing touch, he wore dark-rimmed slightly tinted glasses.

This is not an ideal situation, he determined from behind his *New York Times. This leaves a lot to be desired.*

Fifteen minutes after he sat down, Jack observed a group of five people walk into the hotel, one of whom was a strikingly tall, attractive woman. They quickly dispersed, so he was not positive they were acting in concert. Just as he had feared, Jack was only able to observe one of the men from where he was seated. The woman strode directly up to the counter.

"Who the hell is that gorgeous woman?" Jack muttered out loud. "I'm not sure I've ever seen legs that long."

Jack wasted no time. He bounded to his feet and headed toward the clerk closest to the one talking to the beautiful woman. He was second in line.

Chapter 33

Fortunately for Jack, none of the clerks were able to recognize him because he had initially paid one of the bellmen from the Plaza one hundred dollars to register for him.

"You're sure he isn't in?" the woman said to the clerk. "It's very important that I speak to him."

"Mr. Handler is registered at our hotel," the clerk said, "but he does not pick up his phone. I have to assume he is not in, or is resting. You can leave a message. That's the *best* I can do. He's either not in, or he doesn't want to be disturbed. … Do you know what Mr. Handler looks like? If you do, you might want to take a look in our restaurants and coffee shop. You might spot him in one of them."

"That's a great idea," she said, looking back over her shoulder. "I'll give it a try."

She looked right past me, Jack observed. *She's either a very good actor, or she was not able to see through my disguise.*

Jack was wearing a button camera on his shirt, so when she looked directly at him, he knew that he had captured an image of her face straight on.

He would have immediately sent the picture to Kate to have her run it through facial recognition, but he did not want to attract the woman's attention by using his cell phone right then.

If this woman is in any way associated with Child Protective Services, Jack thought, *then I'm George Clooney. ... But I would bet anything that she was somehow responsible for the CPS complaint.*

"Okay, then," she said. "I would like to leave Mr. Handler a message."

"If you would just step over to that house phone. Pick up the handset, and leave your message."

"Oh, okay. Thank you very much for trying."

The woman then walked toward the house phone. She did pick up the handset, but she held the switch down so that it would not ring the desk. And then she pretended she was talking.

Jack caught her fakery out of the corner of his eye, until his phone vibrated. He looked at the screen, and then said, "Hi, Kate. What's up?"

He smiled at the desk clerk and apologized, "Sorry, I've got to take this call."

"Dad, Henry's plane just landed. What should I have him do?"

Jack thought for a moment, and then smiled broadly.

"Have him head over *this* way. I'll hang in here until he arrives."

Jack turned back around to see if the beautiful woman was still at the house phone, but she was gone. He then looked around the lobby for her entourage, and they were nowhere to be found either.

"Terrific," Jack muttered. "I guess I'll have to kill some time until Henry gets here."

Only a moment or two passed before Jack dialed Roger.

"Hey, buddy," Jack said, "looks like we finally saved one."

"I don't think he's out of the woods, yet."

"What do you mean?" Jack asked. "We've got him registered at our hotel under a different name. Sipos doesn't even know what hotel I'm really at. And, if he hasn't figured that out, he won't know where the judge and his family are, either."

"Don't be so sure. He just invested over two hundred million dollars in The Group. And for that kind of money you can buy politicians, journalists, and a few thousand thugs. … Not to mention a few very professional hitmen. … That's what I wanted to warn you about. Sipos and Reynolds have contracted one of the top killing machines in the world."

"Really? What's his name?"

"Emma. *Her* name is Emma. As far as we know she doesn't have a last name. … Ever heard of her?"

"*Heard* of her?" Jack questioned rhetorically. "We've never been officially introduced. But, I think I just *saw* her. … Who, exactly, is she supposed to kill?"

"Judges, of course. She will take over the actual assassinations—planning as well as execution. But not just judges and justices. Dana has specifically commissioned her to take you out. You, Kate, *and* the boys."

Jack laughed out loud. "And what makes you think that?"

"She just missed you at the Thompson house last night. Apparently you were leaving through the garage with the judge's car, and she was coming in the front door."

"And you know all this how?" Jack asked.

"You know I can't divulge my sources. But have you ever known me to feed you bad info?"

Jack pondered his words for a moment, and then asked, "Is this from Allison?"

"Hell no," Roger said. "Allison doesn't discuss such matters with me. … But, sometimes Dana will let something slip over an unsecured phone line, or a careless email. When that happens, all bets are off. She's free game. I'm sure a lot of bad actors are following her emails, and even her phone calls. … Not Allison's, though. Hers are *totally* secure. I make sure of that. It's my job. But when she … when Dana goes off the reservation, then I can't help her. I know for a fact that Mossad has been reading her email—Dana's, that is. She has her own server here in the condo. And the NSA, and who knows who else, is monitoring her phone calls."

"Any chance of repercussion coming back on her?" Jack asked.

"I can't see that. She's Teflon," Roger said. "Bob, the ex pres., he claims she could shoot a dozen people in Times Square, before witnesses, and she would get away with it."

"That's Allison," Jack said. "But what about Dana? Just how protected is she?"

"Dana is not my problem," Roger said. "Dana never invites me anywhere. In fact, I'm not even supposed to know Dana exists. So, you may assume that when Dana is taking a walk, or riding around in a car, that means I'm not involved. I might as well be in Hawaii, or Paris. *Dana* is not in any way my responsibility."

Jack finally was getting the picture. If he tried to bring Allison down, he would have to go through his friend, Roger. And should that happen, one or both would die.

But, the same rules did not apply if he targeted Dana.

Jack thought for a moment, and then said, "One more matter. Do you have any word on the evidence I sent you—regarding Pelosi?"

Jack had sent by courier the pills he suspected of being warfarin, the empty vodka bottle, and the empty bottle of phytonadione—all items he and Henry had confiscated from the dumpster outside the lodge where Associate Justice Pelosi had died.

"Preliminary tests indicate Pelosi died from a massive stroke—therefore, we should expect the final cause of death will be attributed to natural causes. You can be certain of that.

"However, when we view Pelosi's death in light of a very definite vendetta against certain judges and justices, then we have to look a little deeper.

"First of all, as is common for men his size and age, Pelosi suffered from heart disease—arrhythmia, atrial fibrillation. According to the preliminary report, he has had numerous mini-strokes—technically they're called transient ischemic attacks. What they do is provide all the symptoms of a stroke, but they clear right up without any lasting effects.

"But, two years ago he suffered a fairly significant stroke. It caused some permanent damage. As a result, he has been on warfarin ever since."

"Why warfarin? Why not one of the newer blood thinners?"

"The effects of warfarin are quite quickly reversible. The concern was if Pelosi were to take a fall, and bump his head, he could easily bleed into his skull and suffer significant brain damage. That's why warfarin. Were that to happen, he could be given other medication, such as phytonadione, that would counteract the warfarin and cause the blood to clot. In his case, the word is that he carried phytonadione on his person, so that in an emergency, he could self-medicate.

"That's the story. And there is plenty of reason to think it plausible. He liked to fight. But not box. He participated in a rather exotic sport called *dogfighting*. Really don't know much about it except it's supposed to be a younger man's game. He had engaged in a bout the night of his death, in fact. So, it would make sense that he would have some phytonadione on hand in the event that he received a head injury."

"I'm not sure I totally follow," Jack said. "Tell me if I've got this right. Phytonadione would cause the blood to clot, and if he already had a propensity for having a stroke, a large dose of that medication, in the absence of warfarin, could bring one about?"

"Enough of it would, without the warfarin."

"Did he have phytonadione in his system at the time of his death?"

"We'll find that out with the final autopsy report. I would say that it would take a fair amount to cause a big man like him to have a problem. But I'm no doctor."

"How would that much be administered?"

"It can be dissolved in alcohol … such as vodka."

"So," Jack summarized, "if Pelosi were given enough phytonadione, and deprived of his warfarin, it could result in a stroke? Is that accurate?"

"Given enough *coulds* and *ifs*, and a fair amount of luck, I think that would be correct. … You must take into consideration that, given he had the ability to self-medicate, he accidently took the wrong medication. It's entirely plausible."

"Is that what you suspect happened?"

"I'm Secret Service, I don't deal with that type of conjecture. … I leave that to the philosophers … and some detectives. But, I would like to see just how much phytonadione they find in Pelosi's body."

"Yes," Jack said. "And so would I. …I just thought of something. What if someone switched out his warfarin, and replaced it with that other stuff—vitamin K, disguised to look like warfarin?"

"Hey. Anything's possible. It'd be difficult to prove, but it's possible."

Jack disconnected his call and began a thorough survey of the hotel's lobby and restaurants in order to determine how best to withstand the onslaught he suspected might be launched against him.

"Henry," Jack said after checking his vibrating phone. "I'm in the coffee shop right now. I'll meet you at the front desk forthwith."

Chapter 34

Alexander, who had shed his Hasidic costume for more traditional San Francisco apparel, was meeting with Emma in a private room at a downtown restaurant.

"Glad to see you looking a bit more normal," she said with a smile.

Emma was five feet nine and strikingly beautiful. She walked with grace and had a flair to her that would cause all eyes in the room to follow. She was dressed in a long black dress with spaghetti straps and a side slit to the middle of her thigh. She wore dark stockings with tall leather three-inch-heeled boots. She carried a Versace patent leather tote over her shoulder. It was large enough to carry her weapon of choice for any given day. She had dark brown hair pulled up in a topknot with face-framing wispy bangs cut to lash length, tapered to cheekbone length, and blended with jawbone length layers. Huge golden hoop earrings accented the stylish coiffure. Her eyes were fringed with dark thick eyelashes highlighted by tastefully applied smoky eye shadow.

"I think you were the first Orthodox Jew I've seen in all my visits to the Bay Area."

San Francisco isn't like other large American cities, particularly when it comes to its community of observant Jews. In fact, a three-block stroll down almost any New York street from Midtown Manhattan to Brooklyn would produce a longer list of kosher restaurants than a person would find in the entire Golden City.

Sipos did not respond to her comment. Instead, he just sat there silently scrutinizing each word of an email he had just received from Dana.

"Like I told you earlier, it seems impossible that Handler could be so lucky, or clever. No one should have been able to figure out the names of our last two targets *before* the hits."

"Look," Emma interjected, "I just got here. *I* wasn't responsible for mucking up the Thompson hit. So, I'm not sure what you mean by *our* jobs. So far, the only person with *my* target on his back is Jack Handler … and those associated with him."

"I was referring to the contracts on Proctor and Thompson—the ones Dana and I have been working on. I know you had nothing to do with them. The hit on Thompson failed, and Proctor's almost did. My theory is that there is a leak somewhere at her end."

"How do you communicate?"

"Through highly encrypted email," Sipos said. "And then we use a code. No chance that anyone is able to read them."

"No encryption is perfect," Emma said.

"What my IT guy set up is pretty damn close. It's run through TOR, and then we communicate only through cryptograms, which means even should the NSA, or some other hacker, manage to peel the onion, he would be left with a cryptogram without a keyword. Virtually impossible to decipher."

The name *TOR* is derived from an acronym "The Onion Router."

TOR is an anonymous network which operates in the Dark Web part of the Deep Web. TOR is accessible only through a specialized browser and cannot be tapped by any search engine.

Data entering TOR is routed through thousands of randomly selected encryption relays, with each encryption laid upon the other like layers of an onion.

"There must be an internal leak," Sipos said. "There must be a mole within her organization."

"Her *organization?*" Emma questioned. "Just how big could her organization be?"

"That's the thing. She communicates with me through an encrypted network, and TOR. If she wishes to convey a message to individual members of The Group, I'm not so sure she always uses the secure network. I think she might get careless.

"She does not convene regular meetings of the whole group on any regular basis. Only when there are serious problems. And then, specific details are not discussed—those are always dealt with individually."

"Those names," Emma said, "Thompson and Proctor, they would not have been discussed with The Group?"

"Right. She and I alone discussed the individuals that were to be terminated. The other members of The Group are left in the dark about the hits until afterward."

"How about the contracts? How are they handled? I know that Dana contacted me personally. She said she was on a totally secure telephone connection. Is that true?"

"Absolutely. Even the NSA can't touch it. It is as secure a connection as exists anywhere. The Russians don't even know it exists, much less how to attack it. If she was on her secure connection, then your communication with her was safe. … It's just that sometimes I think she might get careless."

"Could her home or office be bugged?"

"She has it swept daily."

"By whom?"

"By the best," Sipos said, growing a little irritated by Emma's grilling him. "Besides, she never takes or makes a secure call inside a building."

"That's a helluva of thing, isn't it?" Emma said. "When a person can't even make a telephone call without someone trying to hack it."

Sipos just looked at her and smiled.

"One hell of a thing," he said. "You're right about that."

"Must be a mole."

"Damn hard to know," Sipos said. "Ever see the movie, *Tinker Tailor Soldier Spy*?"

"Four times," she said. "I fell asleep during three of them. The fourth time I drank a two cups of coffee with a shot of espresso in them. Finally, I figured out who the mole was."

"Fall asleep now and you'll be dead."

Emma smiled. They had both ordered off the lunch menu, making sure the server was out of range each time they communicated. Sipos was drinking his typical three martini lunch, while she ordered a raspberry-green tea—she had long ago given up alcohol, as her profession required a steady hand.

The room was ornately furnished with gold and black art deco furniture, and walls hand-painted with a myriad of images of the Gatsby era.

"You said earlier that you were working on a plan?" she asked in a hushed voice, leaning close enough to hear him breathe. "Exactly what is this plan supposed to accomplish?"

"I need to find out how Handler is obtaining his information. And then eliminate it."

"If I take Handler out now, won't that solve it?"

"Not really," Sipos said. His brow was now furrowed. "You kill Handler before we know how he's reading our mail, whoever replaces him will still have that advantage. We need to use him to get to the mole, or whatever the source of the leak is, and fix it. And then you can kill Handler."

"I can see that you and I are going to have to negotiate," Emma said. "My contract calls for the termination of Jack and Kate Handler, and two fourteen-year-old boys, Red and Robby. That's it. There's no provision in it for all this screwing around."

"I understand," Sipos said. "What is she paying you?"

"I thought you two worked together?"

"We do. But Dana generally deals directly with the contractors, and she contracts the hits. In most other areas involving finances, I would be more involved. But this is different.

"I am concerned that this leak could blow everything up. That's the *only* reason I showed up at the job last night, or that I'm talking to you right now.

"She does not even acknowledge that she has this problem, much less make any effort to fix it. I'm hoping that you and I can get it done. ... Why don't you tell me what you need to help me get to the bottom of this, and we'll go from there."

"Like I said. I had to watch that damn movie four times before I could figure out what it was trying to tell me. And I'm not stupid. I don't know how long this is going to take, or what will be involved. I don't even know what your plan is. ... Or if it even has a chance of working.

"What I do know is that the longer I stay in one place, the greater my chance of getting caught, or killed. This whole thing is beginning—"

"I get it," Sipos said. "Let's do it this way. I will give you a million U.S. dollars to let Handler live—for now. ... And, once I get this squared away, you come back and do the Handler hit, just like Dana wanted."

"How about this?" Emma said angrily, "How about I kill your sorry ass right now? For interfering in my contract. And then I take care of the Handlers ... and then get the hell out of this shitass town. How does *that* sound?"

Sipos was genuinely worried. He'd hoped that this conversation would lead to a solution to his problem, not present an even more serious situation for him.

"Damn it. You're right!" he said. "You're *absolutely* right. How about I keep out of your way and let you do the work you were hired to do? How does that sound?"

"Look," Emma said. "I would like to help you if I can. ... I will give you twenty-four hours to solve your problem, and then I take care of the Handlers? Will that work for you?"

"That would be fine."

"But, as far as any of this other stupidass horseshit, leave me out of it. I do not even want to be seen in the same state with you, ever again. Starting right now. I will do my job—that's it. ... But, I will take your one million U.S. dollars. Today."

"I'm perfectly fine with that," Sipos said, taking just a moment to digest what she had said. "But just hear me out. Five minutes. Give me five."

I could really use a cigar right now, he thought. *But all of the crazy ordinances. I'll just have to wait. When I leave here I'll hit the rum and cigar room on South Grand.*

"Okay."

"If Handler knew about Thompson and Proctor," Sipos said, "don't you think he also found out about you? And if he did, wouldn't you think that you have been compromised just as I have? … And, when this hits the fan, if we allow it to, you just might have to move to some island in the Pacific, or to Belize, and hide out there for the next twenty years. … Or, maybe you'll end up dead."

Emma was steaming. She knew Sipos was right.

"Tell me your plan," she said after several uncomfortable seconds.

Chapter 35

"You don't look half bad," Jack said to Henry as he greeted his friend at the counter.

"You're lying. I look like crap, and I know it. ... And who the hell are you pretending to be?"

"Let's go over here and sit down for a bit," Jack said, pointing toward a small table with two chairs on the far side of the lobby.

"What have you got in mind for me?" Henry asked as they walked. "I hope it's taxing as hell—something to get my mind off the pain."

"Taking painkillers?"

"Hell no," Henry said. "I thought you knew me better than that."

"This ought to be just what the doctor ordered, then," Jack said.

The two men sat silently as Jack pondered the words he would use to explain his situation.

"I just learned that a very powerful person has taken out a contract on my life," Jack finally said.

"The same one who's knocking off the judges?"

"Right. But it's much worse than that. She is targeting Kate and the boys as well."

"No shit. Why the boys?"

"Good question. My guess is that it's her strategy to draw me out in the open. She obviously isn't worried about anything that the boys, or even Kate, for that matter, might know or do that could hurt her. I'm the one she wants, she's just using the others to control me."

"So, where are Kate and the boys right now?"

"They're here in the city. At a different hotel."

"And, why are we here?"

"Officially, this is where Kate and I are staying."

"Tell me a little bit about this hit."

"The woman I was talking about, she's contracted a high-priced gun to take us out."

"Ever had any dealings with this guy? The gunman?"

"It's a woman. Emma. And she's quite the looker."

"You've actually seen her? Or just pictures?"

"She was here only an hour or so ago. She was standing right there at the front desk."

"Didn't she spot you?"

"I don't think so."

"What's my role going to be?"

"You're going to stay here," Jack said, as he fingered through to the image he'd shot moments earlier. "This is the woman. Emma."

"She *is* good looking," Henry said. "I suppose it wouldn't hurt quite as much if she shot you. As beautiful as she is."

Jack smiled.

"I don't have anything on the guys she travels with. But there are four of them. My guess is that they've been doing this for a while."

"She's going to figure out pretty quickly that I'm not Jack Handler," Henry said.

"Sure she will. And she might follow you around. But if we don't meet up, it will get her nowhere. It could serve as a distraction. Or, it could get you killed. But I don't think she is going to do anyone she won't get paid for. She is a professional."

"I'm up for it," Henry said. "And what's our ultimate game plan here? You must have something in mind."

"I'm thinking that we can gain a little time, initially, and then, perhaps, use you to lure her into a trap."

"So, I'm bait, and she's the mouse?"

"Something like that. But, for right now, I want to make sure that she doesn't hurt Kate or the boys. ... Ultimately, I want to follow this thing all the way to the top. Kill the head. That would be my game plan. To take out Dana, or whoever the hell is on top."

* * *

In a private room at a restaurant barely ten blocks from where Henry and Jack were planning their next move, Sipos and Emma were finalizing a strategy of their own.

Chapter 36

"This is how I want to do this," Sipos said. "Remember, I mentioned Judge Elizabeth Cohen, Ninth District Court of Appeals?"

"I recall. She's not on the list. But she *is* a problem. You were talking about moving her up."

"Yes, I'm putting her on the list, but not for the conventional reason. There're actually two judges, both on the Ninth, that I'm including. And neither of them were on the original list. But both of them are problems. Cohen was one of ours. She's wandered off on her own. The second judge, Judge Clifford Higgins, he was a thickheaded strict constitutionalist from the start. Killing him will just make me feel good.

"The first one, Cohen, I am going to put forward to the ten permanent board members of The Group, and to Dana. Higgins, however, I will present his name *only* to Dana, and ask her not to share it with the board, since Higgins was never one of our groomed candidates.

"If Cohen receives protection, from the FBI or Jack Handler, and Higgins does not, then we will know that the leak is coming from a mole on the board. If Higgins alone gets the attention, then we will know that the leak does not involve the board. At that point we will have to start looking for the mole in Dana's immediate circle—perhaps even an electronic bug. This would be especially likely should both of these judges receive special protection.

"I realize that this is not a perfect plan, but it's better than nothing. I will do my best to expedite the orders so that the plan falls within your twenty-four hour time limit. ... I think you'd agree that your job will be easier, and safer, if we can find and eliminate the source of the leaks."

"Possibly," Emma said. "But, to me, time is the most critical issue. Most mistakes are made when we start overthinking our mission. I much prefer putting the plan together and executing it immediately."

Sipos had already begun his call to Allison's secure connection.

"Al ... Dana. Sorry about that slip. I've got a couple new names for you. I've already discussed them with Emma. But you might want to follow up with her on any info you think could be helpful. Here they are, Judge Elizabeth Cohen, and Judge Clifford Higgins. Both are on the Ninth."

"Well, that's a surprise," Dana said. "We have not discussed *them* before. May I ask your reason?"

"I'd rather not go into it now. We've got the manpower and expertise right now. Plus we are already in San Francisco. But that's all I'm going to say. I just didn't want to surprise you. ... And, one more thing. Please do not mention Higgins's name to the board. He was not one of our candidates, so it follows that they should not be privy to any information regarding Judge Higgins. ... But, regarding Cohen. Please run that name past the board and give them all a heads up to stay clear of her."

"That's all well and good," Dana said. "But just be aware that you will be picking up the entire tab on these two. I won't be covering anything. Is that understood?"

"Absolutely. But I would appreciate it if you would contact Emma personally, through standard channels, and release her to me for these jobs. … And also immediately notify the board regarding Cohen."

"Fine. And I will be sure to let her know that you will be paying her. Not me."

Thirty seconds later Emma received a call from Dana.

"I understand from Sipos that he has a couple jobs he would like you to take care of for him," Dana said. "Is that okay with you? Judges Cohen and Higgins?"

"We've discussed those two specifically and I've agreed."

"Okay, then, just know that he will be paying you directly for everything. Is that understood as well?"

"I'm good with it."

"I'll talk to you later."

"Done," Emma said, turning back to Sipos. "That was short and sweet. She doesn't sound very happy about this arrangement."

"To her, the only good idea is one she comes up with. But I like her decisiveness. At least I always know where she's coming from."

"What do we do now?"

"Nothing, for now," Sipos said. "We wait. I've got two men doing surveillance at each of the new locations. If the FBI or Handler shows up at either one of them, or both, we will have what we're looking for."

"What if it doesn't happen? Do I take them out anyway? And do I still get paid? I'm not about to keep playing around in your petri dish. I do my jobs and get paid. That's how it works for me."

"And that's how this is going to work, too."

"Okay, just as long as we have an understanding."

"This might work to your advantage."

"How so?"

"If Jack Handler shows up at one of these locations, my men will let me know, and you can take it from there. That would make Dana very happy."

"Nothing *ever* makes Dana happy."

* * *

"Jack," Roger said. "Hope I'm not disturbing anything."

"I'm just sitting here chewing the fat with Henry."

"What the hell? I thought he was chasing nurses around the hospital in the U.P. What's he doing in The City by the Bay?"

"Long story. What's on your mind?"

Chapter 37

Because Dana did not like the inconvenience of accessing a secured connection when she initiated calls, especially when she was angry, she would often take a shortcut and skip the safeguards. Therefore, the phone call Dana had just made to Emma was over an unsecured service provider.

Roger's operatives wasted no time in providing him with the details of the call, and he, in turn, immediately called Jack.

"Something very strange just happened," Roger said. "And I don't have a solid reason for my suspicions, but I certainly have some."

"What's up?"

"We just monitored a call placed by Dana to Emma. It sounded like it referenced an earlier call placed by Sipos to Dana. But I don't know that for certain, because he would have observed protocol, and used a secure connection.

"Looks like they have named two more judges for elimination. Both are on the Ninth, just like Judge Thompson. Their names are Higgins and Cohen."

"I'm not familiar with either of them," Jack replied. "How do you want me to handle it?"

"This might just be a case of paranoia," Roger said. "But this smells like a trap to me?"

"For me?"

"For both of us," Roger said. "I'm told that Dana was genuinely perturbed, so I doubt that she is in on it. ... Sounds like something Sipos might have cooked up. Perhaps with Emma's participation.

"If I take the bait and have you or the FBI immediately run out to these judges' homes, it will be clear that someone is monitoring Dana's calls. It would not take long to figure out that it's me. And besides, how likely is it that they would be hitting three judges on the same court? I don't think they would do that. Unless, of course, it is a trap."

"Even if it is a trap, it sounds like it's for real," Jack said, "How can we just allow them to die?"

"We can't," Roger replied. "But we don't have to dispatch the cavalry, either."

"What does that mean?"

"It means that we find another way to thwart the hits—without anyone physically showing up on their doorstep."

"Can't be from me or the FBI. Any ideas?"

"I've been thinking about it," Roger said. "If this is a trap—and I have to say that my gut tells me it is. ... If this is a trap, there will be a time cushion to work with. Whoever is setting it up, they are going to allow for some time to pass. Undoubtedly, these judges are being physically monitored. Someone is watching their houses, and their offices. If they have offices outside their homes. We don't dare go near them, or it will tip our hand."

"Here's a thought," Jack said. "I've actually pulled this off before, and with some success. What we do is suspend a couple, maybe three, propane tanks in trees in the general area where one of these judges lives. Locate them close together, but not too close. And open the valve just a little. Propane is heavier than air, so the gas will disperse and move along the ground with the breeze.

"And then we call the gas company referencing the judge's address.

"The gas company will come out. They will not be looking up, because the standard household natural gas is lighter than air. But they both have the same rotten-egg smell, because sulfates are added to provide a warning. It will take them a while to figure out the cause. It will look like a very generalized underground gas leak. They might even evacuate. It could take them a couple of days to get to the bottom of it."

"Good," Roger said. "That sounds very good. I'll make the complaining calls because I can trick the exchange to look like they're originating locally. … Any ideas for the other judge?"

"Can't be the same thing," Jack said. "Unless, of course, they're neighbors."

"Would you want to live in the same neighborhood as a federal judge?" Roger said through a smile. "Even if you were a federal judge yourself? … I checked. They live on opposite ends of the city. Cohen lives in a small Jewish community. Higgins has a house in the surrounding hills. The gas trick would work for Cohen. Not sure how we deal with Higgins. Not yet."

"Set his house on fire?"

"Too much like releasing gas," Roger said. "Remember, the whole point might be to ferret out the leak. In other words, trace it back to me. Can't allow that to happen."

"I've got another idea," Jack said. "I think you might like it."

"Well, spill it."

"Surveil the area with a drone," Jack said. "Not just any drone. We need one that can hover at five thousand feet. It must have infrared sensors, and a very good HD remotely monitored camera. We locate whoever it is that is monitoring the house, and have the local authorities pick them up. Say they are trying to lure children.

"Once we've eliminated the surveillance, we can get the FBI in to pull the judge and his family out."

"That could work," Roger said. "Do you know anyone with a drone like that?"

"Not in San Francisco," Jack said. "But I know someone who most likely can get his hands on one."

"Call him," Roger said.

"Don't need to. I'm talking to him right now."

"Oh. I see," Roger said, already suspecting where Jack was headed. "The drone you're describing is very illegal. … I might, however, have an alternative solution. … I'll take care of Higgins."

"These are all very temporary fixes," Jack said. "Once they've had a chance to analyze the situation, they'll figure out that the leak is coming from Dana."

"I'd suggest that they've already thought this through," Roger said. "And they have concluded exactly that. But this subterfuge will buy you a day or two. That's all."

"Plus, it will save the lives of a couple judges."

"Exactly."

* * *

"Henry," Jack said after putting his phone in his pocket. "We're going to have a cookout—sort of. One without burgers. Roger has a job for us to do. … It'll be good for you. Get your mind off your shoulder."

After picking up three tanks of propane, and some nylon rope, Jack and Henry headed out to the Cohen house.

"Jack," Henry said. "You hinted at cutting off the head of the snake. I suspect you're referring to Dana, or whatever her real name is. Do you have a plan to pull that off? Because, I'm beginning to feel like we're just chasing shadows. If we know who's responsible for this, why don't we go after them? Does that make sense to you?"

"It sure does," Jack said. "But it's not that simple. Roger is in the middle of this. And, unfortunately, he's already doing all he can to help. And, if I simply go after the head, I just might end up having to go through him. And then, one of us won't make it. Killing Roger is just about the last thing I would want to do.

"I'm not saying that I wouldn't take him out, if that's the only way I can save my family. But I would like to find a way to avoid having to do that."

Up until that point Henry did not fully appreciate the challenge Jack was facing. Henry said to himself. *Roger is the head of the detail that protects the former first lady—Allison Fulbright. Then Dana is really Allison. Damn, Jack's in trouble. ... We're all in trouble.*

Chapter 38

Jack's propane plan worked as designed.

He first spray-painted the propane tanks dark green, and then he and Henry rented a tree-trimming vehicle. They blitzed the neighborhood upwind from the Cohen house seeking out tall evergreen trees. When they had the three tanks in place and opened slightly, they notified Roger and he called in the complaints. Of the three addresses given, the Cohens' was centermost among them.

As a result, the gas company, along with fire emergency responders, evacuated the entire neighborhood—including the two men who had been watching the Cohen house for Sipos.

Roger pulled off the other part of the scheme just as efficiently.

Because Judge Higgins lived so far out in the country, the car with the two shady characters in it was quite easy to spot. Roger himself placed the call to the local authorities reporting an attempted abduction, giving them the plate number, description and location of the surveillance car.

Within five minutes the chopper pilot asked permission to pull out. "Mission accomplished," he told Roger. "Four patrol cars, with six officers. All with weapons drawn. Suspects in custody."

* * *

"Well, Emma," Dana said, "how's that arrangement between you and Sipos working out?"

There was a strong tone of disgust in Dana's voice. She was not pleased that Sipos had stepped on her plans with regard to Emma. She had contracted the beautiful killer to take out Jack and his family. So, when Sipos took it upon himself to present a side deal to Emma, Dana viewed it very dimly.

He should have sought my permission beforehand, she said to herself. *In fact, he should not have even talked to her at all. He compromised our entire operation. And just look what happened. It has become clear that Handler somehow found out about those other two judges—the ones that never should have been on the list. And he warned them off. No one but Handler could have pulled it off like that—making it look like there was a gas leak and all. Sipos screwed this up royally, and now I've got to fix it. He has turned my brilliant plan into a stupid sideshow. And now I'm left to correct his mistakes.*

That was how Dana viewed Sipos's actions—as interference.

And that was also how Emma saw it. If the paycheck Dana had promised her to kill Jack and his family was not so generous, Emma would have gladly planted two .22 caliber rounds in Sipos's skull and moved on.

In fact, she even went so far as to run that idea past Dana—to kill Sipos. But Dana vehemently denied permission.

"Sipos might be careless," she told Emma. "And sometimes he acts stupidly—he's getting to be an old man—but he is dedicated to the cause. And he is very, very rich. We need to let him live because we can use him, and his money. … But his time will come. And when it does—"

"Let's get back to the job at hand," Emma interrupted, not comfortable with listening to Dana ramble on.

"I want you to shelve for now the project with the judges, and to concentrate on terminating Jack Handler, and his family. If I am correct, you have not yet been able to locate him. Is that right?"

"I would probably be in a plane over the Atlantic right now," Emma said, not pleased with the tone or content of Dana's words. "Were it not for your friend Sipos. ... You and he need to just get the hell out of my way and let me do what I do."

Dana was not used to being addressed in such a fashion, but she knew better than to rile Emma up.

"Then be about your business," she said. "I don't want to see or hear from you again until I read Handler's obituary."

Neither of the women said another word. After a few seconds, Dana terminated the call, which, again, was over an unsecured connection.

Chapter 39

Nunchuck and his associate had arrived in San Francisco with the rest of Emma's group to help locate and kill Jack and Kate. Emma assigned them to remain at the Holiday Vista Hotel because that was the location where Jack was supposed to be staying. Even though they assumed that Jack was actually staying someplace other than at that hotel, it seemed reasonable to monitor activity just in case he showed up.

They even checked in themselves, and took turns waiting in the lobby.

It was only their second day when they experienced their first success. Nunchucks was sitting and reading a copy of *Black Belt* magazine when he spotted someone who looked familiar. It wasn't Jack Handler, but, for some reason, Henry caught his attention.

Quickly he raised his smart phone and snapped a picture.

When he ran the image through his facial recognition software it came back with the name "Chuchip (Henry) Kalyesveh, MMA fighter.

Currently an associate of Jack Handler, Private Investigator."

"Chuchip," Nunchuck whispered to himself. "Nine, ten years ago. We were on the same card in Chicago. We both won our bouts. I remember you."

"That's it!" Nunchuck whispered again. "That's my guy."

But by the time the info had come to his phone, Henry was already in the elevator and on his way up. Nunchuck pushed the *Up* button, and then watched the digital readout for the floors. *One guy on the elevator, and there was only one stop—twelfth floor,* Nunchuck determined. *Twelfth floor, and the car headed back down. That's it.*

"Get your ass down here," Nunchuck said when his associate answered his call. "I think I'm on to something."

The associate, Gordon Milton Brower, was not a young man. He was a hardened criminal, having spent twenty-two of his fifty plus years in prison. While no one considered him to be particularly bright, he was loyal. And he did not have a drinking problem. Of all the people Nunchuck knew on the outside, Gordon was the only man he trusted.

"Whatcha got?" Gordon asked.

"It ain't Jack Handler, but it is his friend. His name is Henry. I can't pronounce his real name. He got off on the twelfth floor. This is how we do this.

"We both wait in the lobby, or at least close enough to the elevators that we can monitor them. As soon as we spot him getting off the elevator, you will go up and get off on the twelfth. And just wait.

"I will wait in the lobby. When I spot him coming up, I will call up and warn you. You will then take a position at the elevator. When he gets off, you will get on, but you will hold the door open. And then, you will get back off and follow to see what room he goes in. … I'll take it from there.

"There is one more thing. I could be wrong, but he looks to me to be favoring his left arm. No sling, or anything. He just doesn't seem to be carrying it in a normal way—like maybe he injured it in a fight, or something. … Watch yourself, though. He's one very tough sonofabitch. Even with a bad wing, I think he can handle himself."

Four hours later Henry walked out of the elevator and down to the coffee shop.

"Here's our chance. Head up to the twelfth and wait for my call.

It did not take Henry much time to pick up a coffee and sweet roll at the coffee shop, and head back up.

"Gordon, he is just getting on the elevator. Press the *Up* button, and then do like we discussed. He will assume you are simply waiting for an Up elevator."

Five minutes later Gordon walked out of the elevator and joined his friend in the lobby.

With a big smile he said, "Our guy entered room twelve seventeen. He had the key, and I saw him go in."

"Okay," Nunchucks said. And then he started writing.

"This is what you do," he said to Gordon. "I will go up to his room and wait. When I call you, I want you to go over to the service phone and call his room. When he answers, tell him exactly this, *Kate asked me to drop off a package for Henry at the front desk. But she told me not to go up to your room in case I'm followed. She said you will want what's in the package.* And then hang up. I'll call you later and tell you what to do.

"Got it?"

"No problem," Gordon assured him. "What are you gonna do?"

"Don't worry about that right now. Just read the note to him exactly as I wrote it—nothing more, and nothing less."

Nunchucks took the elevator up to the twelfth floor and took a position right next to Henry's room.

"Okay, Gordon, make the call and read the note. Do not make conversation with him after you read it. Just hang up and wait for me to call you."

Two minutes later Nunchuck heard the phone ring in Henry's room. He could not make out much but he did sense that Henry was not talking. *Must have hung up. Time to rock and roll,* he said to himself.

Just seconds later Henry stuck his head out of the door to see if trouble awaited. But by the time he spotted Nunchuck it was too late.

A single crushing blow across the bridge of Henry's nose drove him back into his room and flat on his back.

Nunchuck did not want to take the chance of killing Henry, so instead of striking him again with his weapon of choice, he tasered him.

While Henry was incapacitated, Nunchuck lifted him into a steel chair and zip-tied his wrists and ankles to it. He then stuffed a face cloth into Henry's mouth, and secured it there by tying a sock around his head.

"I've just got to check out that left arm," he said as he ripped off Henry's shirt. … "Just as I thought. You're injured. Looks like a bullet hole to me. I wonder how you got that." And then yanking him forward by the hair so he could get a look at his back, he said, "And it came out the other side. You're pretty lucky to have survived that. Looks like a high-velocity rifle wound to me. Saw a lot of them in Afghanistan. Is that what you've got?"

Henry was in no condition to talk. But he was coming around.

"You are going to talk to me, my friend," Nunchucks said. "Everyone eventually talks to me. So you might as well do it right away, and save yourself a lot of pain and suffering. Got it?"

Henry did not even look at his taunter.

Nunchuck slapped him on the side of his head, and asked him again, "Got it?"

Henry nodded.

"I'll bet that left arm hurts pretty bad, doesn't it?"

Henry nodded.

"Can you use it at all? I saw you carrying it at your side like you were in a lot of pain. Is that how it is?"

Henry nodded.

"I'll bet that does really hurt. But it could be worse, you know. It could hurt a lot worse than it does right now. Here, I'll show you what I mean."

Nunchuck snapped a pocket knife from off his belt and flipped the blade open. Then, with no hesitation, he shoved the blade into Henry's wound, severing the stitches and causing a major flow of blood.

"Now that really hurts, right?"

Henry, beginning to perspire heavily, nodded.

"That's pretty tender in there, I bet. I only went in maybe an inch, if that. But this blade is nearly four inches long. Now, that would not only be very painful, it might just kill you. … Do you want me to show you what I mean?"

Henry shook his head.

"Are you going to help me out, then?"

Henry nodded.

"Good boy. Good boy. I'm really happy to hear that. … Now, I'm not going to remove your gag. I don't think I can trust you to be quiet. But I am going to let you write me a little note. This is how it's gonna work. I'm going to place a zip-tie on your left arm above your elbow. And then take the tie off of your wrist. You can then write your answers. You can write with your left hand, right?"

Henry nodded.

This could work, Henry began to think.

Henry drew his bicep as close against the chair as he could, ensuring the tightest possible restriction with the zip-tie.

Nunchuck accommodated Henry by drawing the tie tightly around the back of the chair and Henry's lower bicep.

Perfect, Henry said to himself.

Nunchuck cut the tie on his left wrist, placed a magazine on Henry's left thigh, stuck a pen in his hand, and slid a piece of paper under the pen.

"I'm gonna ask you some questions, and you're gonna answer. Got it?"

Henry nodded again, but this time he was squeezing a smile out from under the gag.

"Okay, Henry, here's my first question. Whether or not I hurt you again is *totally* up to you. Do you understand me?"

Henry nodded.

"Do you know where Jack Handler is staying?"

Henry took his time. Writing very deliberately he scribbled three words.

Nunchuck leaned over to read what he had written. As he did Henry exerted all his arm strength against the tie that secured his left arm. Nunchuck had affixed the tie as tightly as he could, leaving the securing part of the tie facing the front. By turning his arm outward, and using all his strength he quite easily snapped the tie. Henry had practiced this maneuver numerous times, always with the same successful result.

He then surgically shoved the ballpoint pen through the soft tissue of Nunchuck's neck, severing his carotid artery. Hot blood began gushing out of the wound. As soon as he felt the blood he released the pen and grabbed Nunchuck by the collar of his shirt, forcefully pulling Nunchuck's face into the hardest part of his own forehead. He repeated that exercise until he sensed Nunchuck's knees buckling.

Henry slowly let the man crumple to the floor, making sure that he would be able to reach Nunchuck's knife with his one free hand.

It took only a couple minutes for Nunchuck's unconscious body to totally bleed out. By that time Henry had freed himself.

Nunchuck's phone began to vibrate.

"Yeah," Henry answered.

"Nunchuck, is that you?"

"Yeah."

"Should I come up now?"

Henry smiled broadly and said, "Yeah." And then, with his right hand, he crushed the phone.

Chapter 40

Kate," Jack said. "I just got a call from Roger. He believes that there is a renewed interest in Dana's desire to see us dead. You're with the boys right now?"

"We're actually at Fisherman's Wharf."

"Let me guess—Ripley's Believe it or Not Museum.

"That's where the boys chose to go?"

"Right," Kate replied. "They wanted to see the sea lions on Pier 39, but someone must have warned them that we were coming, and they all took a hike.

"So, we headed straight down to the Ripley Museum—the Odditorium. The boys are fascinated. It's quite large—two floors of a large building on Jefferson Street, just south of Musée Mécanique. That's the vending machine place. ... As you can tell, there's lots to do here today. I don't think we will see much else on this trip."

"How about Buddy?" Jack asked. "Is he with you?"

"He just got in," Kate replied. "They drove straight through. And, yes, Buddy is sporting his new *Service Dog* vest. That was a brilliant way to get Buddy into the hotel ... and virtually everywhere else."

"Robby came up with the idea," Jack said. "He thought Red should have a Service Dog. And Buddy didn't object. … You probably should hang out in the museum until I get there. From what Roger said, Allison's judge project is on hold until we're dead."

"I don't know if that's good or bad," Kate said. "What's her obsession with harming the boys?"

"It's clever, actually. By putting the boys in the mix, she knows pretty much that I will stick around wherever they happen to be. And you as well. … And that's exactly what's happening. I'm on my way to Fisherman's Wharf because that's where you and the boys are."

"How safe are we right now?" Kate asked. "I had the distinct feeling that we were being followed down here. But I don't know that for sure."

"You're armed? Because, I think that by now she has figured out that we're not staying at the Holiday Vista. … It's only a matter of time."

"That safe, huh? … Of course, I'm armed. But we do need to get a plan."

"See you as soon as I can catch a cab and get there."

Jack was faced with a dilemma. While he knew that Emma and her men would sooner or later launch their attempt on his life, and that Kate and the boys were also targeted, he knew as well that it would be just as dangerous to head back to Sugar Island. At least in San Francisco he was not putting in danger the lives of his Upper Peninsula friends.

So, he decided to do battle in the city where some of the greatest movies of all time were made—Clint Eastwood's *Escape from Alcatraz*, Woody Allen's *Play it Again Sam*, Eddie Murphy's *48 Hours*, *The Maltese Falcon*, and *Dirty Harry* Callahan. Of course, the only movie scene that truly captured Jack's admiration was Steve McQueen's classic chase in *Bullitt*.

But, Jack remained hopeful that the scene he was about to stage would be no more violent than the closing act in Woody Allen's masterpiece.

* * *

Emma had left her men, Nunchucks and Gordon Milton Brower, to surveil the Holiday Vista Hotel after discovering Jack was officially registered there. After not spotting Jack entering or leaving, she correctly concluded that Jack had set the room up as a ruse to misdirect attention away from where he was actually staying.

She then recalled that Sipos had told her that he had arrived on the same plane as the Handlers. That information revealed the exact timeframe she should investigate.

So, she went down to the airport and inquired about two teenage boys, an older man, and an attractive woman. Dana had given her pictures of both Jack and Kate. Soon she was able to find an attendant who had helped find a taxi for a family who fit that description. He even recalled the driver's name, and for a price the taxi driver was willing to tell her the hotel where the Handlers were staying.

The rest will be easy, she thought, *now that I know where they are really staying.*

She had followed Kate that morning to Fisherman's Wharf.

Chapter 41

Emma was a master of disguises. Generally, however, she did not like donning any unflattering garments—even though it might make it easier to gain close proximity to her targets.

But not all targets presented the sort of challenge that Jack did.

She observed Kate and the boys entering the museum, and she concluded that Jack would not be far behind.

She believed that Jack and Kate would have become fairly familiar with her appearance, and that they probably had pictures of her. So, a disguise was definitely in order.

As was always her practice, she did not bring a costume with her. Instead, she would size up the situation, see what props were readily available, and then improvise.

Those teenage boys will be very content to hang out in this museum for quite a while, she surmised. *This is where I stage my attack.* She positioned herself in front of the museum, and observed. Finally, she spotted what she was looking for.

"That ought to do just fine," she whispered to herself, as she followed a rather tall female worker to a secluded area where city employees liked to go to sneak a cigarette.

"Pardon me, Miss," she said. "But could you tell me where is the

Musée Mécanique?"

"Sure," the young lady said as she pointed with her cigarette. "If you head straight that way you'll see it. It's big. You really can't miss—"

That's all Emma allowed her to say. Following the girl's cigarette with her eyes, Emma viciously delivered the business end of a leather-covered blackjack to the side of the girl's head. A second blow to the head proved immediately fatal. Emma helped her to the ground and began stripping off her jumpsuit.

Emma then scooped up the lanky young lady's body, dumped it in a nearby unlocked dumpster, and closed the plastic lid.

She complained out loud as she transferred the tools of her trade into the jumpsuit and slipped it on. "Damn, girl. This stinks. You smoked way too much. … Won't be a problem for you anymore, though. I suppose you could say that I helped you quit smoking. But you don't have to thank me."

Emma confiscated the worker's long-handled broom and mechanical dustpan, practiced a few strokes with it, and headed out front to watch for Jack.

Within minutes the unexpected happened.

A young man walked up behind her and asked, "Hey! I've never seen *you* here before. Are you new?"

"Just started."

"Liz usually takes care of this area. Where's she working today?"

"Last I saw of her she was around back."

"Guess I'll see if I can catch up with her. … Wanna grab a cig with me?"

"Sure."

Emma strode along behind the tall but slightly overweight young man until they reached the surreptitious smoking area.

"I don't think she's still back here," he said. "Must be she got assigned to a different area. You got a cigarette I can bum off ya? My name is Skip, by the way."

"Libbie. My name is Libbie."

"Do they call you Lib for short?"

"No."

Emma reached into the pocket and pulled out half a pack of Marlboro filtered.

"You smoke the same brand as Liz. Don't that just beat all," he said taking a cigarette from the somewhat crushed pack.

"Got a light?"

Emma took one of the Marlboros for herself and put it in her mouth. She then slid the pack back into her pocket and pulled out a yellow Bic lighter.

She lit his smoke, and then her own.

"You might smoke the same brand of cigs as Liz, but you're a whole lot better looking—if you don't mind my saying. … I know I have to be careful what I say, sexual harassment and all. … You're not offended, are you? I'll take it back if you are. I was just paying you a compliment. I didn't mean anything."

"I'm not offended. Thanks for the compliment. It's totally okay."

"Wow, that's a relief. I really worry about getting myself in trouble with my big mouth. I really need this job."

"Not to worry. I'm cool. … Maybe you could give me a hand with something," Emma said. "I accidently dropped my newspaper in that dumpster, and I can't reach quite far enough to get it out."

"Sure. No problem. I'll see what I can do."

"Don't tell anyone," Emma said on the way to the dumpster, "but I brought my trash from home. I know I'm not supposed to do that. And

I forgot that my paper was in it. I like to do crossword puzzles at lunch."

"I'll get it for you."

When they reached the dumpster, Skip flipped it back with a single effort.

This guy is very strong, Emma surmised, as she removed a Taser from her pocket.

"Oh my God! That's Liz!"

As Skip leaned over to pull Liz out, Emma tasered him on his side. He was paralyzed.

She then picked up his feet and tried to wrestle him into the dumpster, but his pudgy belly got hung up on the edge and she could not leverage the rest of his body enough to get it in.

"Well, that's going to have to do for now," she said as she removed a six-shot .22 caliber revolver from her pocket, pushed the suppressor to the back of Skip's head, and fired two shots.

He farted loudly as life drifted from his quivering body.

"You would have to do that, wouldn't you?!"

Emma put the revolver back in her pocket and refocused at loading her victim's lower body into the dumpster. After some struggle, she discovered that by placing one of his feet on her shoulder, she could twist the other foot and roll his body on the edge of the dumpster until gravity pulled him the rest of the way in.

"Damn, that was a miserable job," she growled as she removed the spent cartridges, put them in her pocket, and loaded two fresh rounds.

"Okay, Jack Handler. It's your turn. … You'd better not fart in my face!"

As she walked to the front of the museum she felt around in her pocket to confirm that she had three fully-loaded speedloaders for the .22 revolver.

Chapter 42

Dana had not explained to Emma why she had included Kate and the two boys in the contract to kill Jack, but Emma had no problem with it. She had encountered a similar situation one other time in her professional career. In that case, which involved the hit on a mob boss, the patriarch of a competing crime family called for the death of the target's two young daughters and his cocker spaniel, as well as the hit on the boss himself.

When she inquired as to why the girls and the dog had to die, the old man told her that there were two reasons. First of all, he wanted to make a definitive statement. He wanted the target's family all to know who the real boss was, in case anyone might have had doubts.

And, second, he wanted to make sure that the target didn't go into hiding when he found out about the contract. In other words, he did not want the target to think that he could weather the storm and eventually everything would go back to the way it was. Not only would the death of his daughters and favorite dog be a symbolic loss, it would be difficult to go into hiding with a dog and two girls.

Emma didn't care about Dana's motivation. It was just a job to her. In her mind it was that simple. Some women have babies, some deliver them; other women try cases before judges and juries, while others run for public office. For Emma, killing people was what she did—it was as simple as that. And the mere fact that two of her targets were adolescent children was not a significant factor to her.

Actually, in the case of the hit on the mob boss, she felt less emotion taking out the man's two daughters than she did in killing his dog. "What did this poor helpless animal do to deserve this?" she asked herself at the time. "Absolutely nothing."

Pop. Pop.

Killing was her job. Whether it be the shooting of a young child, or the poisoning of an old man, it just didn't matter to her as long as she got paid.

"Well, I'll be damned," she muttered when she spotted Jack entering the museum. "How's that for timing?"

Jack was wearing a tan windbreaker, a light colored pair of khaki pants, baseball cap and sunglasses. His appearance was not any different from what it would have been at any other time.

He looked as though he didn't have a care in the world. But, in that respect, nothing could be further from the truth.

Both Jack and Kate were fully aware that their lives, as well as the lives of the two boys, were in grave danger.

Robby and Red knew that something was up, but, of course, Jack and Kate had not shared any of the details with them.

It was not by chance that the Handlers were hanging around in a building like the museum—the boys had specifically chosen this facility for their family outing. But Jack and Kate had discussed it thoroughly and determined that the museum's layout might afford them the best opportunity to stage a successful stand against an attack. This is how they hoped their plan would work.

Kate would send the boys and Buddy off to a significantly isolated section of the building. The whole facility was fascinating, so the boys could easily entertain themselves out of harm's way.

Jack believed that the killer would wait to make sure that he and Kate were close to one another. This would ensure that both could be taken out in rapid succession.

Emma was aware that Kate was a police detective, and therefore certainly possessed a proficiency with firearms and self-defense tactics.

But, she knew from experience that a drawn firearm is much more effective than one in a holster or handbag. She believed that she would have the element of surprise working in her favor. All she would have to do is get a single round off squarely into Jack's skull, place a second round into his brain stem, and then shoot Kate between the eyes.

That will take a maximum of two seconds, she reckoned. *If I do it right. I need to take a deep breath and relax. Now is the time to put all that training to use.*

To hone her skills, Emma had soundproofed her basement and constructed a pistol range complete with moving targets. Through nearly daily practice she had developed her shooting skills to a level thirty percent greater than FBI proficiency requirements.

She planned to kill Jack and Kate first, and then take out Red and Robby. She would allow one minute to hunt the boys down and kill them. If she couldn't accomplish that in the allotted time, she would punt. *Can't spend too much time in one place,* she thought. *Besides, I'm thinking that all the boys are is bait to attract the real targets—Jack and Kate Handler.*

If everything went according to Emma's plan, she should have her work in the museum completed in a minute and a half, total.

If Kate's instincts were correct—that she and the boys had been followed to the Wharf—then an attack was most likely imminent. Anticipating the attempt, she and Jack sought out the best possible location within the museum in which to frame their stand.

After making sure that the boys were occupied in the Hall of Mirrors, which was as far away from them as possible, she and Jack positioned themselves facing each other in an open area. That would afford them the ability to monitor anyone approaching from within the building.

Jack determined to hold that position for ten minutes. *If the attack does not occur during that timeframe*, he concluded, *then my strategizing was in error.*

They knew that any hit occurring in a facility like the museum would not be carried out with a rifle. That meant that the shooter would need to get in close—generally to within three or four feet.

They did not have to wait long.

Kate had left her sunglass on. This allowed her to be facing in one direction, while focusing her eyes in a slightly different one.

"Tall woman approaching rapidly at my eleven o'clock," she said.

Jack cocked his head slightly to the right so that he could monitor the potential threat using the rear vision reflection in his sunglasses.

"That could be her," Jack said as he slipped a snub-nosed S&W Airweight five-shot revolver from his belt holster. "We have to be totally sure that's her before we take her out. She has to present a weapon."

Emma suddenly sensed that she was walking into a trap. Perhaps she caught sight of the reflection of Jack's eye on the inside of his sunglasses. Or maybe she picked up vibes from Kate's blank expression, or the fact that Kate appeared to be making a move for her weapon.

Emma was not conscious of what tipped her off—she was just following her target-range reflexes.

While she was still nearly twenty feet away she quickly pulled and pointed her weapon. Jack spun to face her, but neither he nor Kate had time to get a shot off.

Emma's .22 caliber round caught Jack on the front of his baseball cap almost squarely in the middle of his upper forehead. The force of the round sent his cap flying right into Kate's face, knocking her sunglasses off and temporarily obscuring her vision.

Jack crumpled to the floor.

His sunglasses, which had become dislodged when the force of the bullet knocked his head backward, bounced on the floor beside his crumpled body.

Emma had wanted her next shot to sever his brain stem, so she took another three steps toward him, re-aiming the revolver as she approached.

She could see that the force of the cap striking Kate in the face had impeded her ability to draw her weapon.

As Emma drew down on Jack for her second shot, Buddy suddenly appeared. The family protector, who had been leisurely hanging out with Red and Robby, somehow sensed Jack's plight. He had bolted from between the boys and made a beeline to Jack's aid. He never slowed down. Sailing airborne for at least ten feet, Buddy hit the wrist of Emma's gun hand with tremendous force. Her pistol went flying as he sunk his canines deeply into her flesh.

Kate pounced on the shooter with both knees, pinning her to the floor while pummeling her with a devastating flurry of fists to her face. She then rolled the unconscious Emma onto her stomach and slapped her with handcuffs.

"Holy cow! Kate!" Robby said. Both he and Red had followed Buddy as quickly as they could. "What's happening? Who's this lady? … What's wrong with Uncle Jack? Is he gonna be okay?"

Chapter 43

Kate did not respond to Robby's question because she did not want to lie to him. She knew her father had taken a bullet to the head and that he was most likely dying or already dead. She did not want to say the words, but she suspected the latter.

Blood was beginning to run a steady stream down Jack's face and onto the floor.

Kate fought the urge to check on her father. Instead, she followed procedure and secured Emma's weapon, surveyed her surroundings for additional threats, and then hurridly dragged Emma by the hair into an out-of-sight space behind a display.

"You two," she said to Robby and Red, "Take Buddy and go back to where you were. Now! Move!"

"But—"

"Now!" she said, with all the authority she could muster.

Robby did not say another word. Both boys turned and headed quickly in the direction Kate had pointed.

Taking cover behind another display, Kate's eyes scoured the museum for anyone heading toward her from the entry.

She waited.

Finally, she spotted a trim young man dressed totally in black. He had just entered the museum and was cautiously heading in her direction.

She scrutinized his every step as he approached. *He's wearing full body armor, except for his face and head.*

At the end of his right arm Kate could make out what looked like a Glock with a suppressor.

She hid in silence and waited.

When he reached down to check Jack's pulse, using Emma's pistol Kate put two rounds into the side of his head. And then, not wanting the man to fall on top of her father, she lunged into him like a defensive lineman, knocking him to the floor nearly three yards away.

After she had hid the dead man's body beside Emma, she again took up a defensive position. From there she scrutinized her surroundings for anything suggesting that there might be another attacker.

After what seemed to her an eternity, she carefully crawled on her hands and knees over to where her father had fallen.

"Oh, Dad," she cried. Tears were running down her cheeks. "What have they done to you?"

She removed her scarf and began blotting the blood off Jack's head. It was then that she noticed that he was still bleeding a copious stream. *That's odd,* she thought. *Could his heart still be beating?*

Immediately she felt his neck for a pulse.

"You're alive! Oh my God, Dad! Can you hear me? … Dad!"

She then took a closer look at the wound on his head. She could not find where the bullet entered his skull. There was a substantial amount of contusion around the injury, and some laceration, but nothing indicating that the round had actually penetrated the bone.

She visually examined her sunglasses that were lying on the floor and saw that they were severely bent at the bridge.

"Something hit me in the face when Dad was shot," she said to herself. "His cap."

Still on her hands and knees she crawled over to the cap her father had been wearing.

Picking it up she exclaimed, "A *ballistic* cap! I did not know there was such a thing."

She felt inside. There she found a badly deformed bullet trapped between the fabric of the cap and a hard plate covering the inside of the front panel. Fitted on the sides and back of the cap she discovered panels of compressed polyethylene.

Just then Jack began to moan. He reached a shaking hand to the bloodied scarf that Kate had placed over his wound.

"Kate. What the hell happened?"

"You've been shot in the head," she said crawling back over to her father. "That cap of yours—it stopped the bullet and saved your life. It looks to me like you've got a pretty severe concussion., but you're going to survive."

"I'll say," Jack said as he started to sit up. "My head is ringing. … Give me a hand. We've got to get out of here. … Where are Red and Robby?"

"I'm sure they're watching from a distance," she said as she lifted Jack's arm to help him to his feet.

Still holding onto Jack to steady him, Kate visually searched the museum until she spotted Red's bushy mop of hair. She motioned emphatically for the boys to join them.

"Who's that?" Jack said pointing with his eyes toward the dead man on the floor.

"Emma's assistant," I would guess.

Several people had begun to gather around, including a pale-faced balding man with a plastic tag pinned to his chest that read *Manager*.

"Ma'am, should I call the police?"

"I *am* the police," she said showing him her badge. "But it would be helpful if you could back everyone off. This is a crime scene. Just keep everyone at a distance of twenty feet until we can secure it."

"Yes, ma'am."

When the boys and Buddy approached, the manager intercepted them and told them that they must stand back.

"They're fine," Kate said. "They're undercover officers. You can let them and the police dog through. Thank you for your help."

"Boys," Jack said, beginning to get a grasp on the situation. "Go to the front entrance. I spotted a wheelchair up there. Run it back here."

"Hang on to that cap," he said, turning to Kate. "Roger just sent it to me. Pretty new stuff. He's going want to see some pictures of that."

As soon as the boys got back with the wheelchair Jack lifted Emma's dead accomplice and set him in it.

"How's the woman?" Jack asked. "She still alive?"

"She's cuffed and probably still out cold. A bit beat up, but she'll recover."

"What's up with your hands?" Jack asked, and then he noticed Emma's bruised and bleeding face.

"Oh," he said. "Let's get her on her feet so we can get the hell out of here. This place is going to be crawling with cops."

Kate and Robby helped Emma to her feet. When she started to talk Kate squeezed her upper arm until she winced.

"You keep your mouth shut," Kate said. "Not a peep outta you or I'll yank your shoulder right out of its socket. Do you understand me?"

Emma's silence signaled that she did.

As they began to make their way through the onlookers, Kate said to the manager, "Thanks for all your help. We've got to get these two to the hospital. I'll send in a crew to take pictures and clean up. Don't let *anyone* touch a thing. Remember, this is an official crime scene, and you're in charge of it until forensics takes over."

"Yes ma'am."

Jack, pushing the wheelchair, brought up the rear. He was still very dizzy, and the wheelchair helped to stabilize him on his feet.

"How'd you get here, Dad?"

"Taxi. How about you?"

"Same."

Kate leaned over and asked Emma, "Where's your getaway car?"

Emma hesitated until Kate jammed her long fingernails into the tall lady's biceps.

"Black Escalade right around the corner," she finally admitted. "Four-ways flashing. Keys are in my left pocket."

As they neared the vehicle they spotted two security guards examining it. They appeared to be calling in the tag number.

Kate presented her badge and said, "Excuse us. Police business."

The guard who got the best look at Kate's badge shot a glance at his partner and shrugged his shoulders.

"Could I see that badge again?" he asked.

"Back off," she said. "This is police business."

After Jack eased the body into the rear seat, he pushed the wheelchair over to the guard that had been doing all the talking.

"Here, make yourself useful," Jack said. "Return this chair to the museum."

The guards stood speechless as Jack and Kate prepared to leave.

They nearly filled the Escalade. Red, Robby, and Buddy took the way back seats. Kate strapped Emma and her dead helper in the rear seats.

"You good to drive?" she asked her father.

"Yeah, let's just get out of here while we can."

Jack turned off the flashers and pulled into traffic.

But he didn't get very far when a patrol car, with lights flashing, pulled alongside and motioned for him to pull over.

Jack smiled and nodded, and then hit the accelerator.

Chapter 44

I don't have time for this shit!" Jack complained.

The patrol car hit its siren and pulled in for the chase.

After running several red lights, Jack said, "This is not going to end well … not like this. Emma, any ideas? Got any countermeasures on this Escalade?"

"These cuffs are killing me!"

Kate had left Emma's hands cuffed behind her when she strapped her in.

"I asked you a question," Jack repeated. "I wreck this truck and we'll all go to jail, or get killed. What have you got for countermeasures? I'm sure you've got something rigged up."

Emma had no idea why the Handlers had not already killed her. *They had every chance to take me out, but they didn't,* she wondered. *They must have something in mind.*

She was not pleased with her situation. But she was still alive, and for the time being that beat all the alternatives she could conceive of.

"Small red button," she finally said. "Right under the dash."

"What does it do?" Jack asked.

"Never had to use it," she said. "But this seems like the perfect time to try it. Just push the button, and we'll see what happens."

Jack hit it once and held it for about five seconds.

He watched in his rearview mirror as a fine mixture of water and oil sprayed a heavy mist behind them.

The patrol car slammed on its brakes and stopped in the middle of the street. The water and oil had totally coated the windshield when the driver turned on his wipers.

"That worked pretty well," he said. "But I'm sure they've radioed in the plate number."

"Doesn't matter," Emma said.

"What doesn't matter?" Kate asked.

"That they called it in. This much I remember. When you hit that red button it also drops off the outside plate. There's another one under it. … The cops have the description of the vehicle, but not the right plate number. So, if you start driving normally, you might be okay."

Kate was irked by her impudence, but kept her silence.

Jack slowed to traffic speed, and then hit Roger's speed dial on his cell, but did not address Roger by name.

"Hey, buddy, I have a passenger in my back seat. Emma something is her name. I can't really talk right now, but I need you to find me a safe house. I'm heading south out of Fisherman's Wharf on 101. Can you come up with something?"

"Give me a minute," Roger said. "Stay on the phone. I'll see what I can do."

Three minutes later Roger said, "Jack. Stay on 101 South through the city, past the airport, and all the way to another airport—San Carlos. Exit there, but go west instead of east toward the airport. The street is Holly.

"Take the first left, which is Industrial Road. Continue down Industrial until you reach Bransten Road. That will be two blocks past Terminal Way. Turn west on Bransten. Down a few blocks, on the right, you will spot a red tractor-trailer. It will have its flashers on, and there will be cones behind it. Drive between the cones, and I'll take it from there.

After Jack disconnected, Emma asked, "Who were you talking to?"

"Who are you working for?" Jack asked, totally ignoring her question.

Emma thought about refusing to answer, but then she thought better of it. *Handler would not be asking me that question if he did not already know the answer,* she reasoned.

"Someone named Dana," Emma said. "But I've never actually seen her face."

"How can I get hold of her?" Jack asked.

"You can't."

"How do *you* communicate with her?"

"She calls me. I never initiate a call."

"What if you have an emergency? How do you get the message to her?"

"I'm not supposed to have emergencies, so—"

"Look, you skinny little shit!" Jack barked. "Right now you're in stink up to your chin. So don't be giving me grief. I ask you a question, and you give me an answer. If you want to keep your teeth and your pretty little smile, then talk to me like I'm your favorite uncle. Do you get what I'm telling you, or do I have to express myself more clearly?"

Emma hesitated a short moment, and then said, "I get it, Mr. Handler."

"Then let's try this again. If you have to get a message to this Dana person, how do you do it?"

"I have a number. It's an exchange in New York. I don't know anything about it. I just call it, and she gets a message, I presume. And then she calls me."

"When do you expect to hear from her again?"

"After I've completed my job."

Jack and Kate both understood what she was saying—that killing them, and the boys, that was her *job.*

"How do you prove that you've successfully fulfilled the contract?" Jack asked. "What does she require?"

"My glasses. Did you pick up my glasses?"

"Yeah," Kate said. "I've got them."

"There's a camera and a recording device built in them. I send her the video, and she releases my money."

"So, do you have video of your shooting me?"

"I'm sure I do. It'll be right in the glasses. But so will that damn dog attacking me."

"We can edit that out, and send it to her. Would that do it?"

"She included a number of items on that contract, but I know the *only* one she was *determined* to eliminate was you. Everything else was superfluous. You're the one she wanted dead. She will pay me on receipt of video evidence, as long as my success gets confirmed by a second source. Can you do something about that? ... And you can't do anything to make her think that you might still be alive. She's got to buy into the story and have no reservations. She is one skeptical bitch."

Jack dialed Roger. "Hey. I'm dead. Emma killed me. We've got to make that story stick."

When Emma brought up the incident involving Buddy's attack, it reminded Kate of something.

"Boys, I still haven't figured out why you disobeyed me earlier—when I told you to stay at the far end of the museum. And then Buddy suddenly shows up, and you're right behind him. What was that all about?"

Robby looked at Red, and then back at Kate. "I'm sorry, Kate. It was truly all Buddy's doing. He just all of a sudden bolted toward you, like he sensed an emergency. We just followed him. It was all *his* idea. We're really sorry about that. But please don't be mad at Buddy."

Kate smiled but did not say a word. She just turned and faced the front windshield. She did not want the boys to see that a single tear was tracking down the right cheek of this tough New York City homicide detective.

Jack continued silently to drive south on 101 for fifteen minutes. He was thinking about how close he had just come to dying.

Finally, he asked Emma, "What role does Alexander Sipos play in this whole thing?"

She was surprised to learn that Jack was familiar with Sipos. *Just how much does he really know?* she wondered. ... *And should I answer this question? If I refuse, or even hesitate, it could be a problem. My Escalade might end up alongside the road with my body in it. If I don't tell the truth, and if he detects deception, same thing might result. ... Face it, girl, Jack Handler holds all the cards, and most of the chips. You've got to tell him what he wants to know.*

"Sipos has been working with Dana regarding the hits on those judges," Emma said. "But as far as the last two—Cohen and Higgins, he masterminded those all by himself. He suspects that there is a leak among Dana's close associates. Those last hits—they were solely his idea. He was trying to set a trap. ... Dana was against it. In fact, she was *totally* pissed about it. Even pissed with me because I allowed him to involve me. ... So, when his trap went south, he folded up shop out here and went back to New York. I think she's still hot. ... If she gets wind that I failed on this job, she will have me killed—no question about it."

Jack again held his tongue for a long, uncomfortable moment—uncomfortable for Emma.

Finally, he said, "Then I guess that we'd better not let her know that I'm still alive."

Emma breathed deeply, and exhaled a sigh of relief.

Wonder what he has in mind for me? she asked herself.

No one talked for the next eighteen minutes—aside from Robby. And that was only to Red and Buddy.

Red, of course, didn't say much either.

* * *

Jack turned right on Holly by San Carlos airport, and then left on Industrial Road. They passed Terminal Way, and turned right on Bransten Road.

Just as Roger had promised, there was a red tractor-trailer parked on the right side. As they approached, two men scooped up a dozen traffic cones, and pulled down a ramp. Jack slowed as he drove up the incline and into the trailer.

The same two men jumped in behind him and secured the Escalade to the floor for transport.

One of them then approached Jack and invited the whole group to ride in the over-sized Kenworth sleeper. "But, please," he said, "leave the dead guy in the Escalade. We'll dispose of him a little later."

Emma struggled to her feet and headed toward the back of the trailer with the group. "Don't you think it's about time to take these cuffs off?" she asked.

Kate grabbed Emma by the arm and led her back toward the Escalade. "Not so fast," Kate said, digging her nails deeply into Emma's arm. "I think you're going to be keeping your friend company for a while."

"You've got to be shittin' me! I'm not breathing that air. That guy stinks. You can't expect me to ride in the back of the truck with him."

"Turn around," Kate commanded as she pulled out the key to Emma's cuffs.

She unlocked the cuffs, shoved Emma in the driver's seat of the Escalade, and cuffed her to the steering wheel. She squeezed the cuffs as tight as they would allow her to.

"There you go," Kate said. "You can talk over old times with your friend. Maybe you should apologize for getting him killed."

Emma was still complaining when Kate slammed the door in her face.

Chapter 45

Immediately upon his arrival in New York, Sipos scheduled a meeting with the ten executive board members of The Group. He chose, however, not to inform Dana of the impromptu assembly.

While the trap that he had set to ferret out the suspected mole in Dana's organization had failed, at least as far as she was concerned, in his mind he was totally successful.

When he learned that the gas leak at the Cohen house was staged, and that his two *observers* at the Higgins house were apprehended as suspected child molesters, he knew that there had to have been some sort of leak. He just could not nail down the source.

He therefore decided to call a quasi-secret board meeting—one without Dana.

He reasoned: *all of the members were aware that several Circuit Court judges, and two Supreme Court justices, had been assassinated. That should be enough to get the attention of even the most apathetic members of The Group, and now that there appeared to be some fairly organized entity working against them, perhaps this would be the ideal time to utilize a less precipitous method for coercing strict adherence to my demands. I will temporarily postpone further hits on judges, and concentrate on motivating the board to take a more aggressive approach.*

Even though he still had not forgiven Emma for not fully buying into his effort to flush out Dana's mole, Sipos decided that he would still like to use her as his enforcer at the meeting.

Generally, Dana was responsible for setting up and conducting these meetings. But, since his goal this time was largely to usurp her authority, Sipos chose to bypass Dana altogether and announce the meeting directly to the ten board members himself.

> Gentlemen: Unfortunately, something has come up that requires our utmost attention. We believe that someone in our organization has breached security—we have a leak. To date, we have been unable to figure out who is behind it. (Please contact me directly if you have any theories in this regard. I will treat your communication with utmost confidentiality.)
>
> Also, some of our operatives continue to meet with substantial resistance in the field. While (as you know) we are taking some dramatic steps to get this matter resolved, I have decided to temporarily rescind all punitive measures directed at our uncooperative placements, as well as candidates. That means you can inform those who have exhibited disobedience, or even disinterest, that they have been granted that proverbial *one more chance.*
>
> And, by all means possible, convey to them the importance of total compliance to each and every directive we hand down. Make them aware that this is temporary, and if things don't change quickly, we will soon come down on them harder than ever. They must be made to understand that we have a lot invested in each and every one of them, and we simply will not tolerate anything other than total loyalty.
>
> I am sure you noted that the words of this note are softer and less threatening than those of my friend at the last meeting. But, rest assured, as Dana pointed out at that meeting, The Group will not

tolerate failure.

Now, I want you to go about your business with a renewed sense of purpose and revived determination. If you have any loose ends to tidy up, I suggest you get on them immediately, because our next meeting will be in exactly ten days.

My desire, at that time, is that we will be able to celebrate lavishly, instead of with remonstrations and threats.

—The Group

Chapter 46

Emma had every right to be concerned—and she was. Nothing has a greater potential for destroying a killer's career than a failed hit. Dana had hired her to kill Jack's whole family, but Emma had accomplished none of it. Had she a cyanide capsule she might have considered biting into it.

Jack knew what she was going through. Not only did he physically have her totally under his control, her future was in his hands as well. He decided to let her stew on it.

As soon as the Handlers were settled into the truck's sleeper, the driver pulled out.

"Where are we headed?" Kate asked.

"South," Jack said. "South and east. Haven't decided for sure yet, but we need to put some miles between ourselves and San Francisco. This truck is great cover, so we need to take advantage of it while we can. I'd say Fresno, or Bakersfield. I'll see where Roger can get us set up. We need somewhere that will be safe to work out of."

Jack's phone buzzed.

"Henry. What's up?"

Henry explained to Jack that he had been forced to kill two men who had successfully tracked him down.

"All they wanted to know was where you and Kate were," Henry said. "Of course, I didn't tell them. And they then slipped and bumped their heads. Now they're both dead. … They might have informed their boss that they *located* me, but that's all they could have reported on."

"Not to worry, my friend," Jack consoled him, "Their boss is cuffed and traveling coach in the back of this rig. … But, if you took two of them out, and we killed one, that still leaves one of her men unaccounted for. I wonder where he could be?"

"Want me to stick around Frisco and see if I can draw him out?"

"That would be smart. No use taking the chance of drawing him down here. I'll have Roger send in cleaners to sanitize your hotel room … probably yet today. … How's your shoulder?"

"I'm fine. Healing up great. Be good as new in no time."

Jack got to thinking about all the stress Henry must have encountered taking out his two attackers.

"I'll have Roger send in a doctor with the cleaners. He can take a look at your shoulder just to be sure it's still healing okay.

"That'd be great. One of those jokers poked his filthy pocketknife around in my wound. Might need a shot or something. … Any idea what I should be looking for—with that fifth character?"

"We have no idea," Jack said. "But I might know someone who does. Describe the two you eliminated. And I'll see about getting you a description of the fourth."

"Nunchucks. One of them carried nunchucks. The other one was older—maybe pushing fifty. Shorter, too. Not very smart. Probably weighed one eighty. Balding."

"That should do it. I'll go talk to Legs and see what she will give up. She does seem to be willing to talk right now. Sit tight until I get back to you."

"Hey, driver," Jack said, opening up the door leading from the sleeper to the cab of the truck. "I need to get back to my prisoner. Can you pull over?"

"No need," he said as he toggled a switch on his dash. "This is a *special* rig. Take a look behind you."

Jack turned to see that a passageway had opened to the trailer. He was looking directly into Emma's wide-eyed astonishment.

Jack proceeded to enter the trailer and take a seat in the Escalade beside Emma. "Got a question or two for you," he said.

"Get me out of here and I'll tell you anything you want to know."

"First things first. I know you had four men assisting you. One of them is sitting right behind you. Describe the other three for me."

"What's in it for me?"

"You're still alive, aren't you? Spill it."

"There are three more. I'll describe them, but you have to promise me that you will give me the chance to call them off. No point in getting them hurt."

"Describe all of them."

"Promise you'll not go after them?"

"I will do my best. But I can't promise anything. Now, talk."

"Nunchucks. He's my best man. He never goes anywhere without his nunchucks. Six two, one ninety. Smart. Handsome. Dark hair.

"And then there's Gordie. He's older—not as old as you, though. No offense. Shorter. Balding. Has a small scar on his upper lip, and he has a crooked nose.

"The fourth one's Alicia Gomez—a girl. She sometimes dresses a little butch. She's thirty. Very pretty. Fifth degree black belt. I don't know what she weighs, but she's very strong. Five five. … I do not want her—"

Jack jumped out of the Escalade and headed back to the sleeper.

"Wait," Emma shouted. "Get me out of here. It stinks, and I have to pee."

Jack did not look back.

As soon as he closed the passageway he called Henry.

"Jack," Henry said. "Your doctor is already here. Hey, buddy, you didn't say anything about this doctor being a chick. And a hot one at that."

"Let me talk to her," Jack said.

"Jack wants to talk to you," he said, handing her the phone.

"Hello, Jack. How ya doin'?" Alicia asked, as she took two steps back and pulled a Glock 9mm from her bag.

"Henry, take a seat. I'm gonna have a little conversation with your boss. You deaf?! Sit your ass down!

"Jack, I've got your big friend here. But I'm afraid he doesn't look so good."

"What have you done to him?" Jack asked.

"Oh, nothin' much. Just poked him with my little needle."

"What'd you inject him with?"

Henry fell backward into the chair. But he wasn't trying to be compliant. He was beginning to feel lightheaded, and if he had not sat down he would have fallen.

"H. Really great heroin. Let's just say it's better than anything he could buy on the street. He's gonna die a very happy man. Even a big fellow like him couldn't handle what I just gave him."

"Heroin!" Jack blurted out. "He doesn't do drugs. He'll have no tolerance for it."

Kate could hear enough of what was going on to know it was serious, so she slid to the other side of the sleeper and dialed Roger.

"Kate?" Roger asked, obviously taken by surprise. He was not used to fielding calls from her.

"Got a problem. One of Emma's associates got to Henry. She pretended to be a doctor. She apparently injected him with some heavy drugs. I heard Jack say it was *heroin*. She might be lying."

"I'll get someone up there right away."

"Holiday Vista Hotel, room twelve seventeen."

"Any idea how much he was given?"

"No."

"Is she still in the room? Is she armed?"

"I think she's still there because Jack is talking to her right now."

"Who is she?" Roger asked.

"One of Emma's associates."

"Then she's a killer. We're going to have to go in hot. Is she alone?"

"I think so, but don't know."

"I'm going to have to work with the local police for this. I don't have that kind of firepower at my disposal—not for such a rapid response. Gonna hang up now."

Kate looked over at Jack and mouthed, "Heroin?"

Jack nodded.

"Got someone here I want you to talk to," Jack said. "A good friend of yours."

He was already headed back through the passageway into the trailer.

"Emma," Jack said. "I've got a friend of yours on the phone. She has something to say to you."

Jack handed the phone to Emma. She sneered at him as she leaned her head into the steering wheel to talk.

"Hello."

"Emma?"

"Yes. Leesha?"

"They're both dead—Nunchucks and Gordy. This bastard beat them to death."

"They're dead? Who killed them?"

"Henry something. He works for Jack Handler. Nunchucks was interrogating him, and somehow he managed to take him out. The same for Gordy. ... I fixed him, though. Shot him up with enough H to kill ten men."

"Hold on," Emma said, placing her hand over the mouthpiece and addressing Jack. "What is she saying? My men are dead?"

"And your girlfriend soon will be as well if you don't do just as I say."

"She injected heroin in your friend. A lot of it. He's as good as dead already."

"Narcan," Jack said. "See if your friend has some Narcan with her."

"Do you have any Narcan?" Emma asked.

"Hell no."

"Tell her to get out of the room right now," Jack said. "She'll have to go out over the balcony, the cops are about to bust down the door."

Jack was not so much interested in protecting Emma's friend as he was in trying to avoid a shootout.

"Can you escape out the back?" Emma asked. "Don't answer. Just do it. The cops are about to kick your door down."

Alicia strapped on her backpack and hurried out the balcony sliding door. She tied a 3/8-inch nylon rope to the railing, and began rappelling to the ground.

Jack grabbed the phone from Emma and called Roger.

"Henry has been given a very large dose of heroin. Ten times standard street fix. Have the responding officers do what they have to do to gain entry. The only person inside should be Henry, and he's unconscious.

"You're sending a doctor in with the cops, right?"

"Yes."

"And he does have Narcan. Right?"

"Jack," Roger replied, "this is San Francisco. Of course he has Narcan. And I already have made him aware of the problem."

"Make sure he knows going in that it's a *heroin* overdose—a *major* overdose. He should give him Narcan immediately. A lot of it."

"I will remind him," Roger said, reading the anxiety in Jack's voice. "Looks like they just entered the room. ... And the doctor has begun administering Narcan."

"He understands the magnitude of the overdose?" Jack asked. "A standard dose of Narcan is not going to do the trick. This was an attempted homicide, so it was a huge dose."

"He's seen a lot of overdoses," Roger said. "If anyone can straighten this out, this is the man who can."

"I'm staying on the phone until Henry's out of the woods," Jack said.

"I understand."

Jack then began addressing Emma.

"Tell me a little more about this Alicia." he said.

"She sometimes works for me. For when I need an extra hand."

"Like these other three?"

"No. Alicia is a very close friend. Very close. We've known each other since ... since college."

"Don't bullshit me," Jack said. "I did some research on you. You've been a criminal all your life. You *never* went to college."

"Prison. I met Leesha in prison. And we've been together ever since."

"Well, I just saved her life," Jack said.

"Only because you did not want a standoff. Not with your friend dying from an overdose. Let's be honest."

Jack reached under his jacket and pulled a Walther .380 out of a belt holster. He pressed the barrel to Emma's head.

"You listen very carefully to what I'm about to tell you. Interrupt once and it will be your last. You tried to kill me. You almost succeeded. You would have killed Kate as well, if you were a little better at your job. But you failed on both counts.

"Now, your little bitch just tried to kill my good friend. And she failed too. … I'm seeing a pattern beginning to develop. Whenever you mess with me or my family, you fail."

Emma's eyes flashed up into his, and she flinched as though to speak.

Jack clicked off the safety, and her mouth snapped shut.

"Here's the deal," Jack said. "Henry dies today, and you die today. It's that simple. But if Henry lives, I will consider letting you live another day. But, at best, you will be guaranteed only the rest of this day. And that is *only* if Henry pulls through.

"Now, the rules governing your life will be different for tomorrow. I haven't decided whether or not I can use you alive. So don't get your hopes up."

Just then Jack heard Roger talking to him.

"Jack, looks like Henry is responding. The doc said that if Henry weren't so big, he probably wouldn't have survived. But he is very confident that we're on the other side of this thing. Henry's going to have a huge headache, but he's going to make it."

"Can you hide him away in a hospital with an armed guard?" Jack asked. "I've gambled with his life way too much lately. Check that wound for infection, too. He said something about one of those guys messing with his wound. I just want to see him get his strength back."

"I'll take care of it," Roger assured him. "I'll put two of my men on him."

"Emma," Jack said thumbing the safety back on. "This is your lucky day."

"Can I talk?" Emma asked.

"Yes."

"You've still got a problem," she said. "But I might be able to help you with this one."

What could she possibly know about a threat against me? Jack wondered.

"*I've* got a problem?" Jack asked, returning the Walther to his holster. "What sort of problem do I have? And what do you think you could do to help me?"

Chapter 47

Emma explained to Jack just how determined Dana was to see him and Kate dead, and that she would not give up until she was convinced that they had been killed. That was not news to Jack. He fully appreciated his situation. But Emma had more to say.

She outlined a plan that she thought would work. Not only would it get Dana off Jack's back—at least temporarily—but it would also allow her to collect on the contract.

It was that second part of the plan that Jack found compelling. Had Emma merely stated that she could help *him*, without any benefit to her, he would not have taken her seriously. But, if she could help him with Dana, while at the same time enriching herself, that might be a plan that could work.

She also convinced Jack that he should bring her out of the Escalade and into the sleeper with his family. Jack agreed to do that for her.

The physical conditions in the Escalade were becoming unbearable. Soon after death, the muscles that control the bladder and the lower colon relax, causing a final defecation and urination. The body in the back of the Escalade was passing through that stage.

Plus, given the lack of airflow, the whole trailer was beginning to stink, particularly in and around the Escalade.

As Jack entered the Kenworth T600, with its 191″ two-bedroom sleeper, he asked the two boys and Buddy to watch TV in the smaller bedroom. And then he addressed Kate:

"Emma has a proposition that I thought we should at least entertain. … Go ahead, Emma, lay out your plan for us."

It was obvious to both Jack and Kate that Emma had thought the whole matter through.

Much of what she said the Handlers already knew. For instance, they were well aware that Dana had contracted Emma to kill both of them, and also the boys. Emma explained that she believed that the reason Dana included the boys in the contract was to ensure that Jack and Kate would be sharing the same real estate when the hit went down. That information only confirmed Jack's theory of why Dana included the boys.

Jack and Kate also knew that the contract on their lives would not go away simply because Emma had failed. There were plenty of talented killers out there, and whoever was next in line for the job would simply step up.

"As long as that contract is out there," Emma explained, "Dana will keep throwing fresh bodies at you until someone makes it happen."

To this point Emma had not told Jack anything he did not already know. Plus, there was more to it than even Emma was aware. For instance, Jack's hands were virtually tied as far as getting at Dana/Allison. As long as she believed that he and Kate were still alive, she would not physically venture outside the watchful eyes of Roger Minsk. That meant for Jack to hunt Dana down and kill her, he would have to go through Roger. And he knew that were he to tangle with Roger, one of *them* would have to die.

Roger had already made that clear to Jack. In spite of the value he placed on their friendship, Roger viewed his task of protecting the former first lady even more highly.

So, when Emma started describing in detail all the ramifications and intricacies of her plan, both Jack and Kate agreed that it was worth listening to.

"I think something like this just might work," Kate said.

"Then do you think you can take these cuffs off?" Emma petitioned.

"Hell no!" Kate replied. But this time extreme animosity was clearly missing in her rejection.

Jack's take on listening to Emma present her plan was, *what do we have to lose? Sure, her plan is lacking in detail. But that's no problem. All I need from her is* a *willingness to participate—and to do so convincingly.*

For the next two hundred miles Jack developed the tapestry to pull it off. Every time he had a fresh idea, he'd call Roger.

"We'll need a junk yard with a vehicle crusher, and a flat railroad car to load it on when we're done. Should have several other crushed vehicles already on it, so we can put ours on the top. … And a very large forklift, fitted with rubber tires—for junkyard use. Most any fully equipped junkyard that ships by rail should do the trick.

"We should be good with everything else. We will need a fresh vehicle for ourselves at the location.

"Can't go back to the hotel, so will need to have our belongings flown to Grand Rapids."

Chapter 48

Immediately after first viewing the video of what she thought was Jack's body being crushed, Dana began planning the binge. And six and a half hours later she was drunk. *Very* drunk. She had not allowed herself this level of inebriation since her days of privacy in the White House.

To ensure her seclusion this time she left the secure confines of her Upper Eastside home and checked into an upscale Midtown hotel as Dana Reynolds. She had done things like this before—venture out as Dana. In fact, whenever she had business to do for The Group, or a face-to-face meeting with Sipos, or some specialty contractor, she would always shed her Secret Service detail, don her Dana persona, and sneak out the back service door.

She had a black Ford SUV stored in a nearby parking garage for when her adventures involved a road trip. But such was not the case this time. She simply hailed a taxi and had it deliver her to the doorman at the hotel.

Dana then placed an order with her friend at a popular Midtown liquor store: One bottle of Lemon Hart 151 proof Demerara Rum, one bottle each of her friend's choice El Dorado white, dark and golden rums, bottles of cherry and apricot brandies (again, her friend's choice), a six-ounce container of frozen lime juice, a copious supply of crushed ice (in a cooler, of course), a bottle of maraschino cherries, a pound of cubed pineapple, a pound of granulated sugar, and a bag of powdered sugar.

And, even though the recipe for her desired cocktail did not call for it, Dana asked her friend to bring a six-ounce bottle of Grenadine—a red syrup with a sweet/tart taste. While most bars did not use Grenadine in their Zombies, Dana thought that its deep red color contributed to the atmosphere of celebration. And this night, she believed, was her night to celebrate.

Dana was in the mood for a *large* pitcher of Zombie cocktails—six ounces of which is generally adequate to render comatose a three-hundred-pound NFL lineman.

Initially, she intended to get drunk by herself. That was the way she preferred to drink, especially if all she wanted to do was get totally soused. And, at least in the early stages of her planning for this bender, that's exactly what she had in mind.

She had very few real friends. In fact, she had none that she would wish to get drunk with. Bob, her husband and the former president, did not drink much. When he wanted to get high it was always with cocaine. However, once he turned sixty, he determined to cut back dramatically on his drug use because he had read too many articles on early onset Alzheimer's and dementia—how drugs and alcohol use was suspected to be contributors to the debilitation.

If she were to sit down and make a list of names—of the people during her whole life with whom she was comfortable enough to allow herself to get stupid drunk—she could easily inscribe all of them on a three by five index card, and still have plenty of room to include "possibles."

On this day, as she waited for the liquor store delivery, she sat down and actually began creating just such a list.

James Colson would be at the top of the list. He was a trusted aide, and personal friend, during and after her White House years. James was very smart, and he knew how to honor a confidence. Whatever she said to him never went further. And he never lied to her.

Unfortunately, she eventually concluded that he knew too much, and therefore had to be terminated.

Another friend whom she trusted implicitly was Roger Minsk—the Secret Service agent who currently headed up her detail. She knew him to be a trusted friend of her husband's, as well as to her. And, much as was the case with James, Roger treated her with dignity, and never broke a confidence.

Roger, however, was never a candidate for the office of "drinking buddy." First of all, he had a job to do that required utmost sobriety. She knew that he would never touch alcohol in her presence because it would be totally unprofessional, and if there was one word she would use to describe Roger, that word would be *professional.*

She then wrote the name Donna Frisk. Donna was her current chief of staff. Donna knew more about Allison's personal life than any other human being. At least, that's what Dana thought. Yet, Donna did not have a clue about her Dana persona. Donna was Allison's lover and confidant. And, as such she was intimately familiar with Allison's likes and dislikes, and the way she wanted to be perceived by the rest of the staff. As Allison's sexual partner, Donna was obviously more than just her *Girl Friday.* Yet, aside from sex and proper protocol, Donna knew virtually nothing about Allison. So, if Allison or Dana were to go out on the town, or even wish to get drunk in private, she would never be comfortable doing so with Donna.

So, Dana crossed Donna's name from her list.

Ironically, the third person that came to mind was Jack Handler—whose death was the whole reason for her celebration. She and the former president would frequently sneak out of the White House, always with Roger Minsk's help, and meet up at Jack's DC hideaway apartment to strategize. Usually James Colson and Roger Minsk would join them. These meetings lasted several hours, if not all night long, and would generally leave one or more stretched out on the floor with several empty bourbon and Scotch bottles. Roger, of course, was always the *designated driver*.

She enjoyed drinking with them, mostly because Jack and her husband always seem to be communicating on the same wavelength. And, like her husband, Jack knew how to keep secrets. Secrecy was, after all, an essential aspect of their relationship, because after many of these *get-togethers*, a list would emerge, and on that list would be the names of the people who would have to die. Not only did Jack know where all the skeletons were buried, he had laid most of them out himself.

Dana could possibly have listed more, but she couldn't bring herself to do it because she was stuck on Jack's name—or, perhaps she was struck *with* his name. Just as in the case with James Colson, Jack was an old and trusted friend, and the mere thought of his being dead elicited a strong melancholic mood verging on depression.

And so, in the end, there were only two names on her list—Roger Minsk and Bob Fulbright. Getting drunk with Roger would never work, so she crossed his name off.

She could call Bob. He would probably meet her, if for no other reason than to find out what she had been up to. That is, of course, only if he were not playing poker with Roger, or "dickin' some bimbo," as she referred to his promiscuous bent. But they would really have nothing of common interest to discuss in that all he wanted to talk about was his girlfriends, and she hers. And, besides, Jack Handler was one of her husband's oldest and most trusted friends.

Wouldn't do to call Bob, she determined.

There was one more possibility—Alexander Sipos. While they were certainly not friends, they did have a great deal to talk about. And they had a common agenda—control of the entire court system, from the District Courts of Appeal, to the Supreme Court.

"Sipos probably does not yet know that Handler is dead," she said out loud. "I'm sure he will be pleased to hear that news … and he might even want to celebrate the news with a *fantastic* rum cocktail."

"Are you in New York?" she asked, having called his cell. "Great! I have some very good news. I would really like to tell you in person, if you can get away for a while this evening. … Ever had a Zombie?"

Chapter 49

For quite some time Sipos had been growing disenchanted with Dana. While he had not founded The Group, for the past eighteen years he was directly responsible for its oversight. And, no one could argue with its success. Not only was his organization responsible for the appointments of dozens of federal judges, and at least two associate justices, he had scores more in the pipeline.

It was not until meddling Dana and her philandering husband decided that they needed to take a more hands-on approach that the program had begun to unravel. But that was not the worst part of it. While Sipos believed he could work around her incompetence and still make the project productive, he was becoming totally convinced that through her careless use of phones and email servers she had compromised the integrity of the entire program.

He now believed that there was a mole in her office. And if that was not the case, then some sinister player had totally hacked her emails and phone. *How else could my every move be so accurately forecasted?* he asked himself. *And when I try to set a trap for the culprit, Dana undermines it. I must do something about this before she destroys The Group.*

So, when Dana invited him over to get wasted, he eagerly accepted the offer—not because he wished to get drunk with her, nor was he terribly interested in what was on her mind. He would happily meet with her in the hotel, but for purposes of his own.

"Allison," Sipos said. "Is it okay for me to call you by your real name tonight? No one's around to hear it. Would that be okay with you?"

"Sure. Why not?"

"And your big secret. Are you about to announce your candidacy again? Is that what's up?"

"No. Something much more interesting than that," Dana said handing Sipos a Zombie. "But first things first. Before I reveal my secret, I want you to try my special cocktail."

"I propose a toast," Sipos said, raising his glass. "To the continued success of The Group."

"To The Group."

"Now, I'll bet you want me to elaborate on the story I used to get you over here. Right?"

Sipos did not answer—he only smiled broadly.

"I'll get this set up," Allison said as she set her drink down on the bar. "It'll only take a minute. Do try your drink."

He took a small sip of his drink.

As soon as she turned her back, Sipos removed a large capsule from his pocket, opened it, and poured the contents into her drink. He then dumped half of his drink into the sink and replaced it with ice.

"All set over here," she said a few moments later. "Come take a look."

Sipos picked up her drink and handed it to her.

"Okay," Sipos said, "let's see what you've got."

"Recognize this man?" she asked when the first image of Jack Handler appeared.

"Sure do," he said. "That's your friend and mine, Jack Handler. Right?"

"Now watch this," she said as the slide show depicted Jack's being shot. "What do you think of that?"

"Well, I'll be damned! Looks to me like Handler just got popped in the head. That's what it looks like."

When she was finished with the videos she commented that both Roger and her husband believed them to be legitimate, thus confirming that Jack and Kate were dead.

"That's why I called you over to celebrate," she said. "The Handlers are now *definitely* dead. They won't be interfering in our lives ever again."

"Well," Sipos said, "that certainly does call for another toast."

"Your drink is almost finished," she said. "Give me your glass and I'll freshen it up for you."

"Thank you," he said. "But only if you have another one as well."

"I am going to tie one on tonight," Allison replied walking back toward the bar. "I have enough Zombies in the pitcher to knock out the entire front line of the Redskins."

"I doubt that I'll be good for any more," he said as she poured them each another drink. "I've got a meeting in the morning."

For the next few minutes Sipos carefully registered everything she had to show him. While he did not let on, he became very skeptical when there was no video showing the hit on Kate. Also, he had her run back the image of the bullet striking Jack's cap. Again, he did not comment, but he observed that the cap that Jack was wearing did not look to him like an ordinary baseball cap. And when the second video showed Jack sitting in the SUV with a baseball cap on, it was clear to Sipos that it was a different baseball cap from the one Jack was wearing when he was shot. That did not make sense to him, but he did not point out the discrepancy.

"Are you convinced that the video is genuine?" Sipos asked. "It would be easy enough to create something like that on a computer, maybe using a video editing software. Have you a second source to verify it?"

"Like I said, I had Roger examine it. You remember Roger? The head of my Secret Service detail. He had his people examine it, and they determined it was the real thing—no tampering. It would have been better were we able to have had the body autopsied. But that just can't happen. ... not at this point. But, I do have Jack's shirt—the one he was shot in. Not only did it contain his blood with his DNA, along with gunshot residue, Kate's DNA was also present. I think that evidence, along with the videos, settles it. The Handlers are dead. ... At any rate, I paid Emma. And she's a pro. She knows better than to screw around with me."

Sipos lifted his drink and feigned taking a sizable swig.

"Hold that thought," Allison said, setting her drink down on the bar. "I've got to powder my nose."

As soon as he heard the bathroom door close, Sipos removed the powder from two more capsules and poured them out into her drink while stirring it with a spoon.

He then took a small brown bottle out of his pocket containing more capsules. He opened three of them and poured the contents into the pitcher.

Half an hour—and a dozen toasts—later, Allison decided she would like one last Zombie. Sipos poured it for her.

She was able to drink most of it before she declared loudly that, "I gotta take another piss."

This time she made it only halfway to the bathroom before she crumpled to the floor, narrowly missing a glass-topped granite table.

"I'm not sure I'm gonna make it," she slurred.

Sipos slipped on a pair of latex gloves and went to her aid.

"Where's your purse?" he asked.

She lifted her head up from the floor as though elevation might help her remember.

"I dunno. On the bed? My purse is on the bed. Why do you want my purse?"

Sipos did not answer until he had returned with her purse and a glass of water.

"Let's see what you've got here that might help. Here's a bottle of warfarin. You must take your medicine."

Sipos was already aware that Allison had received a prosthetic heart valve several years earlier and was on warfarin. In fact, the powder that he had been pouring into her drinks was also warfarin. He thought that if he could overdose her on a drug she carried in her purse, it would appear self-administered.

He rolled her over on her back and lifted her upper body to a semi-upright position. He poured out six pills into his hand.

"Open up, you're overdue for your medicine."

Allison had difficulty swallowing from that position, but after several attempts she managed to get them down.

"Let's see what else we have here," he said, rummaging through her purse with his free hand.

"Looks like Valium. A couple of these might help you get some rest."

He gave her two Valium pills and had her drink some more water.

Sipos elevated her slightly to allow the medications to reach her stomach. He then laid her down on the floor.

"Maybe if you get a little rest," he said. "That might make it all better."

He then methodically moved about the room erasing any evidence that might suggest he had been in Allison's hotel. First, he dumped out the remaining Zombie mix and rinsed out the pitcher. He then washed out the glass he had been using, placed it back in the cupboard, and finally, he wiped down everything that he had touched.

He went into the restroom and emptied his pockets—six empty capsules, and the remainder of the warfarin he had used to spike the drinks. He dropped the empty capsules into the toilet, as well as the contents of the bottle, and flushed twice. He slid the empty bottle back in his pocket.

He looked around the room until he found the thermostat. He turned it up to eighty degrees.

"That should help my girl sleep," he mumbled.

He then examined Allison. He shook her several times and told her to wake up, but she was not able to react.

He rolled her over on her stomach and positioned her head to the side, exposing her left temple.

And then, gripping a heavy glass lamp that was sitting on the table, he hammered her hard on the side of the head. He took the lamp into the bathroom and washed it down, and then laid it beside the table.

By striking her a single time, rather than several, he concluded that the authorities would assume that she merely fell and bumped her head. While he could not know for certain, he believed he might have struck her hard enough kill her immediately. But, if not, he was confident that he had produced a concussion, and probably some bleeding inside her skull.

Knowing that warfarin worked a lot like rat poison in that it blocked the liver from producing the proteins necessary for blood to clot, Sipos believed that Allison would bleed profusely inside her skull. And, given the large amount of warfarin she had ingested, she would either die from pressure on the brain, or at the very least suffer a severe hemorrhage stroke.

As for the Valium—he thought that might make her sleep through the whole process.

If it all worked out as he planned, Allison would either be dead—which was his first choice—or severely disabled by the stroke. And, it would be determined to be an accident. In either case, she would no longer be able to interfere with him and his work.

Before he stepped out of the door, he pulled his scarf up over his mouth and nose—just as he had worn it when he entered the hotel, placed the "Please do not disturb" sign on the door, and then he left.

Five blocks from the hotel he stopped at a trashcan located on a street corner and discarded the empty bottle.

Chapter 50

"Jack," Roger said. "I've got some very big news for you."

"Yeah."

"Allison has suffered a stroke. She was off on her own playing Dana. For some reason she decided that she would tie one on, and she ended up getting totally soused, fell and bumped her head, and had a stroke."

"She was celebrating," Jack said laughing. "She was applauding her success—killing Kate and me. That's *exactly* what she was up to."

"I suspect you're right. … She showed me the video. Pretty convincing."

"Pretty convincing, but you didn't buy it?" Jack asked. "What did we miss?"

"The video was fine. But that cap you were wearing—I gave that to you. … I'm not too sure how you guys managed to disarm her before she got any more off, but it was clear to me that had she been successful she would have confirmed it with video."

"Bob didn't buy it either?"

"I told him about it, but I didn't show it to him. He knows Allison—she's going to believe what she wants to believe, to hell with the evidence."

"Well," Jack said. "It obviously convinced her, and that's all that really counts. … Any idea how severe the stroke was?"

"We don't know yet. She had been totally off the grid for over twelve hours before my agents knew anything was up. She apparently kicked them out, telling them that she wanted some privacy and that she was going to bed. She then snuck out the back.

"When I heard what happened, I checked her cell log and found a call to a local liquor store, and they told me where they delivered her order. She was registered at the hotel under Dana Reynolds. No surprise with that, right?"

"Right."

"Well, it *appears* that she got herself very drunk, and fell down. It looks like she hit her head on a table. Gave her a serious concussion."

"Was she alone?"

"What are you getting at?"

"I'm serious," Jack said. "I wasn't there, and neither was Emma. But don't you suspect that she could have had some help?"

"As far as we know right now she was by herself. … This is a bad one, Jack. She might not make it. The doctors have relieved the pressure on her brain. It might be a day, or it might be weeks before we know anything. That is, if she even makes it.

"You knew that ever since her valve replacement she's been on warfarin?" Roger asked. "You also know what that can do with a concussion? If she survives, there is likely going to be some significant brain damage. That's what I'm being told."

"Is this going to reflect on you?"

"Of course," Roger said. "I might be reassigned, even if she survives. She was my responsibility. The fact that she kicked us out does mitigate the matter. But, bottom line, she was injured on my watch. … Bob remains a major asset, of course."

"Back to my question," Jack said. "Was she alone at the time?"

"It looks that way," Roger said. "At least nothing has turned up yet to suggest otherwise. … It does seem strange that she would be celebrating like that by herself. But, she has done stuff like that before. She's not a terribly social person. We both know that. And I don't think that there are very many people who would enjoy drinking with her. She's just not a nice person. … But don't quote me on that."

"Who's investigating?"

"The FBI."

"How hard are they going to look?"

"They'll do a good job. If she had company, they will get to the bottom of it."

"Well, for what it's worth," Jack said. "I think that someone tried to kill her. I just know that it wasn't me. At least not this time."

"Really?" Roger said. "What makes you think that she might have had some help?"

"How much do you know about Alexander Sipos?" Jack asked.

"In general terms, or about this incident specifically?"

"Did you know that he has become disenchanted with Allison? He thought that she was careless … to the point that she was posing a threat to The Group."

"And you know that how?"

"Emma has been helping us."

"Really?"

"You didn't know that?"

"I figured she had to be in on the making of that video," Roger admitted. "But I didn't know to what extent you were collaborating. … What are we talking about? Is she all in?"

"I wouldn't go that far. She wanted to collect from Dana—for killing me."

"Did she get paid?"

"Oh, yes," Jack said. "When you signed off on the video, Allison released the funds. She's too smart to stiff a hitman. Besides, I think she was eager to celebrate my demise, and she couldn't justify the celebration without first paying for it."

"But what's that got to do with Sipos?"

"Besides me, who has motive?"

"You mean, besides you and *Bob*?" Roger asked with an air of humor.

"That was way too messy for Bob," Jack said. "If he were to want her dead, it would be two bullets in the head, on a street corner … when *you're* not around. Besides, he doesn't want her dead. But, I'm not so sure that's the case with Sipos. … Maybe we shouldn't be too concerned about who might be responsible. I just know that my being dead will take some of the pressure off. It would be interesting to know if Sipos was with Allison at the hotel. If he was, then he has seen the video, and might think that Emma has killed me."

"For what it's worth," Roger said, "a man fitting Sipos's general description did visit a guest at the hotel. He had his face covered with a scarf, but body size and build, and what we could see of his face, it did look like him. Facial recognition failed because of the scarf. … But, I'm intrigued as to why you think Sipos would soil his hands by killing Allison. He has all the money in the world. Why would he not hire it done?"

"Emma says that he is very much a hands-on guy. Take, for instance, that failed attempt on Judge Thompson. She told me that Sipos was actually in a nearby observation vehicle when she went in the front door. Can't get much more involved than that. … If he decided that the time had come for Allison to go away, Emma is convinced that he would do it himself. And that he would convincingly make it look like an accident."

"You actually discussed that with Emma?"

"She told me about the trap he had tried to set up to ferret out the mole in Dana's organization. By the way, Emma has never met Allison, or seen Dana's face. She has no idea that she's been working for a former first lady. ... Anyway, she told me that Sipos was very unhappy with Dana, and that he feared she was doing serious damage to his project. I think he might very well have had something to do with Allison's bump on the head."

"Sipos is a very savvy guy," Roger said. "If you're right and he was at the hotel with Allison, then he has seen the videos Emma sent to her to make her case."

"Exactly," Jack said. "I think that he was about the only person she knew who she might celebrate this success with."

"That being the case," Roger continued. "Then he must have developed an opinion regarding Emma's recordings. I saw immediately that they were bogus—"

"Yes you did, Roger. But you knew beforehand that I was still alive. Remember? It was you who saved my sorry ass."

"Yes, of course, but even so, when I observed the video *objectively* I had a problem with it. Sipos is smart. I think he would be skeptical. Allison saw what she wanted to see. She wanted you dead. She hired a professional to kill you. And then she viewed recordings strongly suggesting that the hit had been successfully made. *What's not to love about that?* I'm sure that's what she asked herself. ... But, Sipos, I'm not so sure he would have bought it."

"I see what you're saying," Jack said. "But, Allison and Emma had conducted business before. I think Allison trusted Emma enough to accept her evidence—perhaps without doing her due diligence. There is no question that Allison bought it. She paid on the contract. … As far as Sipos is concerned at this point, if he did have something to do with Allison's injury, then whether or not he accepts Emma's video is inconsequential—at least in the short term. He is going to be making every effort to avoid being found out. This means that he will be denying that he ever saw the video. If he did try to kill Allison, that would suggest that Emma was right—Sipos feared what Allison was allowing to happen even more than he feared me. If I lie low for a while, at least long enough to see how Allison is going to fare, this could all work out.

"I still can't quite understand why she would bring the recording to you for evaluation. She knows you and I are friends."

"She doesn't question my loyalty. And she shouldn't. As long as she remains Allison, the former first lady, I am totally in her corner."

"Where does Bob come down on all of this?"

"Generally speaking, he doesn't *want* to know," Roger said. "In fact, that will probably be the case more now than ever. I don't think anyone can predict how this is going to turn out for Allison. If she survives, she could be a totally different person. … There's a lot of blood trapped inside her brain, and it's never going to go away. If she survives she just might become a very different person. … On the bright side, this is good news for you. There's no question that you are no longer on her radar—not for the foreseeable future. It's a gift. Do you know what you're going to do with it?"

"I've got to get back in the game of destroying Sipos's court fixing scheme. That's what this was all about from the beginning. … I think I have a plan."

"Care to explain?"

"*Explain*?" Jack quipped. "I'll do more than that. Consider yourself enlisted … actually, a better word would be *drafted*."

Chapter 51

Jack needed a base of operations from which to launch his war on Sipos, and he was convinced that because of the recent murders of the Lundgruns and the Fletchers, Sugar Island remained too hot. *But the river house in Grand Rapids, that would work,* Jack concluded.

A few years earlier Jack had purchased a home located on the Grand River just north of Grand Rapids in Michigan's Lower Peninsula. Officially, the house was registered as belonging to the "Legendary Trust," with Ted Klanoski listed as the trustee. Klanoski, generally known as Legend, was a faithful associate of the Handlers. While their closest friends knew about River House, no amount of Googling could ever produce a connection. The same anonymity could not be enjoyed with regard to the Sugar Island Resort. So, River House it was.

The challenge for the Handlers was in maintaining secrecy as they carried out the move. That's where Roger came in.

"I need to charter a jet," Jack requested of his friend. "But it must stay off the grid."

"Jack, old buddy," Roger replied, "Do you have any idea what you are asking? The only way I can round up something like that is to go through Bob Fulbright. And you are regarded as the one indirectly responsible for putting his wife in the hospital."

"I'm moving Emma in with us, for the time being. She's a witness to a number of federal crimes. Wouldn't that put a special wrinkle in procurement?"

"Emma? Did I hear that right? You're moving a professional killer in with your family? Is that like what the Godfather intended when he said to *keep your friends close, but your enemies closer?* … Have you discussed this with Kate?"

Jack did not answer Roger's question.

"Don't have time to drive, and I won't put Buddy on a commercial flight. I need a charter, and it has to be on the QT. What can you get me? … Oh, and I need it by the end of the day. … Also, would you arrange to have Henry and a doctor share the ride? He's had enough excitement. I'll feel better if I can look after him. And Kate can make him a pot of chicken soup."

The Handlers, along with Emma, continued south to Los Angeles and there boarded an LAX flight to Grand Rapids.

"Did I read that correctly?" Emma asked as she prepared for takeoff. "Did it say *Sipos Enterprises* on the side of this 747?"

"That's right," Jack said, smiling at Kate.

"Is that like in *Alexander Sipos*?" Emma asked.

Jack then looked back at Emma and said, "Sometimes it just works out like that. We have a mutual friend, and he called in a favor. But it is not something that we talk about."

The mutual friend Jack was referring to was, of course, Former President Bob Fulbright.

About halfway through their flight, Jack walked back to where Emma was seated.

"We need to talk," Jack said taking a seat across from her.

Sipos had this 747 set up as closely as possible to the President's Air Force One. Directly above the flight deck was the Presidential Suite. That's where Jack, Kate, the two boys, and Buddy had been seated.

Directly behind that was the Presidential Office. There Henry and his doctor watched TV.

Kate had handcuffed Emma to the table in the combination conference/dining room, which was located directly over the wings. Even though Emma had not resigned herself to the restrictions placed upon her, she consoled herself with the realization that she was still breathing. *At least I'm still alive,* she thought.

"Don't you think it's a bit silly to keep me cuffed like this?" Emma complained. "Where exactly do you think I'm gonna go?"

Jack did not respond to her question. Instead, he asked, "What's the deal with your girlfriend, that Gomez girl? Did she have any direct connection with Sipos, or with Dana?"

"No. She always takes her orders directly through me."

"How about right now? Any idea what she might be up to?"

"She will remain at the hotel in San Francisco until she hears from me."

"Does she have friends in the area?"

"I'm her friend. She's very loyal."

"Do you have a way to contact her?"

"Cell phone."

"I need you to call her, then," Jack said. "Have her catch a flight to Grand Rapids. Then you and I will have a little talk with her."

"You need to get these damn cuffs off of me, or I ain't—"

"You ain't what?" Jack interrupted. "What exactly are you *not* going to do? Look, I'm not going to keep playing with you. ... This is a special flight. There is no record of you being on it. I would be able to pop you and put your body in a plastic bag, and dump it in the trash. And that would be the end of you. I suggest you listen to me carefully and do exactly as I tell you."

Emma fixed an empty stare at the top of the conference table. A small tear had formed in the corner of her right eye.

Chapter 52

"That's her," Emma said to Jack when she spotted her friend and associate, Alicia (Leesha) Gomez, walking toward them from the arrivals gate at Gerald R. Ford International Airport. He was struck with just how tiny Leesha was. *She looks like she could still be in junior high,* he silently noted.

Jack was convinced that the talk he had had with Emma on board the flight from LAX to GRR was transformational. It might have been the tear in her eye as she sat cuffed to the conference table, but something about her countenance that day persuaded Jack that he would be able to work with her, at least for now.

The way Jack later described Emma's transitional experience to Kate was, "Looks like she had her *come to Jesus moment.*" Jack was referencing the New Testament narrative in which the Spirit of God knocked Saul to the ground on the road to Damascus and asked him "Saul, Saul, why are you persecuting me?" Saul got up a changed man and began preaching the gospel of Christ.

Jack had chosen the Grand Rapids airport for the meeting with the

Gomez girl because he knew that there he would be the only one of the three packing a gun.

Emma arose from her seat and briskly walked toward her friend. Tears were in abundance as they shared a long embrace. Jack remained seated at a round table with five chairs. After a short but intense conversation Emma led her friend back and joined Jack.

"Jack Handler, this is Leesha," Emma said as she approached.

Jack stood and reached out his hand. Leesha, hesitating slightly at first, returned the gesture.

"Ladies, please sit down," Jack said.

And they did.

Emma spoke first.

"I explained to Leesha a little of what is going on," Emma said to Jack. "Perhaps you could fill her in on some of the details."

It was obvious to Jack that Emma was finding it difficult to discuss the matter with her friend.

"Be happy to," Jack said. "For starters, Miss Gomez—"

"Leesha, call me Leesha."

That's good, Jack observed. *The young lady does not lack self-confidence.*

"Leesha. I am about to make you and Emma an offer. And I want you both to know from the start, that if you decide you do not want to accept it, you are free to part company with me, and go about living your lives."

Emma flashed a look at Jack and said, "You are including me in that *free to go* deal?"

"Absolutely. If we decide that we should not work together, then both of you are totally on your own. I won't bother you again, as long as you stay out of my way."

The expression on Emma's face told the story. First, she looked deeply into Jack's eyes, and then at Leesha.

"No strings?" she asked.

"Only if you make it your goal in life to stay out of my way. If you come after me or my family again, I will kill you both. So, to live or die, it will be entirely up to you."

"Let's hear what you've got to say," Emma said.

Leesha followed Emma's lead and was fully attentive to Jack's every word.

"I don't imagine that either one of you are aware of Dana's accident. Is that correct?"

The two women shared a nonplussed eye encounter, and then Emma said, "I'm not aware of any *accident*. I just know she paid me. But I've not heard anything else from her."

"Dana suffered a major stroke. She apparently got very drunk when she found out that I'd been killed. She fell against a table, suffered a concussion, and ended up with severe bleeding on the brain. It could be some time before we find out just how much damage was done."

"That sounds very serious."

"It is," Jack said. "Could be fatal. And if she survives, there will most certainly be some lifelong problems."

"Who is she, anyway?" Emma asked. "I'm sure that is not her real name. She must be some kind of billionaire business mogul, or a front for one. Do you know her real name?"

"That's unnecessary information. She calls herself Dana. That's good enough for me. And it should be for you, as well. The less you know about your clients the safer you are. I'm sure you know that.

"The reason I shared that info about Dana's injury was to show you that you need not think that you have to hide from her as the story

gets out that I'm still alive. Her recovery will most likely be lengthy and fraught with peril. She will have trouble getting around—losing her balance easily. Her speech may be slurred. And her cognitive functions will be diminished. Perhaps greatly so. ... And the damage is irreparable. I have read that injuries such as Dana sustained can even lead to Parkinson's Disease."

"So," Emma asked. "How do you think I should proceed?"

"As though nothing happened," Jack advised, "I'll lay low for a while to allow the whole thing to blow over."

"You led me to believe that you had a job for me," Emma said. "Is that correct?"

"I have a *proposition* for you, that's correct. And I could also use Leesha's help."

"Interested?" Emma asked, placing her left hand on her friend's right forearm.

"If *you* are," Leesha said, "I would like to hear some specifics."

"We'd like to hear what you have to offer," Emma said, as she turned to face Jack.

"The job will pay five million total—one up front, four on completion. It involves eliminating a well-known personality. This individual does not hold public office, nor is this person involved in entertainment or sports. I will determine the time and means of implementation, and you will carry it out. That's all I will tell you. Take it or leave it."

Earlier Jack had secured the funds for this operation from Bob Fulbright, Allison Fulbright's now vengeful husband.

"We are free to leave?"

"At this point," Jack affirmed, "you are totally free to walk away. However, once I name the person, and spell out the details of the hit, you are committed."

"Give us a minute to discuss this," Emma said as she stood. "We'll just take a little walk."

"Good idea," Jack said. "Talk it over. … I'll grab myself a cup of Starbucks. Would you ladies care for anything?"

"I think we'll be fine," Emma said.

"Leesha, you should take your book and backpack. If we decide not to take this job, we're going to catch a taxi and get the hell out of here."

Emma made sure that Jack heard her say it. He smiled at her as he headed toward the coffee shop.

Five minutes later Jack arrived back at the table. Emma and Leesha were both already seated there.

"Well, Jack Handler," Emma said quietly, "we don't take checks."

"We'll discuss details back at the hotel," Jack said as he stood to his feet. "Gather up your stuff and let's go."

Chapter 53

With Emma's acceptance, the relationship morphed into one of client/hired gun, and Jack sought to separate himself and his family from all subsequent interactions.

"That's your car," Jack said as they passed by a brand new black Chevy Tahoe. "The keys are inside the fuel door."

They had just pulled into the parking lot of Airport Holiday Hotel.

"Your suite number is three eighteen," Jack said, lifting a black nylon duffle out of the back of his Tahoe. "Let's head up there and I'll fill you in on the details."

When they arrived at the room, Jack picked up the phone and ordered three of, "Whatever special the kitchen is offering. ... And send up a fresh pot of coffee with it."

He set the duffle on the bed and unzipped it. He held it open so Emma could inspect. On the top was a single bundle of twenty dollar bills, while the rest were bundles of new one hundreds.

"One million, I assume?" Emma asked.

"One million exactly," Jack confirmed.

The three of them then sat down around a table.

Jack started, "The target is Alexander Sipos."

Neither of the women signaled familiarity with the subject—Leesha because she had never heard of the man, and Emma because to do so would have been unprofessional.

"We believe he is at his Upper East Side apartment in Manhattan right now," Jack said. "Have either of you ever been to this apartment?"

Both shook their heads.

"Emma, are you able to contact him?"

"I never did have his phone number," Emma said. "When he was running the scam on Dana in his effort to uncover the mole, he gave me an email address. But he told me never to actually send anything. This is what we did. I would log onto that email account, and create a draft message to myself. He would later log onto the same account, and read the draft message. The message would never be sent. I don't know how effective that would actually have been at creating anonymity, but he seemed to think it worked. We didn't detail much using that email. We would set up a time for him to call me."

"What computers did you use to access it?" Jack asked.

"Always a library or internet café."

"Do you think that connection might still be in effect?" Jack asked.

"No reason to think otherwise," Emma said. "I still have an open contract—thanks to you. Judge Thompson, San Francisco. I inherited the job when you took out the previous contractor. … Plus, he asked me to stay in touch should I come up with something regarding Dana's mole."

"Sipos is a smart guy," Jack said. "And he has a lot of friends. We have to assume that he has figured out that I'm still alive. He probably even saw the video you sent to Dana, and knows that it's bogus.

"So, you should start right out, even in the email, admitting that you were forced by me to fudge the hit. … That I actually put the video together and sent it to Dana. Tell him that Leesha helped you to escape from me, and that you've not been able to get hold of Dana *to make it right*. Do not let on that you know about her injury. See if he brings it up.

"Regarding the hit on Judge Thompson, tell Sipos that while in captivity you learned where I was holding the judge, and that you could get to him. See if he would still pay on that contract.

"Most important in this whole exchange is to blame me for collecting from Dana for the hit on me, and to make Sipos believe that you know where Judge Thompson is, and that you know how to get to him. ... That just might interest him."

"What about the mole?"

"What about the mole?" Jack asked. "Do you have any theories about that?"

"I don't think that there has to be a mole," Emma said. "Sipos told me that Dana did not always use a secure cell phone, or a secure email server. If either one is true, there'd be no need for someone working on the inside. Any good hacker, or even just an interested third party, could read everything she wrote, and anything she said on her cell phone. Could be that Dana was just very careless."

No one talked for a moment, but then Emma started up again. "What if. ... What if he tries to hire me to hit Dana? How do I respond to that?"

"I doubt that she will be on the table. But, should it come up, reject the offer. Dana is in the hospital, and she will be recuperating for a long time. Could be years. You might express again that you still want to make things right with Dana. That you will either return the money to her, or consummate the contract. But you want to communicate with your client first. Don't let on that you know how serious her injuries were. ... But, at the same time, assume he knows all about it, and that he might test you.

"It's only reasonable to think that he still desires to have Judge Thompson go away. If that is indeed the case, then it would also be reasonable to assume that your contract would still be in play. In reality, you would be justified in tracking down and killing the judge without any further contact with the client. There is no time limit. However, since our objective is not actually to consummate that hit, it makes good sense to contact Sipos in order to gather other information."

"Such as?"

"Our sources tell us that Sipos is in New York right now. If you can convince him that it would be in his best interest to establish communication with you, we will be able to determine his exact location by tracing his cell phone."

"What if he disregards my email?"

"He won't," Jack assured her. "Sipos will be forced to react to your overture. Either he will want to call the Thompson hit off because he fears the heat is too intense, or he will want to move forward. Either way, we can locate him when he uses his cell.

"I want you to tell him that the judge is hiding in New York. Chances are that if we happen to be wrong, and Sipos is not in Manhattan, he will go there just to be close to ground zero; in much the same way as he set up shop in San Francisco when he thought the Thompson hit was going down there."

"New York is where they have that organization. Dana had me show up there to instill some fear in the members of the board. It was so weird. She wore a mask the whole time. She looked like that English prime minister. I think she thought it was funny."

"Really?" Jack said. "What sort of organization?"

"I really don't know. She referred to it as *The Group*. I don't know if it had a real name."

"Do you recall anything about the nature of the organization?"

"I was not there during most of the meeting. She called me in when she had finished addressing them. She basically told them about me.

"There were ten of them—all men. She told them that I would kill them if they did not do a better job. That's about it. She had me bring in an Uzi to impress them. I hate automatic weapons. They are so messy. Scary as hell, but pretty much useless for what I do. They're good for intimidation, but that's about it."

Emma was nervous. They had finished the coffee that room service had sent, and so she got up from the table and began making a pot of coffee using the small pot and packets in the room.

"Anyone besides me care for a cup of *crap* coffee?" Emma offered.

She had no takers.

"Was this like a board meeting?" Jack asked.

"That's how I would characterize it. It was very unusual though. Before I even entered, there were two armed men, one at either side of the only door in the room. They were carrying automatic weapons—Kalashnikovs. ... And, right on the table where Dana was standing, there was a Glock. I assume it belonged to her."

"Can you remember anything else? Think about it."

"Like I said, I came in as the meeting was wearing down. Dana said something like, 'Emma, here, will be dealing with you, with any of you, who let me down.' She then explained that the Uzi fires thirty rounds a second. And that I'd be cutting them down with my Uzi if they got out of line.

"That *thirty rounds a second* was a bit of an exaggeration, but it got their attention.

"There is one more thing," Emma continued. "Dana threatened the men that if they did not keep those *in the pipeline* under control, bad stuff would happen. At first I thought she was talking about a literal pipeline, like an oil pipeline. But then she talked about judges. So, I guess, I really don't know what she was talking about."

"Any idea when they might have another meeting?"

"No," Emma said. "But now with Dana temporarily out of the picture, Sipos might want to do something to solidify his authority."

"We don't want to wait any longer," Jack said. "Draft an email and let's see what happens. ... Here, use this burner."

"What should I say?"

"Generally, how did you phrase it when you wanted to talk to Sipos?"

"Only happened twice. I drafted, *Seeking guidance on legal matter*. He interpreted that to mean I needed to talk to him about a hit on a judge."

"How soon after that did he call you?"

"An hour. Maybe a little longer. But not much. I assume he receives some sort of notification on his phone when someone logs on to that email account. Not sure how that works."

"Can we have him call this phone?"

"Sure, I can just leave that number on the draft."

"I've got to make a call," Jack said, excusing himself and leaving the suite.

Jack then called Roger and gave him the number from the burner phone. "And, Roger, I need you to pinpoint the location and record all calls coming into that number for the next couple days. Make it three days."

"What is this about?" Roger asked.

"I just learned some interesting facts about Sipos and his court packing system. It appears to be far more pervasive than I had ever imagined. The organization even has a board of directors. I think that Dana was serving as its chairman."

Jack disconnected the call and re-entered the suite.

"Let's just try that same message," he suggested.

Emma then drafted this message with the phone number of the burner, *AS— Seeking advice on legal matter. —E*

Less than five minutes later the phone rang.

"Holy shit!" Emma blurted out. "That was fast. What should I say?"

Chapter 54

"Hello," Emma said.

"You wanted to talk to me?" said the digitized voice.

"Yes. I have been trying to reach Dana, but she's not returning my calls."

"I heard that she is a little under the weather. Is there something I can do?"

"Possibly. I am afraid I collected a fee from her under false pretenses, and I want to make it right. I was coerced into sending a fraudulent communiqué to her against my will. I did not complete the project in question, and I wanted to let her know."

"I understand. She will not be engaging in any type of activity for some time."

"What happened?"

"She had an accident. That's all I can say."

"I see. There is also the matter of the project I had started earlier. The one involving you."

"Cancel it."

"I now know exactly where that treasure is hidden, and I would be happy to complete the job."

"Not now, but I do have another matter that requires attention."

"Well, if I'm temporarily freed up regarding the other two, then I could help you. Where should I meet you?"

"First let me tell you what it entails. Dana related to me that you met with the board of our organization during the last meeting. I trust that is correct?"

"Yes, she had me step into the room for the last few minutes of a meeting."

"In her absence, I would like you to join me at an emergency meeting of that same board. In the same role as before. Except you will be present throughout the meeting, not just the end. Could you do that?"

"Yes, I could, but I have no idea what you expect. I do not even know the first thing about the business."

"You don't have to. I'll do all the talking. ... At some point, I will stand and point at one of the men. When I do, I want you to shoot him. Be as clean about it as you can. I don't know, maybe use a smaller gun. I don't know. I haven't even decided which of them you will hit. But I need to make an example out of one of them."

"When do I do this?"

"The meeting is set for tomorrow afternoon at three."

"Same building as before?"

"Same room. Can you find it okay?"

"I will be there. But, isn't there something we're forgetting?"

"One hundred K for showing up. Five hundred if I decide to use you."

"Five hundred K before the event. And another five hundred afterward."

"I made my offer. It's a fish in a barrel."

"Sorry, looks like I can't be of help. This is *not* a case of a fish in a barrel. I'm leaving nine witnesses. That's not a good way for a girl like me to do business. … When do you think I might get back in touch with Dana?"

"Don't bother with her for a long time. Maybe for good. The woman had a serious hemorrhagic stroke. She might never recover. … Be in the lobby at two forty-five. I'll pay your fee."

"See ya there," Emma said as she hung up.

Jack was smiling.

"Are you always that big of a hard ass?" he quipped.

Emma didn't answer, but Leesha did.

"That's typical Emma. She doesn't get pushed around."

"Look," Emma said. "You told me yourself, Sipos is not stupid. If I had seemed too eager for this job, he would have smelled something. Leesha will go with me and collect the down payment in case it goes south."

"We don't have much time to work out the details," Jack said.

"Details? What details? Sipos already laid out how this is to go down."

"Hope you didn't forget that you're working for me," Jack said. "Not him."

"What are you saying?" Emma asked. "Isn't this Sipos job for real? Don't I get to collect from him?"

"Absolutely. Collect from him. And once you do, you can do my bidding. I'll lay out in detail what that involves as soon as we get your travel accommodations resolved. But nothing happens if we don't get you to New York on time."

Chapter 55

Emma and Leesha walked into the Sipos Building at precisely two forty-five. Both were wearing tight-fitting dark blue jumpsuits with *Express Building Maintenance* logos on the front left.

"*She* does not stay in the building," Sipos barked as he pointed at Leesha.

"She'll leave with the down payment."

"Right," Sipos said, signaling for his associate to deliver the satchel containing the money.

"Wait for me at the hotel," Emma said to her friend. "I'll get there as soon as I can."

"The board members are waiting for us. I will be sitting at the head of the table. There is a chair for you directly behind me. I will introduce you before the meeting starts. Of course, they have already met you. I think I know who the target will be, but I'm still not sure at this point. Just be ready. When I stand and point at one of them. That will be your signal to *cosmetically* take him out."

"This job is not cosmetic. I will shoot the man in the head. But he is going to bleed. Blood happens in this business. The mess will be someone else's problem."

"Right. I get it. You have the gun with you?"

"Of course. It's in my bag."

"Well, I suppose it's time to go up."

Sipos was nervous. His hands were shaking, and beads of perspiration had broken out on his forehead.

"You should relax," Emma told him. "These board members should not see you sweat. … And, another thing. When I was here with Dana, she had two dudes stationed inside the room, one on each side of the door. They have to go."

"They stay," Sipos said. "They're my sergeants-at-arms. They're present at every meeting."

"They go. I will not have another weapon behind me. They go or I go. … I will be your sergeant-at-arms. Figure it out. But they cannot stay. … In fact, I do not want them on the same floor. When I take my seat behind you, I will remove my weapon from the bag and place it on my lap. The members will get the picture. You can state that I am serving as the sergeant-at-arms when you introduce me."

"I always carry my Glock," Sipos said. "That's not going to change."

"Not as long as you stay in front of me. How about the members? Any of them armed?"

"No. I have them screened on their way in. Only you and I will be armed."

"That works," Emma said. "Shall we rock and roll?"

Sipos blotted the sweat from his brow with a tissue.

"Let's do it," he said.

When they got on the elevator Sipos used his thumbprint to activate the button for the boardroom floor.

"How about coming back down?" Emma inquired. "Do I need your thumb to access the down elevator?"

"No. There's no security on down elevators."

As they were exiting the elevator at the penthouse Emma hit the ground floor button before she stepped out.

"Why the hell did you do that?" Sipos growled as he pushed the button to return the elevator.

Emma did not respond.

As they approached the boardroom Emma said, "You need to take care of your soldiers."

She took a seat and waited outside. The door was closed but she could hear what was being said.

"You two are excused for the day. Check your weapons into the vault, and you are free to go. You will be paid for the full day."

As they passed Emma the one closest to her said, "I remember you. You're Dana's friend. The *bitch* with the Uzi. What the hell are you doing here?"

Emma did not respond.

"Are you our replacement?" he said.

Still Emma did not acknowledge his presence.

"Let's get the hell out of here before the boss blows a gasket. Come on."

"No," the belligerent one said. "I asked the bitch here a question. She needs to answer me. Are you gonna be replacing us at all the meetings? *Bitch*. Is this gonna be your gig from now on?"

When Emma again did not respond the man reached his hand down to lift her face upward. Just before he touched her, Emma struck him with a lightning-fast left uppercut in the groin. As he doubled over on top of her she pushed him backward with her right hand on the top of his head.

"Get this piece of shit out of my face before I do some serious damage."

His partner grabbed him under his left arm and nearly tossed him into the waiting elevator.

"You all should remember Emma," Sipos said as he addressed the board. "In Dana's absence, she has agreed to sit in on our meeting. She will serve today as the official sergeant-at-arms."

As he spoke Emma removed an Uzi with a thirty-two round magazine from her bag. The Uzi was also equipped with a suppressor.

"Hey, lady," a young board member said. "That's a bigger gun than you had before. What's up?"

Sipos almost stood to call him out, but he caught himself just in time.

"Shut up!" he said. "I've got the floor."

"Gentlemen," Sipos said. "There is an envelope in front of each of you. It has your name on it. In just a moment I will ask you to open it. It contains the names of all the candidates with whom you have worked. And, it also lists the judges whom you have been assigned to monitor. Beside each of those judges there is a number—one through ten.

"A one indicates that the judge has ruled consistently within the guidelines we pass down. And ten is just the opposite. The higher numbers, five and above, are unacceptable. If you have a judge on your list with a five or higher, you are not doing your job."

The same man who had earlier commented on the size of Emma's Uzi raised his hand.

"Yes," Sipos said.

"I can see how you can scrutinize a poor performance by a judge that I brought along through the whole process. I can appreciate that. But, to hold *me* responsible for an appointment made years before I came on board—that I have a problem with. I cannot take—"

"Noted," Sipos interrupted. "Now shut up and let me finish.

"I believe Dana made it clear that you would have a limited amount of time to fix your problems. But I don't think she was specific. I am here to tell you that in one month I want to see that each of you has lowered his score by at least one point.

"And the following month—the same thing.

"That should not be difficult. Every one of you could improve.

"Beginning in three months, we will start taking these problematic judges off of your hands. We will have to. But, don't think that just because we remove a judge from the list, it will in any way make you look better. Just the opposite. If we are forced to terminate one of your judges, that places a black mark on your record—one which will be impossible to outlive.

"Keep in mind the millions of dollars we have invested in each of these judges. When you fail to keep them in line, it diminishes the whole organization.

"Each of you has been lavishly compensated for your efforts through the years. In some cases, those rewards have proved justified. Some of you have done a commendable job—but mostly in the past. A few of you should consider your contribution to The Group as adequate or above. I have no doubt that you know who you are.

"But, just because you do not score badly on this test—and it is a test—you should not become complacent. Each one of you could improve."

"May I say something," the same mouthy man said.

"Go ahead," Sipos said, clearly becoming agitated.

While the two men were conversing, Emma removed a pair of goggles and latex gloves from her bag and put them on.

"None of us have opened these envelopes yet. So, I don't know if I am passing your stupid test or not. I don't yet know my so-called *score*. I would just like to go on record as stating that this whole testing shit is a bogus exercise. I don't think any of us should be willing to accept it. It has to be totally unscien—"

Sipos then abruptly stood to his feet, pointed at the man's nose, and said, "Shut the hell up!"

That was the signal Emma had been waiting for.

Chapter 56

The eyes of all ten board members followed Emma as she stood to her feet.

Sipos, glancing backward briefly to verify that Emma was about to engage, then turned his back to her and covered his ears.

But, instead of shooting the protestor, Emma pressed the suppressor to the back of Sipos's neck, pointed it slightly upward, and fired.

Sipos slumped to the floor.

"Quiet!" she commanded. "The next one who makes a peep gets the same thing as your boss."

And then, pointing the muzzle of the Uzi toward an interior wall, she said, "Now, all of you, move over against that wall. Leave the envelopes on the table. ... I count nine envelopes. Whoever has the tenth, toss it on the table."

One of the men had not realized that he was still holding his envelope. Immediately he came to his senses and flipped it onto the conference table.

Emma smiled at the group as she switched her Uzi from single-shot to fully automatic fire. The board members did not know what she was doing or what to expect.

What followed was carnage. Using 9mm Parabellum rounds, Emma fired an extended volley into the ten men. All were struck in the chest with at least a single bullet. Some were hit multiple times.

Emma gripped the table and pulled it out from in front of the fallen victims. This gave her an unencumbered view of them, allowing her to switch the Uzi back to single-shot mode. In a very calculated manner she took aim at the head of each man.

Pop, pop, pop, etc.

When her Uzi emptied, she put in a fresh magazine.

Soon she had become the sole survivor in the room.

What she did not notice when she pulled the table back was that one of the envelopes had fallen to the floor.

Once confident that all the men were dead, Emma removed her jumpsuit and goggles, and tossed them on the floor.

She then scooped up the envelopes, not noticing that one was missing, and put them in her bag.

Using a can of cigarette lighter fluid that she had packed in her bag, Emma thoroughly sprinkled the liquid on the pile of garments that she had been wearing, and ignited them. She then removed her bloody gloves and tossed them in the fire.

Her plan was to wait until the fire set off the alarm, and then exit the building with everyone else.

It worked perfectly. Within two minutes the fire alarm sounded, and out she went.

Of course, the elevator had shut down when the alarm was activated, so she had to walk down forty flights of stairs. But that was not a problem for Emma. Should she have had to, Emma could have run up forty flights—thanks to her extraordinary level of fitness.

By the time she reached the main entrance, she had to wait in the mass of humanity that had lined up in front of the six exit doors. It took a minute, perhaps a little longer, to reach the sidewalk. But those few moments were not wasted as it gave her the chance to make a phone call.

"I will be exiting the building soon," she said. "I'm twenty feet from the doors, and the line is moving smoothly."

"Turn north, left, as you leave," Jack said. "They're going to be blocking off the street in front for fire trucks. Walk two blocks directly north and wait on the southwest corner, down fifty feet from the light. Look for a yellow taxi. Leesha and I borrowed one. I know there are a lot of taxis. We'll be watching for you."

Just as she exited and turned north, the security guard whose balls Emma had just busted recognized her.

"There she goes," he said loud enough for his friend and Emma to hear.

She pretended she did not hear him.

"Hey you," he said, even more loudly. "Hey, bitch. I know you hear me. Where do you think you're goin'? You come back here, we wanna talk to you."

She kept walking, now even more rapidly than even the most seasoned New Yorker walks.

The two men ceased calling out to her, but she did not believe that they had given up. She confirmed her concern as she approached the angled windows of a nearby building entry. She spotted their reflection in the glass.

She slowed her pace slightly to allow them to catch up. Still watching them in store windows as she walked, she timed her attack perfectly.

A crushing right backhand across the bridge of the nose of the man closest to the street immediately took him out.

With that same right hand she delivered a powerful roundhouse punch to the throat of the other man. He, too, dropped with a crushed larynx.

She again picked up her pace, but did not run.

Unfortunately, Emma did not catch the walk light at the first intersection. But that did not stop her. She walked straight across anyway, holding up her left hand to stop both taxis and delivery trucks. Her height, confidence, and sexy legs made her crossing virtually effortless.

When she arrived at Jack's taxi, he reached across and opened the door for her.

But, she was not alone. Two uniformed officers had witnessed the two men attacking her, and they were approaching Jack's vehicle as quickly as two obese middle-aged men could possibly move.

"Hold it right there, Miss," they shouted as they drew their weapons. "We've got some questions for you."

Jack hit the passenger window button and presented a badge indicating that he was a special agent in the FBI.

"Federal officers working a case. Get the hell back!" he shouted.

Both officers stepped away as Jack sped off. One of them was writing down the tag number while the other was on his radio reporting what had just gone down.

Traffic was heavy, but Jack managed to make his way through it for two blocks. There he pulled to the best double park he could accomplish, and turned on his four-ways.

Emma removed the Uzi and the second magazine and left them on the floor of the vehicle. She took care not to touch it with her hand.

It was then, when he looked back to tell Leesha to get out of the taxi, that he made a startling discovery. Jack had never before seen Emma's young friend without her sunglasses. But right at that moment, because it was dark in the taxi, Leesha was wearing her sunglasses low on her nose so she could peer over them. *Oh my God,* Jack thought. *The girl's got one green eye, and one blue. How very unusual.*

"Let's go," he commanded, opening his door into traffic. Horns blew and taxi drivers cursed as the three of them quickly walked west. Within half a block a white SUV approached from the rear. The driver, with his left arm dangling through a loose-fitting sling, blew his horn twice and pulled toward the curb.

"Jack!" the driver shouted with his biggest *Henry* smile. "Could I give you and your friends a lift?"

Chapter 57

Jack wasted no time in hustling Emma and Leesha out of the country. Using forged passports—provided by Roger under the names Carol Warren and Janet Cano—Jack routed them through Switzerland, where the remaining four million dollars awaited them. After their visit to a Swiss bank, they made their way to Brussels.

Once he had seen the women off, Jack caught a flight to Grand Rapids, and returned to the river house on the Grand; while Henry flew into Chippewa International Airport in Sault Ste. Marie, MI. From there he drove to Sugar Island.

"Dad," Kate said when he arrived. "Everything go as planned?"

"Pretty much. We actually ended up with more than we'd hoped for."

"Really? How's that?"

"Emma was supposed to only take out Sipos, but she improvised—considerably improvised. She was concerned about leaving eyewitnesses, so she eliminated the entire board of directors of the Sipos organization. There were ten of them."

"She shot ten men?"

"Eleven, counting Sipos. With Allison laid up with her stroke, the entire upper echelon of their court-packing cadre has been eliminated."

"Will that put an end to it?" Kate asked.

"Not necessarily. There are a large number of candidates working their way through various law schools, and others already gainfully employed in the legal profession, eagerly anticipating federal appointments. Other members of the organization, which I have just learned is officially called The Group, are employed by some of the top universities in the country."

"How do you know all this?"

"Emma had the presence of mind to gather up a whole treasure trove of information before she left the boardroom."

"Where is she now?"

"She and Leesha should be arriving right about now in Zürich. From there they travel to Brussels."

"Funny how that all worked out," Kate said. "In the beginning we would have liked nothing better than to have put a bullet in her head, and now, she has turned out to be a major asset for us. Who could have predicted that?"

"Even though she was very helpful in this Sipos deal," Jack said, "I like the idea of having that woman a big ocean away. She is smart, and very deadly. … But I will admit, I could not have pulled off the hit on Sipos any better than she did. Great outcome. … That having been said, she came *very* close to putting that round in my brain. I'm good with never seeing her again."

"That was my fault," Kate said. "That shot she got off in the museum.

I should have had your back."

"It was not your fault. Who could have anticipated her shooting from that distance—with a *pistol*? It's unheard of.

"Bottom line—you and Buddy saved my life. That's all that counts.

"I spent most of the flight studying the materials she picked up. Very interesting. Some of the professors they have in place have been at it for thirty years. Granted, they might not all have been part of The Group for that long, but it is clear that this is not a new organization.

"It's probably even safe to say that many of them pre-date Sipos's involvement. ... That is, there was most likely a loosely-knit organization in place when Sipos stepped in."

"So," Kate asked, "do you think that it could continue to function without Sipos, Allison, or the board?"

"I think it might—at least for the short term. There had to have been some sort of hierarchy of leadership before Sipos took over. It's possible that they could continue on almost seamlessly. And given Sipos's unpleasant personality, the old guard might be happy to see him and his board gone."

"We're going to deal with them, aren't we?"

"Probably. But I don't know exactly what we *could* do. If we knew who the main leaders were, we might do something with them. But there appears to be so many names. I have nine lists—Emma missed one—and there are between twelve and twenty names on each list. We can't just take out a hundred and fifty lawyers and judges."

"Really?" Kate quipped. "That sounds like an opening for a bad lawyer joke. ... Why don't you run it by Roger? He always seems to have fresh ideas."

Chapter 58

Jack and Kate had just settled in at the river house and were preparing to brainstorm the lists of operatives contained in the documents Emma had lifted from the scene of the Sipos hit, when Kate's cell buzzed.

She looked at her phone, frowned, and then said to Jack, "I'm not ready for this, but I suppose I'm going to have to take it. It's Christina Baldwin—CPS.

"Christina. It's Kate. How are you?"

Kate had just poured two coffees from the freshly brewed pot and was hoping to have a moment without interruption for her investigation.

"I trust you're back from vacation," Baldwin said. "I'd like to set up an appointment to meet with you, Jack, and the two boys."

"We're not back yet, sorry."

"Then tell me where you are right now and I will send a car to pick up the boys. You have delayed this long enough."

Kate had turned up the volume so Jack was able to hear both sides of the communication.

"Dad, did you catch that last mile marker?"

"No, I don't think they post mile markers on county roads," Jack said loudly.

"Not really sure exactly, just know that I've got very poor cell reception here—between one and two bars. Tell you what, why don't we get together tomorrow afternoon, at our house on Sugar Island, at three in the afternoon. Does that work?"

"I suppose," Christina said. "But—"

With the appointment set, Kate disconnected the call, and immediately turned her cell off.

"Better turn yours off, too," Kate said. "Or she will be calling you next."

"Okay," Jack said, cycling his cell off. "Let's see what we can make of these lists. … First, let's see if we can find some familiar names. We should start with Supreme Court justices."

Kate opened the envelopes one at a time and flattened the pages out on their dining room table. Once all nine lists were placed neatly in a line, they began to scrutinize them.

"Check out lists four and six," Kate said. "They end with current Supreme Court justices—Chief Justice James Sutherland, and Associate Justice Craig Merkel—Sutherland's name is in parenthesis and italics. Merkel is in italics only. Sutherland is already dead. He's the one who crushed his throat lifting weights. Maybe when a judge is written up for death, his name is parenthesized.

"Could that possibly be? Is it possible that two Trojan Horses made it to the highest court in the land?"

"I think we have to assume that is the case," Jack said. "But, notably missing was Associate Justice Anthony Pelosi. And yet he made the kill list. Could be that he was not one of the Trojan Horses. Maybe he was just considered a bad influence. He was very popular, and Sipos may have felt he had too much power. He was the chief spokesman for the constitutionalists. … I think maybe they just wanted to get rid of him to open up a seat for one of their guys."

"This is so incredibly evil," Kate said. "Sipos had both Pelosi and Sutherland killed, didn't he? All to open up positions on the bench for his select candidates. That's what's happening, isn't it?"

"Looks that way," Jack agreed. "Both justices are constitutionalists—Pelosi more than Sutherland. It seems to me that Sutherland did not start out that way. But the older he got, and the more he hung around with Pelosi, the stricter he grew. I'm not that big a student of the Supreme Court, but I do recall a time when Sutherland was voting with the looser constructionists. Could have been Pelosi's influence.

"If we're interpreting these correctly, we have two currently seated justices marked as Trojan Horses on these nine lists—one of them is dead, the other, Craig Merkel, is still alive. Who do you suppose is included on the tenth—the list we don't have?"

"Perhaps there isn't another Trojan Horse," Kate suggested. "We have seven lists that do not contain the names of Supreme Court justices. Only two that do. Maybe the tenth one, the one we don't have, maybe it does not contain the name of a Trojan Horse justice."

"Let's hope you're right," Jack said. "But, unfortunately, we can't know that for certain.

"Now, go to the top of each list," Jack said. "Sipos is the first name on every list. That must indicate that he is at the top of the food chain. That's to be expected. But beneath Sipos is another name. It's different on every list, and it stands apart, just as Sipos's does. And it is the same name as on the outside of its respective envelope. No doubt that was the name of the board member who received this list."

"And they're all dead."

"That's right," Jack said. "There then follows a short listing. It's similar on each of the sheets. It contains from two to four names. … I wonder who they might be? I'm not familiar with any of them."

Kate immediately began Googling.

"Dad. Check this out. The three names on the first sheet. They're all old guys. Well-placed in a single major law school. All of them. And the same is true of the second sheet. Both of them are law professors at different law schools—this one's an Ivy League law school. I'll bet that it will be the same in all instances. These would be the talent scouts, so to speak. The mentors? They would locate the prospective candidates, and then be responsible for nurturing them along through the process. I'd bet that's it."

"And then after them," Jack noted, "there is another set of names. This set contains from three to nine names on each sheet. They will most likely be the candidates themselves."

"And then the next to last grouping," Kate said. "They would probably be judges in the lower courts. These would most likely be the real Trojan Horse—the ones already sitting on the bench. … All of them have numbers after their names. What do you suppose those numbers mean? They range from one to ten."

"A rating system?" Jack suggested. "Maybe that's what the numbers—"

"I think you're right," Kate interrupted. "Check this out. Two of the judges that were killed had ratings of nine or ten. It must mean that the higher the number, the worse the rating. Do you think?"

"You know what this looks like to me?" Jack asked. "I think that the ten so-called board members were really little more than enforcement operatives. Their job was to keep the candidates in line—before and after appointments to the courts. And if they failed, then Sipos would implement more drastic measures. That's how it looks to me."

"They are subverting the entire court system," Kate stated as she crossed her arms and pushed away from the table. "The *entire* federal court system, top to bottom."

"I think that's it," Jack agreed. "Their principal target is, of course, the Supreme Court. Unfortunately, because we are missing that tenth list, we cannot tell how many Trojan Horses there are among the associate justices. There could be several listed on that missing sheet—we just don't know."

"If we did a background study of the currently-seated associate justices," Kate suggested, "to see if they were mentored by any of the professors named on these lists, that might provide some insight."

"It could, but it would not be definitive," Jack said. "There would be no way to determine motivation. I think we are stuck, at least for now, with the associate justices who are currently serving. But, we can make this list available to the Senate Judiciary Committee for consideration of future appointees to the federal courts."

Jack and Kate sat at the table quietly for several uncomfortable moments. Finally, Kate broke the silence.

"Tomorrow, three o'clock," she said. "We need to prepare ourselves for that meeting. I think it might be hostile."

"I'm quite sure it's going to be hostile," Jack said. "I don't think that Baldwin knows how to talk to people. Everything about her has to be *in your face*. That's all she knows. We'll have to be there for the meeting, but don't expect a positive outcome."

"Dad, you're usually more positive about stuff like this," Kate said.

"I'm just being realistic," Jack replied. "This woman does not always have the best interests of the child at heart. That's more than just my opinion. I've talked to several in the community about her. Once she gets her dander up, there's no stopping her. She's like a runaway freight train. I'm sorry, but that's the general consensus of those I've talked to.

"Unfortunately—and I hate to admit it—she has a decent argument this time. With the Fletchers being murdered, and the Lundgruns, I can actually appreciate her concern."

"Yeah," Kate said. "I get the same feeling. But, there is one thing we can do to help our case. We can get the house spotlessly clean. We haven't been in it for nearly a week. It has to be very dusty. And it should be aired out. … If we left right now, we could be there in six hours, and I could get started cleaning it up."

"I've got a better idea," Jack said as he called Henry.

Chapter 59

Christina Baldwin, while only in her fifties, did not wear her age well. Granted, she had lived through some difficult times—which no doubt took their toll on her appearance. When her husband was diagnosed with stage-five lung cancer six years ago she totally gave up trying to care for herself. She had battled a thyroid disorder since high school, but after her husband's death she rejected all treatment. That, along with uncontrolled eating and a steadfast refusal to exercise, resulted in her ballooning her five-foot-two frame to over two hundred pounds.

At this point in her life, her job had become her only reason for living. The fact that she had spent the past twenty-six years dealing with children that were not her own had left her with a jaded view of life. During the early years of her career she and her husband had talked of having children. But days turned into months, and then to years. By the time he was diagnosed they had pretty much decided not to have children of their own—the troubled children of others would have to satisfy her maternal needs.

Outfitted on this day in a well-worn navy suit, chunky pair of black shoes, and thick compression stockings, with her signature black bag tucked under her arm, she stormed into the Handlers' house like a bulldozer. Her countenance spoke volumes. She was ready to pull the boys out and make the Handlers pay for their irresponsibility.

"I need to talk to the boys privately," she said. "Shall I take them to their bedroom?"

Jack and Kate nodded their approval and she said, "Okay, boys, lead the way."

After shutting the door behind them, she asked, "Boys, how do you feel about the Handlers? Do you feel like they actually *want* to have you living with them?"

"Well, sure. They're great," Robby said. "Did they tell you that they didn't want us here?"

"I haven't asked them yet," she said. "Red, do you agree with Robby? Do you feel like they really want you around?"

Red nodded.

"And I," Robby said, clearly not comfortable with Baldwin's question, "*we* think they *really* like us. I'm sure they like us."

"How did it make you feel when you learned that the Fletchers had been killed?"

"Sad. They were cool. Jim took us fishing and stuff. … And Mary, she was always nice to us. She made us feel welcome. She made special stuff for us, like cookies and other stuff."

"You used to stay with them a lot, didn't you?"

"Yes," Robby said, wiping tears from his eyes. "They were great."

"Now that they're gone, and the Lundgruns are gone as well, when Jack has business, where are you going to go?"

"Millie and Angel Star live in the Soo, real close to the ferry. We could even walk to their house."

"Have you talked that over with Jack and Kate? Would they expect you to walk onto the ferry and over to the mainland? Wouldn't they be willing to drive you?"

"They would drive us if they could. But in an emergency, we could go on foot. … They asked us what we thought about it. Red and I really like Millie and Angel. So it would be fine with us … to stay there if Uncle Jack had business."

"That's very nice," she said, as she pivoted. "But do you really feel *safe* here? After all that violence. How can you feel safe here anymore?"

"We feel safe. Uncle Jack and Aunt Kate take good care of us. Nothing bad has ever happened to us here. They watch out for us."

"Do you worry that someone might harm you like they did your babysitters?"

"*Babysitters?* We ain't babies!"

"The Fletchers. Are you ever concerned that something bad could happen to you like it did to the Fletchers?"

"Uncle Jack talked to us about that too. He said it was just one of those terrible things in life, and that it was over. The men who hurt the Fletchers would never hurt anyone again. I guess they got arrested. He said we should remember the good things about staying at the Fletchers. Remember how nice they were. And cherish their memory. But not worry about it ever happening again. Uncle Jack is pretty smart. And honest. He doesn't lie to us. And neither does Kate. If they say everything is okay, then we believe them."

"Then you feel safe?"

"Yes I do," Robby said. "How about you, Red? Do you feel safe?"

Red nodded.

"Would you boys mind playing outside for a little while, I would like to talk to Jack and Kate."

"Sure," Robby said with a grin as he sprang to his feet.

Looking over at his friend, he said, "C'mon, Red. Let's go *play* outside, like the lady said."

Christina's use of the word *play* struck both boys as humorous. *We don't play*, they were thinking. *Playing is for babies.*

Christina walked the boys to the door and watched them as they raced toward the river. Buddy brought up the rear.

Jack and Kate were already seated at the dining room table. Christina walked back and joined them. Kate was a little nervous. Jack was apprehensive but remained big-picture confident. He had thought the whole matter through and had resigned himself to the likelihood of a less-than-optimal short-term resolution.

"Jack, Kate," Christina said. "I hope you can appreciate the seriousness of this situation."

Just as I thought, Jack said to himself, *the board, or committee—or whatever she calls the real decision-making entity, they have already made their decision and everything she is about to say today now is mere formality. I just hope Kate can brace herself for what is coming down. It's not going to be pretty.*

Christina's tone made Kate even more nervous.

"First of all I would like to commend you on all the positive things that have taken place since the boys took up residence in your home. They both seem happy and well adjusted."

Neither Kate nor Jack reacted, even though Christina clearly anticipated a response.

"We reviewed the boys' school records, and they were outstanding. Both boys are on the honor roll. And their principal tells us that both Robby and Red are well adjusted and, in fact, are two of the most popular boys in the school."

"Damn," Jack said, not able to resist tossing in a barb, "We sure as hell have to do something about that!"

"Dad," Kate said. "Let's hear her out."

"Mr. Handler. I appreciate the fact that you and your daughter truly care for these boys. And it is obvious that the feeling is mutual. The boys love you like their real parents. Understand, this is very—"

"Can't have that either, can we?" Jack interrupted. "And they don't love us like *real* parents—we are their parents.

"I'm pretty sure I know where this conversation is going, don't I, Ms. Baldwin. You are about to pull these boys out of our house and place them in foster care. Am I right? Haven't you already made that decision?"

"I am truly sorry, Mr. Handler," Christina said, forcing the words through an affected smile. "But it is our job to protect the children we serve."

"Let me ask you a question," Jack said. "How many foster homes have you people found for Red through the years? Before he moved in with us?"

"I don't know specific numbers," Christina said, pausing before answering. "I do know that he had been placed before."

"Well, I do know. Red saw the inside of six foster homes before coming to live with us. And he ran away from all six. In the weeks and months before we met him he was living on his own in the woods on Sugar Island. And your organization had given up. You just let him fend for himself. He was barely fourteen years old. You left a fourteen-year-old child to gather his own food, find his own shelter, and procure his own clothing. That's how effectively *you* cared for him when you had your chance."

"Things have changed. We are better staffed."

"And what, exactly, does that mean? *You're better staffed.* Does that mean you are better able to go out and bust kids in the woods?"

"I understand your frustration."

"I don't think you do. What you are about to do is *not* in the best interest of these boys. They would be much better off left with us. We love them. They love us. They are happy. I don't think that there are two more settled and secure teenage boys in their entire school. And you are about to rip them out of the home that has provided the foundation for their success. It just doesn't make any sense."

"We have a number of fine foster homes in the county. And this would not have to be permanent. We will review the whole—"

"I'm sure you do, and I'm sure you will be reviewing options. But these two boys are doing just fine right where they are. You will not be doing them any favors by forcing all this stress on them."

"We have to do what we consider is in the best interest of the children. I do not know exactly what it is you do for a living, but whatever it is, it has placed these two boys in an untenable position. Two entire families, both friends of yours, and caregivers for the boys, have recently been murdered. In one instance, it was the boys who discovered the bodies. That is no way to raise children."

"We didn't kill them," Jack said. "Those were terrible tragedies. But we saw the boys through it, and they remain well adjusted. It's just a fact of life that sometimes shit happens. That's why they make up those stupid tee-shirts. Sometimes bad things happen to those we love. That's the situation with our friends. But the boys have made it through this tragedy. It does not make sense to pull them out of a home where they are secure, and toss them into a stranger's home. You will be doing damage to them, not helping them."

Kate totally agreed with what her father had been saying, however his aggressive demeanor made her uneasy. She was not sure how the social worker would react to her father's firm words.

But, Jack had a plan. He was correct in his assumption that Ms. Baldwin had walked in their door fully aware that the decision had already been made regarding Robby and Red—that the two boys would have to be removed from the Handlers' home, and placed in temporary foster care.

Jack knew that while he would not be able to overturn *that* decision, he might be able to influence the boys' temporary placement. That's what he was angling for.

"I would like you to consider this," Jack said, no longer so assertive. "Millie Star has applied with the county for license to do foster care. She had previously been licensed in Mackinac County, so I think it just might be a matter of transferring the license. I don't know how that works, but I don't think it has to be a big deal."

"*That's* where I heard that name," Christina said. "Robby had mentioned a friend of yours named Millie Star. Now I recall seeing the paperwork for her license. … I don't know what the status is, but I do know that we are looking for good foster parents. And she is under consideration."

"Well," Jack said. "She's the best. I'm sure you will like her.

"This is what I propose; what if the boys move in with her until this whole matter gets sorted out? That way the boys will remain in the same school district. And they already know Millie."

Christina took a little time to digest Jack's suggestion. Jack could see that his assertiveness had put her on the defensive, and that she was truly considering his proposal. So he kept his mouth shut. Finally, she spoke.

"This is the best that I can do. I will have to take the boys with me today. They should pack up a few clothes and other essentials. We will see if we can expedite this Star lady's license. If it all works out, and I think it might, we can move the boys in later this week."

"And where would they stay in the meantime?" Jack asked.

"Temporary foster care. We have a number of families who take in transitional children. They hold them until a more permanent placement can be found."

"Not good enough," Jack countered. "Let's do it this way. I'll take the boys over to Millie's house later today. She will then work with you on finalizing the license. That way you get what you want—a *safe* home for the boys, and they will not be traumatized. I'm sure you can work that out with your superiors."

"I came here with strict orders to remove those boys from your home, today. I don't know how—"

"And that's exactly what you are doing," Jack said. "You are removing the boys from this house and placing them in temporary foster care. That's *exactly* what this is accomplishing. It's just skipping the part where the cops have to repeatedly go out in the woods looking for these two Tom Sawyers. Do it this way and you will save the county a lot of money and embarrassment. … Of course, you could always lock them up. You do have a juvenile detention facility, don't you?"

"These boys don't qualify for lock-up."

"Well, they just might before you're done, if you miss this opportunity," Jack said.

Christina thought for a moment and then said, "I'll see what I can do."

"Terrific," Jack said, walking Christina to and through the door. "I am so glad you're our boys' caseworker. It is just wonderful to work with truly qualified professionals. We will have the boys over to Millie's by dinner time, and she will visit your office tomorrow."

"Dad! What just happened?" Kate asked as she sat back down at the table.

"I'm not quite sure," he said. "But I think we need a beer."

* * *

"I can't believe that you backed the camper in this close to the channel," Jerome, a skinny middle-aged chain smoker, complained to his partner. He was clenching a filtered Marlboro in his teeth, and had a second one tucked behind his left ear. "Another foot and a half and this sonofabitch would have toppled right in the St. Mary's."

"But it *didn't* fall in, did it?" countered the man in charge. "It's right where I wanted it. ... And if you intend to smoke that thing, you damn well better do it outside. That shit raises hell with my optics."

"I ain't gonna smoke inside. I never do."

"Don't even light up within fifty feet of me. I hate the smell. And it burns my eyes."

Jerome scowled at his boss but did not respond.

The boss, known since his Army Ranger days in Afghanistan as *Zero*, short for zero tolerance, was diligently at work adjusting and calibrating his equipment, centermost of which was an *Accuracy International* sniper rifle with a 8.59mm barrel.

Jerome walked up behind him and peered over his shoulder.

"Do you really think you can hit anything on the other side of the channel? That's got to be a mile or more."

"It's under two thousand meters, and entirely over water. That's well within range. ... But that's not your concern. All you have to do is sit on your fat ass and fish. And if we have company, or a freighter is approaching my line of fire, that is when you speak up. That's it. Period."

"How long are we going to be here? It's boring."

"Until she tells us that it's a go. Or tells us to pull out. She's paying the bill, so she's calling the shots."

Just then Jack opened the door and stepped out on the porch to call the boys in.

"Shut up!" Zero commanded. "He's in my sights."

Precisely at the optimum moment he feigned pulling the trigger.

"Bang," he mouthed. "One, two, three, four. Bullet strikes—Handler's dead."

One hour later Zero received the text message he'd been waiting for.

"Proceed with operation anytime after 0 700 EST tomorrow."

Chapter 60

The next morning Jack and Kate were sitting at the breakfast table discussing their plans for the day when the morning sun reflected off something shiny across the St. Mary's River.

"That's new," Jack said, walking over to a window to get a better look.

"What's that?" Kate asked.

"Something's reflecting the sun from the west—from the other side of the river. Haven't seen it before."

At first Jack used his binoculars, but soon opted for a tripod-mounted telescope the boys used for identifying freighters.

"Whoa!" Jack spouted. "That's not good."

"Really?" Kate said. "Let me take a peek."

"Is that what I think it is?"

"If you think it's a sniper and a lookout, then you'd be right."

"Henry," Jack said after he'd called his friend. "Directly across the river from the house, we've got a camper with a shooter inside. There appears to be at least one other person—a lookout about fifty feet south of the camper."

"How shall I handle it?"

"Grab the Ford truck—the one with the *steel* plow—and pick me up by the main entrance."

Jack then snapped a holstered Glock to his belt and went out through the back door, which would not be visible to the sniper.

"Slide over," Jack said. "You take the Glock and I'll drive."

By the time they reached the ferry, using Google Maps Henry had located the only possible access to the point from the mainland, and they sped off toward it.

"There was a lookout about fifty feet south of the camper," Jack said. "No telling what he will do as we approach. He might stand up and fight, he might flee, or he might join his buddy or buddies inside the camper. When I give the signal, if I give the signal, I want you to stick that Glock right up under his nose. … Put these on."

Jack handed Henry a baseball cap and a pair of sunglasses.

"This could be the Feds," Jack said. "But I doubt it. That lookout did not look much like a federal officer to me. But, just in case it is the Feds, we should try to avoid injuring them. They don't forget quickly."

"Here," Henry said. "This looks like the trail. They should be back in there about two hundred yards, maybe less."

"Looks right. I can see fresh tracks."

As soon as the lookout spotted the approaching Ford he made a beeline into the camper.

"That simplifies matters," Jack said, as he neared the front bumper of the Jeep that was still attached to the camper.

"Fasten your seatbelt and prepare for impact," Jack said with a huge smile.

Jack did slow down dramatically, striking the Jeep at barely over five miles per hour. But it was fast enough. Even though the brakes on the Jeep were set, he easily shoved the camper and its attached vehicle well out into the St. Mary's river.

"I wonder if that's one of those *amphibious* campers?" Henry said.

"Could be," Jack said, now laughing out loud. "But I'm pretty sure that Jeep doesn't float."

"Hope they can swim," Henry said, as Jack slammed the Ford into reverse.

"We're not going to wait around to find out," Jack said. "Hand over that Glock. What's a convicted felon doing with a firearm, anyway? Shame on you."

* * *

"What do you suppose that was all about?" Kate asked, after Jack and Henry returned. "I did watch it all through the telescope. There were a total of two men who made it out of the camper before it went down. They both managed to get to the bank."

"Too bad they survived," Jack said. "Did the whole thing sink—camper and Jeep?"

"Yes. Part of the Jeep was showing above the surface for several minutes, but eventually the current grabbed it and pulled it out into the deeper water."

"That camper must have been weighted for it to have sunk like that. They might have rigged it with weights for stability."

"Do you have any idea who they might be working for?" Henry asked.

"Did they look like Feds?" Kate asked.

"Like I told Henry," Jack said. "They looked more like contractors than Feds. But, I suppose, you never know. Sometimes the Feds hire private contractors. ... My best guess is that they were hired by someone like, like that Dana woman."

"I thought she was out of commission," Kate said.

"Well, so did I. I'll check with Roger and see if he has any idea about what's going on."

Kate picked up her phone and called Millie.

"Hey, girlfriend," Kate said on her voicemail. "Jack and I are heading down to Grand Rapids on business for a few days. Could you make sure the boys do not come over to the house while we're gone? We've had a little incident—we're both okay. But we want to keep the boys away until we can sort it out. … Of course, don't mention anything to them. Or to that social worker."

"Dad. I hope that made sense to you."

"Perfectly. We've got to create some separation between ourselves and the boys. And between ourselves and Sugar Island, for that matter. … What do you say? Let's go wreak some havoc in Grand Rapids."

Jack then turned to Henry.

"You stick around the resort and keep things right-side-up," Jack directed his friend. "And be here if Millie or the boys need something. Don't allow them to be anywhere near the resort, however. … I don't think there'll be any blowback on the flotilla we scuttled. They will probably dive on the wreckage yet today and remove evidence. And then get the hell out of Dodge. That's what I'd do."

"Roger," Jack said after having dialed his friend. "We had a little adventure up here a couple hours ago."

"Really. Why does that not surprise me? What happened?"

"I spotted a sniper across the channel this morning."

"How'd you manage that? All the way across the St. Mary's, and you just *happened* to see a man with a gun? Sure you're not getting a little paranoid in your old age?"

"I'm paranoid. You got that right. But I just happened to catch a reflection that I had not seen before."

"From his scope?"

"No. From his camper. He was set up in a camper. I put a telescope on it and made him out. Him and his lookout, or spotter. … Anyway, Henry and I snuck over there and shoved them in the river—camper, Jeep, the works."

"That's a lot of money you destroyed," Roger said chuckling. "The shot he would have to make is over a mile. For a distance like that he was probably using one of those Accuracy International sniper rifles—a 50 cal., or more likely the 8.59mm. Those are very big bucks. Someone's going to be a little distressed about that."

"Any idea who might have sent them?"

"All the usual suspects. You've made a lot of enemies for one man in one lifetime. … But, that having been said. Did you know that Alexander Sipos has a son? And that he had begun to work with his father?

"For years they had been estranged. The old man was impossible to get along with, and the boy, Alexander Jr., was more interested in chasing skirts than he was in joining the family business. Well, in the past year or so, with the old man getting older, the son finally jumped in with both feet. I heard that he was furious about the death of his father. Or, at least he was acting like he was. I got it from a good source that he did not get along with the old man, and that he was content that he did not have to put up with him anymore. But, he has put the word out that he wants to know who killed his father. So far, there's not been anyone stamping your name on the hit.

"Some have even suggested that Dana might have been behind it. But, given her condition, I seriously doubt that she orchestrated it—at least not directly. That Emma woman. I understand she's still knocking around."

"About today," Jack said. "Do you think it's out of the question that the Sipos kid might be behind the incident across the river?"

"Possible. But Alexander Jr. is no kid. He is in his late forties."

"Okay, anyone else?"

"Like I said, you'll have to round up the usual list of suspects. You've got a lot of enemies. ... But, I will keep my ear out for any chatter."

Jack turned to Kate after he disconnected and said, "Let's get out of here right now. Apparently Sipos has a son in the business, and he might be wanting some revenge."

Chapter 61

Jack and Kate hit I-75 South at ten A.M., and were crossing the Mackinac Bridge before lunch. They had not had much to say—both were heavy in thought.

Finally, Jack broke the silence.

"We might not survive this onslaught. Do you get that feeling?"

"It's pretty intense," she said. "Out in San Francisco, I thought you were dead. I knew the bullet hit you in the head, and you went down. For a few moments, I was sure you were dead."

"Roger had just sent me that cap. If I'd received it two days later, that would have been it.

"And that sniper this morning. What are the chances? If he would have taped up that window as he should have, I would never have suspected. Way too many close calls. … Now, with that younger Sipos after me, eventually my luck could run out. We need to figure out something more permanent for the boys. I think that we need to talk about making Millie their legal guardian, and we can have them whenever we want to—which would be all of the time, once this shit gets settled. I think that would be the prudent thing to do, for their sakes."

"I don't want to talk about that right now," Kate said. A large, lonely tear was running down her right cheek. But she did not touch it because she did not want her father to know that she was crying.

"I am not willing to think about your luck running out. I won't accept that. You are smarter and more careful than anyone I have ever known. It wasn't luck that has kept you alive."

"I understand what you're saying," Jack said. "But let's face it, had it not been for Buddy in Frisco, I'd be dead. ... We do have a bigger concern. And that involves the boys—we've got to take some precautions. ... Moving forward it is critical for us to concentrate on dealing with the Sipos court packing conspiracy. If something were to happen to us, like it just almost did, these assholes would be free to continue on with their scheme. We need to destroy the whole plot once and for all, and to do it quickly. And that means, for the time being, we've got to make sure the boys are safe."

Kate removed a tissue from her purse and blotted her eyes—her signal that it was time to move on. After she discarded the tissue, she slipped on a pair of latex gloves.

"I'm looking at one of these sheets," Kate said. "One of them that Emma lifted when she attended that board meeting. Anyway, I'm looking at this sheet and I'm thinking, this is a totally toxic piece of paper. Toxic for everyone involved—even for you and me."

"*Especially* for you and me," Jack said. "If we were to be caught with these lists, it would tie us to Emma's hit, and there would be no way to explain our way out of it."

"With that in mind," Kate said, "there are two ways for us to use them. We could simply go down the lists and terminate everyone who is named. ... The scorched earth approach."

"Won't work," Jack said. "Not practical. Altogether too many individuals. I know you are not serious about that. ... What else do you have in mind?"

"The other option—if we could find a way to publish these names without revealing *our* identities," Kate offered. "That would explode their organization and put them out of business."

"I've been trying to find a way to do that, too. But, no matter how we approach it, someone, at some point, is going to have to authenticate the documents. That's the problem. Whoever does that goes to jail … or gets murdered."

"I've got an idea," Kate said.

"Let's hear it."

"We know that those documents exist on someone's computer. Sipos, for example, he brought them into the meeting, they have to be on his computer."

"Hack his computer?" Jack said. "Is that what you are suggesting?"

"How does that work?" Kate asked. "You know—all those documents from WikiLeaks. If we could somehow get Julian Assange to authenticate and release them without revealing his source."

"Hacked emails are relatively easy to authenticate without revealing sources. But random documents are just that—random. Without someone swearing as to their origin, they are just pieces of paper, or unattributable files."

"So, then," Kate said, exhibiting her desperation, "are we just stuck? Is there nothing we can do?"

Jack looked over at his daughter and smiled. Their eyes met briefly before he returned his attention to driving. The track of her tear had dried, but Jack's radar still spotted it.

"The stakes are too big to fail," he said. "If we lose this battle, or fail to engage effectively, we lose the courts for a generation, maybe longer. That happens, we lose the republic. … So, to answer your question, there are a few things I can and must, do. But, I do not want to share them with you. You need to be able to plead ignorance. … You're young. You have a career. It's critical that you protect that career. The boys need you to be there for them … for the long term."

"They need you too, Dad. You're the only father figure they've got."

"I agree. And I will do everything I can to come out of this as intact as possible. But I'm old. You're young. It is far more important for everyone concerned that you protect yourself. And I'm going to do everything I can to ensure that."

Neither of them spoke for several minutes. Finally, Kate broke the silence.

"Okay, so you won't share your plan with me. But, is there anything I can do to help?"

"What are the chances that the board room case will fall into your lap? … Back in New York?"

"Pretty good, actually. The captain texted me yesterday and asked if I could come back a couple days early. He wants to hit this case with everything he's got. He's setting up a special team—a task force—and he wants me on it."

"Do it."

"But, what if the evidence doesn't lead exactly where we might want it to?"

"You go where the evidence leads. Do not obstruct in any way. I might call you from time to time, just as I always have.

"I do have a question for you," Jack said. "I see that right now you are wearing latex gloves. Have you ever touched the envelopes Emma gave us without using gloves?"

"Never. She gave them to you, and you gave them to me. I always wore gloves. Neither my DNA nor my fingerprints would be on them.

How about you?"

"I wore gloves. So, if there are any prints on the lists, they will belong to Sipos, the board members, and whoever might have prepared them to start with. Perhaps Emma, but I doubt it because she is quite careful.

"This is what I want you to do," Jack continued. "Open up the glove box. You will see a digital point and shoot camera. Lay these sheets out one at a time and photograph them. Don't use your cell, because you should not have these images on your phone. And then slide them back in the envelopes. When you're finished, take the memory card out of the camera, and find a safe place to store it when you get back to New York. If everything goes south, that could be useful. ... You'd have a devil of a time explaining it, but at least you will have a copy.

"That's about all the deeper I want to get into this with you right now. You'll have to be the judge as to what you share with me regarding your investigation. I might have some stuff for you that you will find interesting.

"There's a burner cell in the glove box. Take it with you. I will explain later how you are to use it."

The next morning Kate caught a flight from Grand Rapids back to New York. As soon as Jack had seen her off, he called Roger.

Chapter 62

I need you to look something up for me," Jack said to Roger. "I need a full set of fingerprints, palm prints too, if possible."

"Whose prints?" Roger asked.

"Alexander Sipos, the younger," Jack said.

"Do I want to know what you're going to do with them?"

"I don't think so," Jack said with a chuckle in his voice.

"They're going to be on file someplace," Roger said. "It might take a day."

"Just make sure they're perfect," Jack said. "Some agencies do crappy work with fingerprints. I can wait an extra day for quality."

"I'll see what I can do. Do you have a drop dead date?"

"ASAP, of course," Jack said. "But, like I said, the crisper the better."

"The FBI has pretty high standards, I'll try them first."

Immediately after Jack arrived at the river house he slipped on a fresh pair of latex gloves and began setting up a quasi-sterile work area on the dining room table.

First, he spread out a freshly laundered bed sheet. He then placed on the sheet the nine envelopes containing the lists of names, an unopened bottle of latex milk, two dozen unopened printed circuit boards, an ultraviolet etching machine, a Canon EOS 5D Mark IV DSLR full-frame camera, a camera tripod, a MacBook Pro laptop computer, an Epson professional printer, an unopened box of latex gloves, an eye dropper, a fine point black permanent marker, and an unopened tube of E6000 clear adhesive.

True to form, within the hour Roger emailed a near perfect set of the younger Alexander Sipos's finger and palm prints.

Jack had anticipated relatively low grade photocopies of fingerprint cards, but Roger had sent him high quality JPEG images taken directly off FBI computers.

"That's terrific!" Jack said out loud. "Won't even need the camera."

He opened the images in Photoshop, reversed the color of the image, so the raised fingerprint was white and the background of the image was black, and then he reduced the size of the images to the size of an average man's fingerprint. He inserted a PCB (printed circuit board) in the UV etcher, and created a three-dimensional fingerprint reversal of Sipos's right index finger. He then did the same for the other nine fingers, and two palm prints, labeling each with the permanent marker.

Once he had the twelve boards etched, he removed the computer and etching machine from the work area.

He then placed the first PCB in front of him, and poured in an ample amount of latex milk into the etching. He set that one aside, and repeated the process for each of the remaining boards.

After allowing time for the latex to dry, he peeled the flexible latex prints from the boards and trimmed off the excess. He then removed a new set of latex gloves, and using the E6000 adhesive, he glued the latex right hand finger and palm prints appropriately on one of the latex gloves. He labeled it *AS Right*—AS standing for Alexander Sipos.

He did the same for the left hand, labeling it *AS Left*.

After the adhesive had the proper amount of time to dry, Jack slipped the gloves on.

"Okay, Mr. Sipos," he said. … "I am now effectively Alexander Sipos Jr. And that's not going to work out very well for you, I'm afraid."

Then, wearing the Sipos Jr. gloves, he set the first envelope in front of him. As was the case with all but two of the envelopes, it had blood spattered on it. He opened the bottle of distilled water and poured the cap full of water. Using the eyedropper, he dropped a single drop of water on each of the fingertips of the right hand. And then he distributed some of the water to the fingers of the left hand by touching the ends of the fingers together.

With the slightly dampened fingers of the right hand, he touched the dried blood on the first envelope. It quickly rehydrated enough so that he was able to leave fingerprints on the outside of the envelope, as well as on the list inside.

He repeated this process for each of the nine lists, taking care to make sure there were fingerprints deposited on each list as well as on each envelope.

He then removed the gloves, and put on a pair of new latex gloves.

Laying one list on his work area at a time, he photographed them individually, along with the envelope the list was found in. He then placed the lists in their respective envelopes.

Once that task was completed, he placed all of the envelopes in a large USPS envelope, addressed it to Roger Minsk, applied stamps to the envelope, and placed it in a mailbox outside a large grocery store.

"Done," he said out loud as he drove off. "Mr. Sipos, you are now a principal conspirator in the death of your father, and the ten members of his board of directors."

Jack then called Roger.

"Okay, buddy, you are about to receive some evidence via USPS. Handle it with extreme care. You ought to guard against leaving your fingerprints or DNA."

"Do you want to tell me what I should be looking for?" Roger asked.

"It will be a large envelope containing nine additional envelopes. Each of those envelopes will, along with the contents of those nine envelopes, evidence the fingerprints of Alexander Sipos Jr. You will find blood on the outside as well as the inside of some of those nine envelopes as well. The blood will be that of various members of the board of directors for Sipos's court packing organization.

"It appears that Sipos Jr. was jealous of his father's success, and resentful of his father locking him out of the project, and so he arranged for his father and the members of his board to be murdered.

"There will be additional evidence of his plot as soon as I can figure out how to fabricate it."

"Damn good thing this is a secure line," Roger barked.

"Hey, I'm not going to even try to fool you. Never have. Not going to start now.

"These lists are dynamite. They contain the names of those working in the organization—which was officially known as The Group, by the way. You will learn the names of all but one of the dead board members, as well as those in positions of influence at various prestigious law schools.

"The lists include the matriculating candidates selected to become Trojan Horse appointees to the Federal courts—from Federal Courts of Appeal, all the way to the Supreme Court. They're all there.

"Obviously, there is nothing I could possibly do personally to make use of these lists. At least nothing that would not end up with me dead or in prison.

"So, you can claim ignorance as to why you were selected to receive them, and the fingerprints and blood spatter will provide legitimacy.

"I think it could very well work."

"Did you say there were nine envelopes?" Roger asked.

"Yes, and that's the bad part. The tenth envelope was left in the board room and was probably burned up in the fire."

"So, there are a number of operatives who remain unknown?"

"That's right," Jack said. "But not only operatives, we can be fairly certain that the missing list would contain the names of candidates and currently appointed judges as well. ... There could even be the names of current associate justices on the missing list. We just don't know."

"And that would probably be enough to seed the project for future growth. Would you think?"

"I think it would," Jack agreed. "But, that does not diminish the importance of what we do know. At the very least, we have the names of the overwhelming majority of the culprits. Plus, if we can do away with Sipos Jr., and the listed operatives, it will go a long way toward limiting the influence The Group can exert—possibly for generations."

"I agree. But, the potential damage that could be caused by having even one of these so-called Trojan Horses on the highest court, I just can't see you leaving so large a loose end," Roger said.

"In the late nineteen hundreds there was a marketing genius named A.L. Williams, and he wrote a book entitled, *All You Can Do is All You Can Do, but all you can do is enough.* I read his book in one evening. I found it to be an amazing lesson in self-acceptance. Sometimes a person just can't accomplish everything he might like to. But, if he does his best, it's okay to leave it at that."

"I know you will do your best, Jack, you always do."

Chapter 63

That evening Jack visited a local coffee shop in downtown Grand Rapids. He put on a pair of latex gloves and removed from the bottom of his briefcase an envelope containing the burner cell that Emma had earlier used to contact Sipos the senior, and with it he wrote an email to the same secret address that Emma had accessed.

Jack drafted the following email, but did not send it: *AS—Successfully eliminated your father and his associates as you directed. Awaiting further instruction —E.* As before, he included the phone number from the burner phone as the callback number.

He then called Kate using his own cell phone.

"Hey, Kate," he said. "I want you to make a call from that burner phone I gave you. The number is the only one programmed into the cell. You should do it as soon as possible. Stay on it for five minutes. But don't utter a sound. And then hang up. You should not make it from your apartment. Go to a local restaurant or coffee shop to make the call. And then destroy the phone totally. Even dispose of the pieces."

The reason Jack chose Kate to make the call was because she was back in New York, and the junior Sipos's offices were also in that city. Should tracking be done, the results would provide evidence consistent with what would be expected of a call placed by Sipos the younger to

Emma.

Jack waited for her call to vibrate his burner cell. He accepted the call but, like Kate, did not verbally respond. As Jack had requested, Kate also remained silent.

After she disconnected, Jack used duct tape to attach the cell phone to the bottom of the table. He then left the coffee shop.

Once back at his river house, Jack called Roger again. He gave him the number of both burner cellls, and told him about the email address used to convey messages via unopened draft emails between Sipos and a hitman.

"It would be a good idea to track these cells down before the batteries go dead," Jack said. "Also, there might be a fairly extensive history of communication between client and contractor. The client being Alexander Sipos Jr., and the contractor, an unnamed gun for hire.

"I think that once you turn the other materials over to the FBI, you should provide this info as well. As a Secret Service Agent, you won't be required to reveal your contacts. But if you were forced to, I'm sure you could attribute it to an *anonymous source.*

"I would think that these two pieces of evidence should provide sufficient grounds for the FBI to convince a federal attorney to convene a Grand Jury."

"The bloody prints alone ought to be enough," Roger said. "But the email draft would provide additional support. It's always good to have more than one piece of evidence."

"Okay, then. I'm leaving that part in your capable hands."

"Did you say *that part?*" Roger asked. "There's more?"

"Roger, you know there *always* has to be more. It's just that it is not always good for you to know too much about some things."

Chapter 64

It's just a damn shame, don't you think," Lindsay said. "After all the boys have been through. That they can't even live where they want? And you and Kate. … It's got to be tough for you as well."

Lindsay's full name was Det. Lindsay Hildebrandt, Grand Rapids Police Department. Jack first met Lindsay during the investigation to find a missing girl. The girl, Angel Star, daughter of Millie Star, had been kidnapped from the Grand Rapids Public Library, and Lindsay had been assigned to the case.

Like Jack, Lindsay had lost a spouse to violent crime, and although she was nearly twenty years younger than he, the two of them were forming a bond that transcended shared professional interests. Every time Jack spent significant time in Grand Rapids he made every effort to contact Lindsay. They never called it *dating*, but that's exactly what it was becoming.

Jack had not grumbled to Lindsay about the boys being removed from his house. She had simply asked about them, and he told her the story.

"Hey," Jack said. "I don't mean to sound like I'm complaining. We both believe that it's a very good thing that the boys have a place to go where they feel so comfortable. Millie is a great friend—both to Kate and me, and to the boys. And with the tragic loss of the Lundgruns, and the Fletchers, we are truly blessed to have Millie willing to step up."

Lindsay was familiar with Millie and Angel, having formed a tight bond with them during the investigation to rescue Angel from her abductor.

"Well, it's nice that you view it in such a positive light. I'm sure the boys sense your optimism and it helps them get settled in."

"Anyway, I didn't call you to bore you with all my domestic issues," Jack said. "I was hoping that if you were free tonight you might like to grab a beer with me. I'm planning to be in town for a few days, so we could make it a different evening, if that would work better for you."

"Tonight would be great," Lindsay said. "Shall I meet you someplace?"

"How about I stop by and pick you up, and we can decide then where we want to go?"

"Give me a call when you're close and I'll meet you at the street. Parking is a mess around here."

While parking was always an issue near her building, the real reason she did not want Jack to come up to her apartment had more to do with one of her nosey neighbors than anything else.

The divorced sister of Det. Calvin Brandt, who was one of Lindsay's co-workers and an archenemy of Jack's, lived across the hall. The last thing Lindsay wanted to deal with was fielding Brandt's inquisition for the next two weeks.

"Be there in about a half an hour," Jack said as he checked his cell. Roger was calling.

"Roger," Jack said, as he accepted the call. "What's up?"

"Jack, I think this is almost a first," Roger said. "All seven surviving Supremes are in emergency session discussing the shit that's been happening. I think the acting chief justice is trying to set up some contingency plans, on how to function with only seven members."

"Good luck with that," Jack said. "They're meeting right now?"

"As we speak."

"Hey, Rog, it's been nice working with you on this. Keep me up to speed. Okay?"

"Absolutely," Roger said. "It's just too bad it had to get to this point with the court—with so much unresolved. We still don't know if there remain any Trojan Horses in their stable."

"Well, it is what it is," Jack agreed. "... I guess you could say that what we engage in is not an exact science."

"I suppose you've got a contingency plan, right?" Roger said. "To ferret out any bad justices?"

"Roger, how does this sound for a contingency plan? Why don't you see if you can get away? Legend and I are going to do some fishing on the Grand River. At our river house. Join us. We'll have a great time."

"I just might take you up on that. Sounds like a hell of a contingency plan to me."

"Just do it. I'll get Henry down from the island. We'll stock the bar, and kick back for the week."

"Sounds good. Count me in."

After disconnecting Roger's call, Jack removed a specially marked burner phone from his jacket pocket and dialed a number he had never called before. On the fourth ring a tone sounded. Jack looked at the phone and carefully depressed and held the star and the asterisk at the same time.

"Damn! I wish there were some other way," he said to himself but aloud. "But we just can't afford to tolerate even a single supreme sleeper. … Better to start over."

A solemn countenance captured his entire demeanor as he held the buttons down for an inordinately long time. Finally, after nearly a minute, he released his grip on the phone and removed the battery. He then headed into the city to pick up Lindsay.

Instead of heading west down West River Drive to US-131, which was Jack's usual route when driving into Grand Rapids from the river house, he remained on Northland Drive, a course that took him across the Grand River. In the middle of the bridge he rolled down the passenger window and flung the burner cell that he had just used through the opening and into the river. He smiled as he rolled up the window.

By the time he and Lindsay had ordered their beers, a banner was scrolling across the bottom of the television set above the bar. It read, "A massive explosion has rocked the Supreme Court Building in Washington DC. It is not immediately known if there were any justices in the building at the time of the explosion. Stay tuned for details as they become available."

Jack observed the bulletin out of the corner of his eye, but Lindsay was already too deep into her beer to notice.

"Henry," Jack said, responding to his vibrating phone. "Thanks for calling back. I have an important job for you. I want you to get down here to Grand Rapids as quickly as possible. I heard the fish are biting."

Epilog

"What in the world is going on in here?" Kate asked. She had just walked in on the two boys, and Buddy. The three of them were in the basement of the Handler house on Sugar Island.

Robby and Red were on all fours. They were joined at the mouth by a small ball, which they each held tightly with their teeth.

Buddy sat about six feet away. He was watching intently. Every twenty seconds or so he would let go with a loud whine.

"Really!" Kate commanded loudly. "What's going on here?"

This time the boys responded to her. They each released their grip on the ball and fell to their backs on the floor.

"We're dogfighting," Robby said.

"Dogfighting?" Kate repeated. "I've never heard of it."

Red reached between them, scooped up the ball and tossed it to Kate.

"Ewww!" Kate squeezed out of a scrunched up mouth. "This is absolutely disgusting! What is *this*?"

"It's a dogfight ball," Robby told her. "Uncle Jack gave it to us. He said if we wanted to be famous lawyers someday, we should learn how to play the game."

Kate examined the spit-covered ball for only a few seconds before disgustedly tossing it back into the fray.

"He told you what?" she said, walking over to the bar sink and washing her hands.

"Uncle Jack said that the last person to play the dogfight game with this ball was a member of the U.S. Supreme Court. And that if Red and I got really good at the game, maybe we might be nominated by the president … to be a federal judge, or maybe even an associate justice on the Supreme Court."

"And you believed him?" Kate asked rhetorically.

"No. Not really. But it is a pretty fun game. … You want to try it?"

"I don't think so," Kate said laughing. "Maybe you should challenge Buddy. He might be good at it."

"We already did. Several times. And Buddy always won."

"Well, I guess that settles it," Kate said just before turning to leave. "Looks like Buddy's going to be sitting on the bench one of these days."

Just as Kate turned to leave the room, Robby called to her.

"When are we going on that hike?"

"Which hike?" she asked, turning to face him.

"To Duck Lake," Robby said. "You know, the old Chase Osborn estate. You said you would take us there."

"Buddy," Kate called. "Come here."

Buddy sprang up and ran to her with tail wagging.

Kate bent down over him and sniffed his mane.

"No more skunk odor," she said.

"How about tomorrow? Shall we take the hike then?"

* * *

The next day Christina Baldwin stopped by Millie's house unannounced.

"I'm here to conduct an interview with Red and Robby," she said.

"I don't recall setting up an appointment," Millie said. "Am I missing something?"

"We don't always announce when we are coming. I hope it's not too big of an inconvenience. I would just like to talk to the boys for a couple minutes, and then I'll be on my way."

"That's going to be difficult to do," Millie said. "The boys aren't here right now. Maybe you could come back Monday."

"Well, then, I'll go to where they are. You do know where they are. Right?"

"Kate is in town for the weekend, and the boys are over at the Handlers' house."

"Really? At the Handlers'. ... Okay," Ms. Baldwin said, obviously very perturbed, "then I'll go over there and talk to them."

She abruptly turned and walked away in a huff.

Millie tried to call Kate to give her a heads up, but Kate had turned her phone off because the Osborn Estate was only a few miles from the Canadian border, and she did not want her phone to roam internationally.

When Ms. Baldwin arrived at the Handler house she pounded angrily on the door, but no one answered. Kate and the boys were off on an adventure, and Jack was still in Grand Rapids closing up the river house after spending several days fishing with Roger, Legend and Henry.

Ms. Baldwin was having a bad day, and not being able to locate the two boys made it worse.

She went back to her car to wait.

Nearly an hour later she succumbed to her anger. She opened her black bag and removed Millie's pending license. "Prissy little bitch," she said out loud. "If you would have allowed me to conduct this final interview with the boys, I would have approved your home for placement. But now, I'm afraid it's gonna be tough shit for you."

In a fit of rage she tore up Millie's paperwork. And she was not satisfied with just tearing it up a single time. She continued to rip up the pages into smaller and smaller pieces.

She started her car and pulled around to drive off. As she did, she ran over some rocks that had been placed near the house to mark the edge of the driveway. Her car hung up on them.

Back and forth she rocked her car until it broke free, and then she sped out of the driveway as fast as she could drive.

Just before she reached the ferry she opened her window and started tossing the pieces of paper out of it.

Once they were all gone, she called the sheriff's department.

"I need some help out here on Sugar Island. I need you to pick up a couple of juveniles. At the home of Jack and Kate Handler. The names are Robby Martin, and Red … don't have a last name. Both are fourteen years of age. They are not where they were supposed to be. I need them placed in detention for the rest of the weekend. I'll deal with them on Monday."

As soon as she disconnected the call, she went into a rage. "Damn them! Damn them all! Snobs! Everybody thinks they are so much better than me," she continued as she fumbled her shaking fingers through a crumpled pack of Marlboro filters that she kept in the center console. Finally, she managed to separate one, guide it to her mouth, and light it.

The first long drag burned her lungs, but was amazingly cathartic. To her sick mind, the pain it caused was like that brought upon her by every other person in her life.

"Fancy pants Kate Handler. And Millie Star. They do not understand just how much power I've got. I'll show them. A weekend in detention will serve them all just fine. I'll bet they pay attention to me after a weekend behind bars. Especially that smartass Jack Handler. He's the worst of the whole bunch. He thinks he's so smart. I'll show him who's smart.

"One weekend in detention. That won't hurt anything. After that, on Monday, I'll fix it. I'll go out to Millie Star's house, and lay down the law. She can resubmit her paperwork, if she still wants to join our program. … It'll be fine. They need to understand just who it is calling the shots."

By the time Ms. Baldwin had driven off the ferry, the sheriff's deputy was getting on. They waved.

The deputy drove up to the Handler house and knocked on the door. Jack was still not home, but Henry was driving in—he had just arrived back from Grand Rapids and had stopped to do some work in the boathouse.

"Can I help you?" Henry asked.

"Yeah, Henry," the deputy said. "I'm looking for Red and Robby. Have any idea where they might be?"

"I do. Kate took them on a hike to the Osborn Estate. I don't expect them back for a few more hours."

"Okay, I'll take a drive back there and see if I can find them."

This was an old story for Red. He had spent two years, off and on, running away from the law. He knew every good place to hide on Sugar Island. As soon as he saw the deputy heading his way he bolted. And Robby, he was not going to leave his friend on his own. So both boys ran away. There was nothing Kate could do.

Jack and Kate spent hours searching the woods for the boys, but to no avail.

Jack began leaving food and warm clothing in the boathouse, hoping that they would show up and take it. But it didn't happen.

A week passed, and then a second, but still no word from or about the boys. Jack was furious with the caseworker, but he knew that his hostile attitude would not serve any purpose, so he simply tried to be as supportive as he could.

* * *

The day after he arrived back on Sugar Island, Jack and Henry drove onto the mainland and were relaxing at the end of the bar over some beers at Moloney's Alley on Portage.

After their third round, Jack leaned forward over the bar and whispered.

"Something's been eating at me ever since I got myself shot up on Highway 28."

"What's that?" Henry asked.

"That second spare tire," Jack said. "The rental those nimrods were driving had a second spare tire behind the rear seats. And it was covered in mud. But the one hanging beneath was clean. I had a good look under the vehicle during the shootout. … Who ever heard of a rental vehicle carrying two spares?"

"And, your point?"

"That's basically it. They went to a lot of work to replace the spare tire with a new one. … I'd like to get a closer look at the one hanging underneath."

"Wouldn't be so hard to do," Henry said. "They've impounded the vehicle and have it stored right out back of the sheriff's office."

"Really?"

"Saw it there myself."

Jack peeled off a twenty, slapped it on the bar and said, "Whaddaya say we go get ourselves arrested?"

"Why not. It's closing time anyway."

"You drive," Jack said. "I'll do the honors. Besides, if that spare contains what I think it might, you'd have a tough time lifting it with your bad shoulder. … Drop me off, and give me fifteen minutes. We just might have something else to celebrate tonight."

* * *

Three days after Roger returned to New York from the fishing trip, Jack received a call from him.

"Roger," Jack said answering his buzzing phone. "What a pleasant surprise."

"Maybe yes, maybe no," Roger replied.

"What's up?"

"At least two items of significant interest to you, I believe."

"And they are?"

"First of all," Roger said, "some of my buddies at the FBI are telling me that the explosives used at the Supreme Court Building were quite similar to those that took down Detroit International Airport—diesel fuel and fertilizer. There was one major difference, however. The detonator used was not dynamite. Instead they used TATP. That's curious, don't you think?"

"Very," Jack agreed. "Are they ready to issue a report? Did anyone take credit?"

"Of course, ISIS immediately claimed credit. But the FBI's not so sure about that. Something that big, usually they pick up some early chatter. But not so with this."

Roger suspected that Jack would not be interested in talking much about the bomb, so the silence that ensued did not surprise him.

"You said there were a couple items of interest?" Jack finally said.

"Allison just had an interesting visitor."

"Allison, or Dana?"

"Allison. I haven't seen or heard from Dana since the stroke."

"Do I know who came calling?"

"I think you might. A petite young lady by the name of Janet Cano."

"Describe her."

"One hundred pounds, give or take. Blondish. Maybe thirty. Quite pretty."

"How about her eyes. Did you see her eyes?"

"I did. Left eye was green. Right one blue."

"What was the substance of the visit?"

"I don't know. If they communicated beforehand, they did so using a secure connection—not Dana's public provider. … But, if Allison's demeanor said anything about the nature of the visit, I think she found it quite disturbing."

"What is her condition—Allison's?"

"Physically, she is in pretty bad shape. She has to use a walker to get around. Wears diapers, and thick glasses. Her eyes don't move together. Her speech is slurred. And she shakes uncontrollably … almost all the time, she shakes. She hasn't been out of the apartment since she came home from the hospital."

"How about her mind? Has her thinking been affected?"

"If she takes her meds, it seems to clear up her thinking. But, most of the time she lets it go. She hates her doctors. She has fired three of them. If he pushes her to take her meds, she fires him. So, I'd say she might be at about seventy-five percent most of the time."

"How about her memory?"

"That's been improving right along."

"Does she remember her stroke, and the events leading up to it?"

"She recalls that Sipos was with her that night. She even remembers getting hit with the lamp, and that it was Sipos who struck her with it."

"You told her that Sipos is dead?"

"Yes. That came as a relief to her, I think."

"How about me? Has she ever mentioned me?"

"That's the really strange part. Right up until this visit with the Cano girl, your death was just about all she talked about. Allison was very pleased that you were dead. But, she has not mentioned it since her visitor left. … Do you suppose that means what I think it might mean?"

"I suspect so."

"And, one more thing. Allison had me help her transfer funds—one million dollars into a Swiss bank account."

* * *

Three days later Roger called Jack again. This time to report that Judge Lawrence Thompson, and his wife Dorris, were both killed in a freak one-car accident less than a mile from their home.

He also told Jack that Allison had him help her make another transfer of funds. Again, it was for one million dollars, and again, the money was moved into a Swiss bank account—the same bank account as before.

"She has seemed to be in a particularly good mood of late," Roger told him. "Can't figure out exactly why that it is. At first I thought it might have something to do with the murder indictment of the younger Sipos. But when I asked her about it, she seemed totally disinterested in the case. Must be something else is tickling her fancy."

After Roger's call, Jack walked over to the window that was facing the St. Mary's, lifted a pair of binoculars from the table beneath the window, and peered out over the channel.

"Emma," he said out loud. "I do wonder where you are right now, and what you're up to."

He then pulled the curtain closed and walked over to his favorite chair. It was a dark brown leather recliner. He pushed himself back until his legs lifted.

He looked over at the door. Buddy had taken the same position as he had every night since the boys ran away. He was lying on the rug with his nose nearly pasted to the crack at the bottom of the door.

"Buddy," Jack said. "Come here."

Buddy arose slowly and walked over to where Jack was sitting. Every step seemed labored. He stood next to him and placed his head on Jack's lap. Buddy's big brown eyes looked up at him as if to say, "Where are my friends? When will they come back?"

Jack stroked Buddy on the head.

"I just don't know what's happening, Buddy, I just don't know."

The two of them remained there for a very long time. Finally, Buddy took a long, sad sigh, and walked back over to his position in front of the door. He circled twice and lay down. But before he assumed his customary nighttime position—with his nose pressed against the bottom of the door—he looked back at Jack again as if to say *goodnight.*

Jack acknowledged the glance, and then leaned his head back. Eventually he drifted off to sleep. He had not been to bed since the boys ran away, and he had determined to spend every night right there until they returned.

In the morning at sunrise, Jack and Buddy would begin their search again. They would spend the whole day knocking on doors and searching empty cabins. And then, at night, they would return to their regular positions—Jack in his chair, and Buddy by the door.

And there they would wait.

Sometimes during the night Jack would awaken with a start. Thinking that he heard a noise, he would have to go to the boys' room and check their beds. Once he realized that he had only been dreaming, he would go back to his chair, and there wait, ready to welcome the boys should they return during the night.

Main Characters in the "Getting to Know Jack Series" (The Cast)

This book, *Dogfight,* is the third book in the second Jack Handler series—*Jack's Justice. Ghosts of Cherry Street—and the Cumberbatch Oubliette (Ghosts)* was the first book in the series.

While many of the characters encountered in this book have already made appearances in one or more of the previous Jack Handler books, if you want a deeper understanding about what makes a player tick, you can refer to *The Cast* to answer additional backstory questions.

Main characters are listed in quasi-chronological order.

Jack Handler:

Jack is a good man, in his way. While it is true that he occasionally kills people, it can be argued that most (if not all) of his targets needed killing. Occasionally a somewhat sympathetic figure comes between Jack and his goal. When that happens, Jack's goal comes first. I think the word that best sums up Jack's persona might be "expeditor." He is outcome driven—he makes things turn out the way he wants them to turn out.

For instance, if you were a single mom and a bully were stealing your kid's lunch money, you could send "Uncle Jack" to school with little Billy. Uncle Jack would have a "talk" with the teachers and the principal. With Jack's help, the problem would be solved. But I would not recommend that you ask him how he accomplished it. You might not like what he tells you—if he even responds.

Jack is faithful to his friends and a great father to his daughter. He is also a dangerous and tenacious adversary when situations require it.

Jack Handler began his career as a law enforcement officer. He married a beautiful woman (Beth) of Greek descent while working as a police officer in Chicago. She was a concert violinist and the love of his life. If you were to ask Jack about it, he would quickly tell you he married above himself. So, when bullets intended for him killed her, he admittedly grew bitter. Kate, their daughter, was just learning to walk when her mother was gunned down.

As a single father, Jack soon found that he needed to make more money than his job as a police officer paid. So he went back to college and obtained a degree in criminal justice. Soon he was promoted to the level of sergeant in the Chicago Police Homicide Division.

With the help of a friend, he then discovered that there was much more money to be earned in the private sector. At first he began moonlighting on private security jobs. Immediate success led him to take an early retirement and attain his private investigator license.

Because of his special talents (obtained as a former army ranger) and his intense dedication to problem solving, Jack's services became highly sought after. While he did take on some of the more sketchy clients, he never accepted a project simply on the basis of financial gain—he always sought out the moral high ground. Unfortunately, sometimes that moral high ground morphed into quicksand.

Jack is now pushing sixty (from the downward side) and he has all the physical ailments common to a man of that age. While it is true that he remains in amazing physical condition, of late he has begun to sense his limitations.

His biggest concern recently has been an impending IRS audit. While he isn't totally confident that it will turn out okay, he remains optimistic.

His problems stem from the purchase of half-interest in a bar in Chicago two decades earlier. His partner was one of his oldest and most trusted friends.

The principal reason he considered the investment in the first place was to create a cover for his private security business.

Many, if not most, of his clients insisted on paying him in cash or with some other untraceable commodity. At first he tried getting rid of the cash by paying all of his bills with it. But even though he meticulously avoided credit cards and checks, the cash continued to accumulate.

It wasn't that he was in any sense averse to paying his fair share of taxes. The problem was that if he did deposit the cash into a checking account, and subsequently included it in his filings, he would then at some point be required to explain where it had come from.

He needed an acceptable method of laundering, and his buddy's bar seemed perfect.

But it did not work out as planned. Four years ago the IRS decided to audit the bar, which consequently exposed his records to scrutiny.

Jack consulted with one of his old customers, a disbarred attorney/CPA, to see if this shady character could get the books straightened out enough for Jack to survive the audit and avoid federal prison.

The accountant knew exactly how Jack earned his money and that the sale of a few bottles of Jack Daniels had little to do with it.

Even though his business partner and the CPA talked a good game about legitimacy, Jack still agonized when thoughts of the audit stormed through his mind.

Kate Handler:

Kate, Jack's daughter and a New York homicide detective, is introduced early and appears often in this series. Kate is beautiful. She has her mother's olive complexion and green eyes. Her trim five-foot-eight frame, with her long auburn hair falling nicely on her broad shoulders, would seem more at home on the runway than in an interrogation room. But Kate is a seasoned New York homicide detective. In fact, she is thought by many to be on the fast track to the top—thanks, in part, to the unwavering support of her soon-to-retire boss, Captain Spencer.

Of course, her career was not hindered by her background in law. Graduating Summa Cum Laude from Notre Dame at the age of twenty-one, she went on to Notre Dame Law School. She passed the Illinois Bar Exam immediately upon receiving her JD, and accepted a position at one of Chicago's most prestigious criminal law firms. While her future looked bright as a courtroom attorney, she hated defending "sleazebags."

One Saturday morning she called her father and invited him to meet her at what she knew to be the coffee house he most fancied. It was there, over a couple espressos, that she asked him what he thought about her taking a position with the New York Police Department. She was shocked when he immediately gave his blessing. "Kitty," he said, "you're a smart girl. I totally trust your judgment. You have to go where your heart leads. Just promise me one thing. Guarantee me that you will put me up whenever I want to visit. After all, you are my favorite daughter."

To this Kate replied with a chuckle, "Dad, I'm your only daughter. And you will always be welcome."

In *Murder on Sugar Island (Sugar)*, Jack and Kate team up to solve the murder of Alex Garos, Jack's brother-in-law. This book takes place on Sugar Island, which is located in the northern part of Michigan's Upper

Peninsula (just east of Sault Ste. Marie, MI).

Because Kate was Garos's only blood relative living in the United States, he named her in his will to inherit all of his estate. This included one of the most prestigious pieces of real estate on the island—the Sugar Island Resort.

Reg:

In *Jack and the New York Death Mask (Death Mask)*, Jack is recruited by his best friend, Reg (Reginald Black), to do a job without either man having any knowledge as to what that job might entail. Jack, out of loyalty to his friend, accepted the offer. The contract was ostensibly to assassinate a sitting president. However, instead of assisting the plot, Jack and Reg worked to thwart it. Most of this story takes place in New York City, but there are scenes in DC, Chicago, and Upstate New York. Reg is frequently mentioned throughout the series, as are Pam Black and Allison Fulbright. Pam Black is Reg's wife (he was shot at the end of *Death Mask*), and Allison is a former first lady. It was Allison who contracted Reg and Jack to assassinate the sitting president.

Allison:

Allison is a former first lady (with presidential aspirations of her own), and Jack's primary antagonist throughout the series. She fears him enough not to do him or his family physical harm, but she and Jack are not friends. She seems to poke her nose into Jack's business just enough to be a major annoyance.

Roger Minsk:

Roger is a member of the Secret Service, and a very good friend to Jack. Roger is also friendly with Bob Fulbright, Allison's husband, and a former president.

Red:

This main character is introduced in *Sugar*. Red is a redheaded fourteen-year-old boy who, besides being orphaned, cannot speak. It turned out that Red was actually the love child of Alex (Jack's brother-in-law) and his office manager. So, Alex not only leaves his Sugar Island resort to Kate, he also leaves his Sugar Island son for her to care for.

Red has a number of outstanding characteristics, first and foremost among them, his innate ability to take care of himself in all situations. When his mother and her husband were killed in a fire, Red chose to live on his own instead of submitting to placement in foster care.

During the warmer months, he lived in a hut he had pieced together from parts of abandoned homes, barns, and cottages, and he worked at Garos's resort on Sugar Island. In the winter, he would take up residence in empty fishing cottages along the river.

Red's second outstanding characteristic is his loyalty. When put to the test, Red would rather sacrifice his life than see his friends hurt. In *Sugar*, Red works together with Jack and Kate to solve the mystery behind the killing of Jack's brother-in-law (and Red's biological father), Alex Garos.

The third thing about Red that makes him stand out is his inability to speak. As the result of a traumatic event in his life, his voice box was damaged, resulting in his disability. Before Jack and Kate entered his life, Red communicated only through an improvised sign system and various grunts.

When Kate introduced him to a cell phone and texting, Red's life changed dramatically.

Robby:

Robby is Red's best friend. When his parents are murdered, Robby moves into the Handler home and becomes a "brother" to Red.

Buddy:

Buddy is Red's golden retriever.

Bill Green:

One other character of significance introduced in *Sugar* is Bill Green, the knowledgeable police officer who first appears in Joey's coffee shop. He also assumes a major role in subsequent books of the series, after he becomes sheriff of Chippewa County.

Captain Spencer:

Captain Spencer is Kate's boss in New York. The captain has been planning his retirement for a long time, but has not yet been able to pull the trigger. Kate is his protégée, and he almost seems to fear leaving the department until her career is fully developed.

Paul Martin and Jill Talbot:

Two new characters do emerge in *Sugar Island Girl, Missing in Paris (Missing).* They are Paul Martin and Jill Talbot. They do not appear in subsequent stories.

Legend:

Legend is one of the main characters in the sixth book of the series, *Wealthy Street Murders (Wealthy).* In this story, Jack and Kate work with Red, Robby, and Legend to solve a series of murders. Wrapped up in a rug and left for dead at the end of *Wealthy,* with Buddy's help he lives to play an important role in *Ghosts.*

Mrs. Fletcher:

Mrs. Fletcher, one of the caretakers at Kate's resort on Sugar Island, progressively plays a more prominent role as an occasional care-provider for the two boys. And, of course, she becomes embroiled in the intrigue.

Sheriff Griffen:

The sheriff first appears in *Murders in Strangmoor Bog (Strangmoor).* He is sheriff of Schoolcraft County, which includes Strangmoor Bog, and Seney Wildlife Preserve.

Angel and her mother Millie:

In *Strangmoor*, the seventh and last book in the "Getting to know

Jack" series, two new main characters are introduced: Angel and Millie Star.

Angel, a precocious fun-loving redhead (with a penchant for quick thinking and the use of big words), immediately melts the hearts of Red and Robby and becomes an integral part of the Handler saga. You will probably see Angel and Millie in other subsequent books in the "Jack's Justice" series as well.

Lindsay Hildebrandt and Calvin Brandt:

These two significant new characters are introduced in *Ghosts of Cherry Street (and the Cumberbatch Oubliette)*. Lindsay, a rookie detective in the Grand Rapids Police Department, quickly becomes a special person in Jack's life. If you were to ask her if she is dating Jack, Lindsay (who is two decades younger than Jack) would immediately inform you that people their age don't *date*. But she does admit that they are good friends and occasionally see each other socially.

They have in common the fact that they both lost their spouses in a violent fashion. Lindsay's husband, also a Grand Rapids detective, was shot and killed several years earlier. This crime has not yet been solved.

Calvin Brandt, a veteran Grand Rapids detective, does not get along with anyone. And that is especially true of Jack Handler. Jack would be the first to admit that he was not an innocent party with regard to this ongoing conflict.

Chuchip Kalyesveh:

Chuchip generally goes by the name of Henry because he has found most people butcher his Native American first name.

Jack first met Henry in a Federal prison camp where both were serving time. They became good friends when Henry saved Jack's life by beating up four other inmates who had been contracted to kill him. Jack says he has never met another man as physically imposing as his friend Henry.

Now that both are free men, Henry works for Jack at the Sugar Island Resort. And, sometimes, he partners with Jack (unofficially, of course) to help out with some of his tougher private security cases.

Expect to learn more about Henry as the next Jack Handler books roll off the press.

Emma:

Emma (Legs) is a very attractive thirty-someish contract killer. She makes her first appearance in *Dogfight.*

* * *

If, after having read one of my later books, you do not wish to wait for me to complete the next one, you might want to delve into the pages of my earlier Handler series—"Getting to Know Jack." It comprises seven books, most of which are set in Michigan—many in Michigan's Upper Peninsula. Only the first book lacks any reference to the beautiful state of Michigan. That book, *Jack and the New York Death Mask*, is a political thriller set in Chicago, New York City, Upstate New York, and DC.

Even though *Jack and the New York Death Mask* is the first Jack Handler book, many of my readers started with one of my later books. That is not a problem, because adequate backstory is provided inside each of the individual titles to make them great stand-alone reads.

* * *

Here are the Amazon links to my previous Jack Handler books:

Getting to Know Jack Series

Jack and the New York Death Mask:	http://amzn.to/MVpAEd
Murder on Sugar Island:	http://amzn.to/1u66DBG
Superior Peril:	http://amzn.to/LAQnEU
Superior Intrigue:	http://amzn.to/1jvjNSi
Sugar Island Girl Missing in Paris:	http://amzn.to/1g5c66e

Wealthy Street Murders: http://amzn.to/1mb6NQy

Murders in Strangmoor Bog: http://amzn.to/1IEUPxX

Jack's Justice Series

Ghosts of Cherry Street: http://amzn.to/2n3lrRf

Assault on Sugar Island: http://amzn.to/2n3vcyL

Dogfight: